Hayley Clark has worked in UK charities for most of her professional career. Her passion for travel has taken her to far-flung places across the globe, where she has hiked the Great Wall of China, been charged at by an elephant and dived with great white sharks. Hayley is also an accomplished artist and woodcarver, spending days in her 'She Shed' at the end of her garden when she isn't squeezing in penning her latest novel.

Her first novel focuses on friendships and secrets, a theme she will continue to explore alongside romance in her new works.

A huge thank you to my long-suffering husband, who has had to listen to me saying 'when I finish this book' hundreds of times over the last few years, and to my lovely friends, Jackie and Sarah, who provided encouragement and critique and nudged me to get it finished! Also, a special mention to my close friends who have remained supportive and excited on my behalf; I greatly appreciate them buying this book to gift to others even before they have read it.

Hayley Clark

BENEATH THE SURFACE

AUSTIN MACAULEY PUBLISHERS
LONDON * CAMBRIDGE * NEW YORK * SHARJAH

Copyright © Hayley Clark 2025

The right of Hayley Clark to be identified as author of this work has been asserted by the author in accordance with sections 77 and 78 of the Copyright, Designs and Patents Act 1988.

All rights reserved. No part of this publication may be reproduced, stored in a retrieval system, or transmitted in any form or by any means, electronic, mechanical, photocopying, recording, or otherwise, without the prior permission of the publishers.

Any person who commits any unauthorised act in relation to this publication may be liable to criminal prosecution and civil claims for damages.

This is a work of fiction. Names, characters, businesses, places, events, locales, and incidents are either the products of the author's imagination or used in a fictitious manner. Any resemblance to actual persons, living or dead, or actual events is purely coincidental.

A CIP catalogue record for this title is available from the British Library.

ISBN 9781037101007 (Paperback)
ISBN 9781037101014 (ePub e-book)

www.austinmacauley.com

First Published 2025
Austin Macauley Publishers Ltd®
1 Canada Square
Canary Wharf
London
E14 5AA

Thank you to my publishers, Austin Macauley, for taking a chance on a first-time author and for their support throughout the editing process.

Table of Contents

Before   13

1 7 Months Ago June, Carolyn   *15*

2 7 Months Ago June, Kira   *19*

3 7 Months Ago June, Ruby   *23*

4 7 Months Ago June, Sauna   *27*

5 7 Months Ago June, Coffee   *33*

6 6 Months Ago July, Ruby   *40*

7 6 Months Ago July, Carolyn   *45*

8 6 Months Ago July, Sauna   *49*

9 6 Months Ago July, Kira   *55*

10 5 Months Ago August, Carolyn   *59*

11 5 Months Ago August, Ruby   *65*

12 5 Months Ago August, Kira   *70*

13 5 Months Ago August, Carolyn   *75*

14 4 Months Ago September, Carolyn   *81*

15 4 Months Ago September, Kira   *86*

16 4 Months Ago September, Ruby   *91*

17 4 Months Ago September, Sauna   *94*

18 3 Months Ago October, Halloween   *97*

19 3 Months Ago October, Kira   *101*

20 3 Months Ago October, Carolyn	104
21 3 Months Ago October, Kira	108
22 3 Months Ago October, Carolyn	113
23 3 Months Ago October, Ruby	117
24 3 Months Ago October, Carolyn	121
25 2 Months Ago November, Carolyn	124
26 2 Months Ago November, Ruby	128
27 2 Months Ago November, Kira	132
28 2 Months Ago November, Sauna	139
29 2 Months Ago November, Kira	141
30 2 Months Ago November, Ruby	148
31 2 Months Ago November, Carolyn	154
32 1 Month Ago December, Kira	158
33 1 Month Ago December, Carolyn	166
34 1 Month Ago December, Ruby	170
35 2 Weeks Ago December, Kira	177
36 2 Weeks Ago December, Ruby	183
37 2 Weeks Ago December, Carolyn	190
38 1 Week Ago Christmas Eve, Ruby	195
39 1 Week Ago Christmas Eve, Carolyn	198
40 1 Week Ago Christmas Eve, Kira	205
41 The Day Before 30 December, Carolyn	211
42 The Day Before 30 December, Ruby	218
43 The Day Before 30 December, Kira	222
44 12 Hours Before New Years Eve, Carolyn	228
45 6 Hours Before New Years Eve, Kira	232
46 3 Hours Before, New Years Eve, Ruby	237

47 1 Hour Before New Years Eve, Sauna	*241*
48 30 Minutes Before New Years Eve	*246*
49 10 Minutes Before New Years Eve	*249*
50 5 Minutes Before New Years Eve	*250*
51 Now Midnight, Ruby	*252*
51 Now Midnights, Carolyn	*253*
52 Now Midnight, Kira	*254*
53 Now	*255*
54 After New Years Day	*257*
55 After 1 Week Later, Sauna	*258*
56 After 1 Year Later	*259*
Epilogue	*261*

Before

1
7 Months Ago
June, Carolyn

Carolyn sighs heavily as she contemplated the next couple of months. It may only be June, but the prospect of the long weeks of the summer holidays stretching ahead of her only compounded how lonely she felt. Not having to cope with her errant husband's mood swings and petty grievances was normally a blessing. However, as the sun finally started to shine, the kids got more and more restless, and it just brought her situation home to her.

Carolyn was sick of dealing with the responsibility of juggling household chores, kids' clubs and activities all on her own; and quite frankly, she was sick of feeling like a single parent, as Josh built his illustrious career all over the world.

Carlolyn knew that she should be grateful for what she had: a beautiful house in a lovely neighbourhood, two healthy children (who, although they gave her grief on a daily basis, were actually pretty wonderful compared to some other people's brats) and the allowance Josh gave her so that she could have a comfortable lifestyle. She had amazing family and friends. She needed to focus on what she could do this summer rather than thinking about everything that didn't feel possible.

One of the main things she was resented was Josh's lifestyle—the way that he swanned in and out of their lives depending on where his next contract was and how, when he was around, she spent so much time walking on egg shells; she couldn't relax enough to appreciate having an extra pair of hands around to parent the twins. Since Josh had taken another long-distance contract at the start of the year, she had pretty much been a single parent and home alone.

This trip had taken him to somewhere deep into South America, where the only regular contact he had with her and the kids was via some dodgy satellite phone, or the occasional FaceTime when they came back to civilisation for a break and to stock up on supplies.

He had been home once at Easter for a couple of weeks, before he had to hot-foot it back to the middle of nowhere again—happier on his mission to save the environment one endangered plant at a time than at home with his family. His trips had grown more frequent over the last few years, as his reputation as a ruthless and intrepid botanist had grown—sadly, along with his ego and his sense of entitlement.

The last few years, and particularly those during the pandemic, had been some of the most trying for them. Despite her loneliness, the times when Josh was home all the time were even harder for her than being alone. Josh had taken time out between contracts in South America and Papua New Guinea, to work in Europe and with the world seed bank at Kew Gardens.

He had even spent some time lecturing at the Royal Society and at various highbrow universities. The only trouble was that when Josh was working in the UK, he never seemed to fully participate in family life—unlike the first few years they were together, when he couldn't get enough of her; it seemed that now he couldn't wait to get away.

As she carried the next pile of washing from the utility room to the ironing board, she looked up at their wedding photo on the hall wall. She could never understand why Josh had been the one to propose all those years ago—why he had wanted to commit his life to her and start a family when, quite frankly, he wasn't suited to it. It wasn't in his nature to be faithful or to put others above himself.

Carolyn shook her head and frowned again at the photo; she was a mug. Other women wouldn't put up with his reckless attitude to family life, his demanding and controlling behaviour, and certainly not his philandering. The trouble was, what would she do without him? She didn't have a job. She had barely worked after university, except for a junior PR position before she married Josh. She didn't have rich parents to fall back on, and quite honestly, she was a mess.

Her other constant worry were the kids; she worried that they were not getting enough quality time with him. Yes, he had a ferocious temper, was demanding, and sometimes incredibly controlling, but he was still their father, and he did have some good qualities. Josh was bright and intelligent, and so knowledgeable about the natural world; he understood plants and species of life form to an intense degree and was always keen to impart knowledge to those willing to learn. He was also the best ever at bedtime stories.

She smiled to herself; there was no way anyone could outdo his ability to invent the most outlandish worlds and adventures at the drop of a hat. But it still didn't alleviate the fact that he just wasn't around very much; and when he was, she could never be quite sure which Josh would show up.

As she picked up another sock off the laundry pile and let out another sigh, she thought, *Things just never lived up to expectations, did they?* Josh had never been anything but great with the kids, and they loved him. Unfortunately, it was always her who bore the brunt of the darker sides of his personality.

She just hoped that this time, when Josh came back, maybe things would be different. Perhaps they could have a bit of down time with them all as a family—maybe even book a holiday and do things other families enjoyed together, like chilling by the pool or creating sandcastles on a Spanish beach. Carolyn almost chuckled at how unrealistic her expectations were; it was highly unlikely she would get Josh to agree to any of that.

He would tell her she was being selfish, wanting to tie him down to a boring, kid-centric holiday—that if she really wanted to go, he would give her the money and she could go with one of the other mums or her brother's family. She knew that the more that she mentioned it to him and the more desperate she seemed, the more he would close off and shut down, to the point of becoming angry. And she knew where that would lead.

She gave herself a mental shake. She had absolutely no right to be maudlin on a day like this—the sun was shining, and she was looking forward to spending the day with her mum, doing a bit of shopping and then meeting the girls at the club later for a bit of R and R. She might even persuade her dad to look after the twins for a couple of hours; as long as she had fed and watered them beforehand, he could still manage reasonably well to entertain them, despite his recent diagnosis of Parkinson's.

In fact, Amber was surprisingly sensitive when it came to spending time with her grandad—making sure that she asked how he was and not fighting with Charlie quite so much. Carolyn smiled to herself. Yes, there was a lot to be grateful for. She bent down to pick up her gym bag, and just as she was about to shove her towel and cossie inside, she heard an almighty crash followed by a high-pitched shriek.

'AHHH, Mum!' And there it was again, peace shattered.

Well, that was the least of her worries. She could deal with the twins bickering and fighting every day of the week. What she had finally surmised over the last few lonely months was what she couldn't deal with any longer—and that was Josh. Maybe this was the year she would pluck up the courage to do what she had wanted to do for a very long time. Maybe this was the year she would actually leave him.

2
7 Months Ago
June, Kira

Kira thought back to the day she started her new job, smiling as she thought about how different Aaron Spark's gym was from the sweaty backstreet "anyone-welcome" gym she used to teach at. The first time she had walked through the door, in January, she had instinctively felt out of place; all of this money and opulence was such a long way from anything she was used to, and she wasn't sure that she would fit in.

But now, as she slung her gym bag and yoga mat over her shoulder and walked in through the sliding front doors, she realised just how wrong she had been. It hadn't taken long at all for her to be able to greet everyone by name and to get to know the team, who had all been so welcoming to her.

Long gone were the musty-smelling village halls with their squeaky floors and terrible acoustics, where she had started her career in fitness, coaxing elderly ladies through a series of gentle movements in a step aerobics class for seniors. She knew she was privileged to land this position as a yoga—and soon-to-be Pilates—instructor, and to have the time to build up her personal training list as she finished her qualifications and became a fully-fledged PT.

Having a permanent base also gave her somewhere solid to train between classes and clients, instead of having to grab the odd hour here and there, or out on the road as she pulled shifts all over the place to make ends meet.

Not that any of the customers at this health club needed to worry about money like she did. Aaron Spark's gyms were renowned for their exclusive clientele. Started by ex-Olympic Swimmer Aaron Sparks back in the late '80s, his empire had grown out of the boom of the '90s and had now settled as a place for the middle classes to frequent.

Sparks members' hard-earned cash was spent on cookie-cutter BMW 4x4s for her and eco-friendly Tesla's for him—or, for the higher earners, maybe a Maserati or new Porsche. Money was spent on Botox, boob jobs, six-packs, and expensive but tasteless tattoos.

Summer was a time for members to show off tans acquired from time spent on Portuguese golf courses, days spent basking on yachts in Mykonos, or, for the slightly classier, long breaks in the South of France, tanning on the riviera. Girls with names like Sophia, Tally and Melody played chase in the pool with boys whose names were back in fashion like Monty and Arthur.

Kira smiled as she made her way to the locker room, thinking, "Who was she to complain about these rich folk and their *new money* if they paid her wages?" She was happier here than she had been in years, and maybe some of their good fortune would rub off on her.

'Morning, Kira!' A singsong voice made her start as she shoved the last of her kit into the locker and snapped shut her padlock.

'Oh, so sorry. I didn't mean to make you jump.' A petite blonde of around 60, in Lululemons and a purple matching gym vest, smiled warmly at her. 'I just wanted to make sure you knew where everything was and if you needed a hand with anything.'

Sue from reception was the resident whirlwind, keeping everyone on track with bookings, equipment, rooms, refreshments and sorting out customer queries—all with a huge smile and warmth that radiated from her tiny frame.

'Actually, Sue, I'm all good!' Kira smiled. 'I'm just excited that I finally get to take this Pilates class in front of actual people and not just practice the theory. I know the staff here have been helping me by being my guinea pigs, but it's not the same as paying customers.' Kira looked around the locker room to make sure there was no one nearby to hear her say quietly, 'I'm actually really nervous.'

She gave a little shiver as she contemplated an empty Pilate's studio—the regulars not impressed by the change, and their old Pilates teacher moving to an Ashram in India, leaving Kira with a bunch of disgruntled yummy mummies not happy with a new, unknown instructor.

'You have absolutely nothing to worry about, love.' Sue patted her arm reassuringly. 'They were literally fighting each other off to get a spot in your class. It seems that you might be the new flavour of the month.' Sue gave her a slight wink and a squeeze of the arm as she smiled and headed for the changing room door.

Kira let out an audible sigh of relief. At least she wasn't going to die on her arse teaching her first official Pilates class—well, not until they had experienced her brand of Pilates anyway. There was still time for failure.

She gathered up her mat, iPhone, Bluetooth speaker and Sparks water bottle, and headed out to find just how many eager ladies were going to turn up to the midday class. Things were definitely heading up in general—she had a job that she loved, a bunch of friends she felt she could rely on for the first time in her life, and now a shot at the nationals. She treated herself to a couple of small stretches, limbering up in the locker room before she moved to the studio.

Her last big race had taken place on Sunday, a mere two days ago, and her legs still felt a little sore, but she was so pleased with where she had placed. She had been in a few races at the start of the triathlon season in May, but this was the first biggie. As soon as she woke up on the morning of the race, she had a feeling something good was going to happen. Before she had finished pulling all her gels, anti-chafe, gloves, cycle helmet and all the other crap she had to take with her into her bag, she was buzzing.

It was a gut feeling—either this race was going to be one of the best of her life, or there would be some other reason that it would become memorable. She had taken a look at the startling clear blue sky overhead and thought to herself, this could be the day where she finally got what she had been working towards, without the events of the past year overshadowing her achievement.

She had worked so hard for this opportunity, and after Sunday's results, there was nothing that stood in her way of being placed in the top 3 of the women's over-25s category, for the county and her Tri club, and then moving up into the National Triathlon championships. At 28, she was pushing the top of her age group, but as she continued to stretch out her legs one at a time on the changing room bench, she thought about how, although her limbs were tired today, she felt toned and strong.

She knew that she was nearly at the top of her game, and nothing was going to stop her getting there. A lump started to form in her throat as she reminded herself again why she worked so hard, why she pushed herself to do this, and why it wasn't just for her. It was never about the personal glory. It was all for Joanna. She didn't have time to dwell on that now; Joanna was gone.

She forced a smile back on her face, remembering the old adage of "fake it until you make it". Inhaling a deep breath, she shook out her long brown hair and stretched her arms over head, exhaling as she started on tidying her hair into its ubiquitous French plait, before confidently grabbing her stuff and headed out to the studio with a huge smile on her face.

3
7 Months Ago
June, Ruby

Ruby gave a sigh of satisfaction as she unpacked her case files from the small wheeled bag, that she used to carry her heavy court paperwork around, and placed them back onto her desk. She had had a massive win today, and the feeling of triumph had lasted all the way on the drive back from court, as she replayed the look on Mr North's face as the judge awarded Mrs North more than half of her husband's estate, and full custody of their 4 children.

The fact that Ruby had also managed to ensure that Mrs North had a 60% claim over her wealthy ex-husband's future earnings and his pension pot was the icing on the cake, and just went to rub salt into the smug bastard's wounds.

As Ruby made her way upstairs, past the kitsch lemon and pineapple wallpaper on the wall of her compact terrace house and into her bedroom with its equally eye-catching mermaid wallpaper, she recalled Mr North's look of contorted outrage as the verdict had come in.

His pudgy, well-fed face had turned puce as he had spluttered obscenities in their direction, as they left the court and headed for a celebratory glass of fizz at the wine bar round the corner—Mrs North already looking like a woman without the weight of the world on her shoulders. *Yes*, Ruby thought to herself, *victory felt good!*

She smiled to herself as she peeled off her smart white blouse and wide-legged black trousers, happy to take off the colourless façade of her day job and to see the bright colours of her tattoos emerging—bringing her back to her real self in the short time it took her to shed her work clothes.

She admired her body art in the full-length mirror, loving how the stunning interwoven vines, flowers, moons and stars climbed up her body, instantly brightening up the room. She couldn't wait to recount today's saga to the girls later when she met them at Sparks. Carolyn had something she wanted to bend her ear about, so she better hurry up.

Ruby rifled deeper into her wardrobe to grab the loudest hot pink maxi dress that she owned, and then, from the adjoining shoe rack, her favourite green rattan wedges that she knew would instantly make her feel less lawyer, and more "Ruby". She unpinned her shoulder-length hair from its chignon, tipped her head upside down, and spritzed its bright dyed-red length with textured spray, before swooping her head back and topping off the look with a huge fake gardenia hair clip.

Yes, that was better—maybe a touch more cleavage than most people would be comfortable with, and perhaps the dress clung a little tightly to her voluptuous hips than some women would think was decent, but she didn't care. This was the other side of Ruby March that colleagues at the Crown Court never got to see.

As far as they were concerned, she was as sombre and straight faced as the other female lawyers, in their sensible black and grey suits, low heeled court shoes and black tote bags. Maybe a sweep of mascara and a nude lipstick, but always blending in, always being taken seriously.

Ruby moved into the bathroom to grab her make-up bag, slicking on her favourite bright red Chanel lippy to accentuate her full lips, and adding a thick flick of waterproof liquid eyeliner to her eyes. She delved into her jewellery box and selected 3 pairs of silver hoop earrings of ascending size, and threaded back into the multiple holes in her ears, finishing the look by reapplying her septum piercing, with a slightly larger-than-usual hoop with a small Celtic knot at its centre.

She could be who she wanted, both in the court room and out, and no one was going to tell her she couldn't do it. Not her family, not a man, not a judge or fellow lawyers. Though if they saw the real her right now, she had no doubt that it would cause more than a few eyebrows to be raised. But she was good at her job—there was no denying it—no matter what she chose to look like.

In fact, there was nothing Ruby loved more than the opportunity to prove someone wrong, and to face off with some idiot misogynist in the court room, when they plead their pathetic cases about how they were the wronged party in their marriage, that their wives didn't understand but the bitch was happy to spend all his money. There was always more dirty washing and dark secrets that were aired in the court room than one would expect.

Once the mud-slinging started, in Ruby's experience, it did normally tend to be the men at fault, with more indiscretions coming to light. She had seen it all since she started as Junior Counsel 10 years ago: adultery, gambling, debt, drugs, prostitutes, secret lives and secret wives—there was nothing that could surprise her these days.

The girls at the club loved to hear about her latest cases and the disastrous marriages and family issues of people living in the next town, as Ruby made them laugh with her stories. If anything, it gave them light relief from their own lives. Ruby had always made an active decision to practice law in the next city. She didn't want to do, as her friend Carolyn would put it, "shit on her own doorstep". She wanted to keep her professional and private lives as separate as she could possibly get.

No, she wasn't stupid—the last thing she wanted was to bump into any of her clients, or, even worse, their ex-partners, who she had taken to the cleaners, when she was going about her daily business. She doubted very much that they would recognise her, but it was better to be safe than sorry and keep business firmly away from pleasure.

She stuffed her swimwear into her bright purple bag and then remembered that she had promised to take Carolyn a few of her more cast-off outrageous outfits for the twins' dressing-up box. It was so much fun to be a surrogate aunty to Amber and Charlie, and to have the opportunity to fuss over them since she and Carolyn had become friends and grown closer. She absolutely adored them, even if they did terrorise their mum. She and Carolyn had grown really close over the last few years and now had a firmly established routine.

She still chuckled to herself when she remembered how they had accidentally met 5 years ago, when they had both ordered identical caramel macchiatos, but with extra cream and cinnamon sprinkles at the Aaron Sparks café bar. There had been a mini standoff between them at the counter as they both reached for the same drink, before laughing it off and agreeing that by ordering the same strange drink, fate must want them to be friends.

Their friendship had brought her no end of joy—Carolyn's scatty, fun nature, her potty mouth, and her ability to always rope Ruby into helping out to organise quizzes and socials at the club, drawing on her legal expertise for free whenever she needed support for the events or friends needed marital advice in their regular sauna catch-ups.

She checked her watch again and hurried out onto the landing to hunt down a towel, colliding with the firm chest of her boyfriend in the process.

'Hi, babe' she grinned, as Kyle steadied her by the hip.

He reached in for a quick kiss before frowning down at her.

'Where's the fire?'

'I'm late to meet the girls!' she whipped back over her shoulder as she reached into the airing cupboard, faltering on her next question as Kyle started to peel off his workwear.

'Good…day at work?' There was nothing like the tautness of his back and ass to distract her mid-sentence, as he stepped out of his boxers and walked ahead of her into the bathroom.

'Yeah, it was good,' he shouted over the noise of the shower and extract fan. 'Nearly finished the Sullivans' shelving and start on the kitchen tomorrow.' He started to hum to himself as she imagined him lathering himself up with soap.

With a sigh of regret, she hefted her bag up onto her shoulder. It took every inch of her willpower not to drop her bag back on the floor, whip off her dress, and go and join her beautiful boyfriend of two years in the hot, steamy shower.

God, she was lucky. Kyle was just the icing on the cake of her nearly perfect life, and she loved spending as much time with him as possible—preferably naked—but no, not right now. Duty called. She knew the others would be expecting her, and she wasn't going to let them down. No doubt they would be waiting with anticipation to hear all about the case from today, and she wanted to see how Kira's first class as a paid-for Pilates instructor had gone.

They were planning to have a quick glass of wine in the café bar after, if it had been a success, but with any luck, she would still be back in plenty of time to take advantage of her freshly showered man.

4
7 Months Ago
June, Sauna

'This has got to be the best ever new tradition,' sighed Kira as she rested back against the hot slats, stretching her long, slim legs out along the cedar bench and revelling in the dark, womb-like warmth of the sauna. 'Or is it a habit? I never really did understand the difference,' she sighed and leant further into the wood that was starting to soothe her aching muscles.

'Well, I think it's a habit if it's something you do repeatedly, at the same sort of time, each day or week, I guess,' Ruby smiled at her friend as she too stretched out on the bench above her. 'Or is that a ritual? Oh crikey, you would think between the two of us that we would have an answer to that!'

It was so nice, Ruby thought, *to have someone to have these kinds of inane conversations with after a hard day in court, just taking time out with the girls to chew the fat and actually relax.*

'Well, whatever it is, I'm just grateful I have it and get to unwind a little after this week. I swear I was literally shaking before that class earlier,' Kira shared.

'Oh God, I'm so, so sorry,' Ruby interrupted. 'I meant to ask as soon as I saw you in the changing room how it went today. I knew you had your first paying customers. What an idiot!' Ruby blushed in the darkness.

'Seriously, Ruby, it's all fine. You sent me a message last night wishing me luck. I didn't expect anyone to remember,' Kira added quietly. 'However, now we're on the topic—oh my God, I can't believe how well it went,' she pulled herself up into a seated position and let out a little squeal.

'Honestly, such great feedback already, and people on the app booking in for Tuesday. It's such a relief, and I'm just so pleased,' she grinned to herself. All her hard work had been worth it—the extra tuition she had taken online, the endless nights spent practising routines in her living room in front of a full-length mirror, even resorting to filming herself and cringing as she watched it back and tried to improve her posture, her tone, her instruction to the class.

'Ah, that's amazing, love.' Ruby leant down and patted her friend affectionately on the shoulder. 'No one deserves this more than you, and I'm not surprised they're all queuing up to come to your class. The last I heard was that Cassie, who left, just used to put them all through the same boring crap routine every time. She didn't even help the older ladies, who couldn't do all the moves and were struggling.

'The only reason the class was full then was because there wasn't an alternative Pilates instructor. I wouldn't be surprised if they had told Cass to move on after you started to bring in a bit of fresh blood. I'll have to get Carolyn to do a bit of a snoop with Sue—she literally knows everything that goes on around here.'

'I wouldn't want to think that I was the reason Cass left,' Kira frowned. She never wanted to think that she might be the cause of someone's unhappiness or loss of livelihood. It literally gave her the shivers; she was a kind soul at heart.

'Seriously, Kira, you have nothing to worry yourself about. I was only kidding, really, about Cass. As far as we all know, she hooked up with one of the punters. And when he moved to another gym the other side of town, she followed him, as he said he could get her more classes. Then she vanished off to India. Nothing to do with you, chick,' she reassured her friend.

She knew how anxious Kira got about a lot of things and felt personally responsible. She resolved to make sure that she didn't make such flippant comments in the future that Kira could take literally.

It had been a long road for Kira over the last 6 months, and Ruby wanted to let her know that she was there to support her—to help her lovely friend continue to grow back her seriously dented confidence, and to help her to settle more into her role at Aaron Sparks. It was one of the reasons why she had brought Kira along to these regular catch-ups in the sauna, and asked her to meet for coffee with her and Carolyn so regularly. She knew what it was like to move somewhere new and to start from scratch with no friends for support.

She also knew what it was like to have been through trauma and come out the other side. So, if she could be a helping hand for someone as gentle as Kira, then she would. Ruby was about to suggest that she come along to Kira's next class if it helped with moral support, when their peace and quiet was disturbed by the sauna door being yanked open with force and slammed again.

'Fucking hell, what a day! Christ, it's so good to see you ladies!' Carolyn plonked herself down hard on the wooden slats close to Kira's feet. 'Oh, so sorry, I didn't see your feet there!' Carolyn apologised. 'It's so bloody dark in here. You're lucky I didn't end up sat on your lap,' she cackled.

'You would not believe what a complete pain in the ass the twins have been this morning, and then again when I picked them up from dad's this afternoon. Honestly, it's like they are living, breathing devils sent to try my patience at every level. The fucking mess they make—sorry, sorry, I know I shouldn't swear, but they drive me to distraction!'

'You know, Carolyn,' Ruby waggled her eyebrows in Kira's direction, 'no filter at all when it comes to telling you how hard it is being a parent to two little angels.'

Carolyn let out a little giggle. She knew Kira and Ruby were used to her ranting. To be honest, if she didn't have these two lovely ladies to let off steam with, who knew what sort of trouble she would be in? She already drank too much. Maybe she would have to take up yet another vice or become one of those people that rang the Samaritans to just let off steam. Seriously, she needed to get a therapist or something.

'Honestly, it's fine,' Kira interrupted her thoughts. 'I know how hard it can be for any parent of twins. My mum used to tell me and my sister often enough,' Kira smiled through the hot darkness at Carolyn.

'Oh,' Carolyn shot round to look at Kira, 'I didn't realise you were a twin! You must get this then. I bet you and your sister argued all the time one minute, then you're the best of friends. Does it still happen like that now you're grown up?' Carolyn smiled back.

'I *was* a twin,' Kira replied gently, watching Ruby catch Carolyn's eye and give a gentle shake of her head. 'No, it's ok. I don't mind talking about it. My twin, Joanna, died when we were 21. It's a long time ago now, so it's fine, honestly,' Kira hurried to reassure her.

'Well, shit, I'm so sorry, Kira. That must have been really hard for you. I've no idea how that must feel,' Carolyn reached over and squeezed her hand. 'I'm always putting my foot in it, aren't I, Rubes? I didn't mean to upset you in any way.'

'Honestly, like I said, it was a long time ago now, and I'm getting on with things. I think part of me will still always feel like a twin, but we always had our own interests and personalities, as I know your two do.' Kira was always quick to placate and make sure Carolyn didn't feel bad. Talking about Joanna was always hard, but the more she did it, the better it actually felt.

It was rare that she got to talk about Joanna anymore. Her parents had cut off any conversation about her years ago, removing most of the traces of Joanna from her late teenage years from their house, so that the only photos on show they had were from when they were both really small, and you couldn't tell yet which twin was which with their identical outfits and mops of auburn hair.

The fact that they barely even acknowledged Kira's birthday anymore was yet one more reason she had decided to move away, 2 years after Joanna's death, and never really go back.

Her parents still lived in the family home, still went about their daily lives, but from what Kira could see from her short and infrequent visits, they were just existing, not living. When both their girls were alive, they had been different—more aspirational and supportive of both of them in their endeavours, and wanting more for their futures. But then came the cancer, the years of chemo, and the painful reality that Joanna was never going to beat this terrible disease—and that's when they seemed to give up.

Kira shook herself mentally out of the funk. She didn't want her disappointment in her parents' lack of ability to support her emotionally to cloud the lovely day she was having. She turned towards Carolyn, who was looking pensive and unsure about how to answer sensitively.

'Carolyn, honestly, tell me more about the twins. I've met them obviously, but it would be good to know more about them than just how much they drive you crazy!' Kira encouraged.

'Well, they are definitely very different. Honestly, you wouldn't think that they were even related sometimes. But then, occasionally, there seems to be this unspoken understanding between them—like they just conspire psychically, and things just happen, or they have this intuition about each other. I guess that must happen with all twins, but them being such opposites, you just wouldn't imagine it would.'

'One thing they do very much the same though is when it comes to winding me up!' she exclaimed. 'So, if you know anyone that wants a pair of 10-year-olds for the next 6 weeks, while the little psychos are on summer holidays, then they are welcome to them,' Carolyn laughed. 'In fact, I might go get them out of kids' club right now and tell them I'm dropping them at Aunty Ruby's house.'

Carolyn chuckled at the look on Ruby's face, as she pushed her sweaty fringe back off her face. 'I swear they make this thing hotter every time I come in here. I love that this is our secret refuge. Honestly, I think I would actually be checking into an asylum if I didn't have my Tuesday and Fridays hiding in here,' Carolyn sank into a deeper recline on her hot pink fluffy towel.

'I feel it's my personal duty to save Carolyn from herself. Everyone needs a break from real life every now and then, and this sauna is as good a place as any to get away from it. It's so nice you can join us now that you have your shifts sorted, Kira,' Ruby gently nudged the pretty feet below her with her own bright purple sparkling toes.

'Ah, thanks. You've made me feel so welcome the last 6 months. I don't want to crash your time together though. They say three's a crowd,' Kira remarked shyly. It was a long time since she had been asked to be part of someone else's gang.

Since Kira had started training competitively, it was all she could do to keep in touch with her parents once a week, and her friends from school and university had all slowly drifted away after Joanna had died, none of them knowing how to approach Kira when she had all but shut down. This, though—a casual hang out a couple of times a week—maybe she could do that. Her coach and her physio were always trying to encourage her to take some downtime, and to use the sauna and steam room to help her body repair.

Maybe she could just build this into her recovery time and maintain some new friendships at the same time? There couldn't be any harm in it, and if she didn't feel like it, then she could just say that her training was too intense, or that she had an extra class to prep for.

'Don't be daft!' Carolyn squawked. 'Seriously, I need someone other than Ruby to bitch to about my life, or lack of it, and I already know you make a perfect listening ear.'

'Oh, poor you, Kira,' Ruby smiled. 'You don't know what you're letting yourself in for, agreeing to meet with this one twice a week to hear her have a rant,' Ruby smiled over as Carolyn rolled her eyes at her.

'No, seriously, Kira, you're one of us now,' she paused. 'That's if you want to be?' Carolyn looked over at her hopefully.

Kira leant forward from her perch to look between the bright and vibrant red-haired Ruby and the sweaty face with dishevelled bangs of Carolyn, 'Do you know what, ladies?' Her face split with a broad smile. 'I would really like that. Thank you.'

5
7 Months Ago
June, Coffee

'So, how are the classes going, Kira?' Carolyn slid onto the green, squishy couch opposite Kira, who was perched neatly on a cream leather bucket chair.

She had commandeered their usual table in what was supposed to be a quieter corner of the café bar, but was really just the best place that Carolyn had found over the years to people-watch. She argued that its proximity to the soft play area didn't mean that it was hard to hear each other speak at times when the little angels were running riot, but that other people couldn't hear them when they were mid-gossip. She had a fair point.

'Sooo good, actually. It's amazing. Sue was telling me the other day that she even had people asking to go on a last-minute cancellation list for my Sunday session, and they were even happy for her to call them last minute!' Kira squeaked and then blushed deeply, still surprised by the reception her new classes were getting.

'Oh, you should be thrilled! Honestly, there's no need to be modest. You're a fucking success, and that's great! Isn't she, Ruby?' She scooted her butt to the side as Ruby slid in beside her, carefully setting down her bucket of frothy caramel macchiato on the low table and joining in.

'What was that? What did I miss?' Ruby looked expectantly between her two friends.

'I was just saying that Kira here is a fucking success, and she should be proud, not blushing and looking all bashful. She is knocking the socks off this place with people queuing to get a spot in all of her classes,' Carolyn enthused, patting a surprised Kira on the cheek and nudging Ruby in the ribs a little too hard for comfort.

'Ouch! Carolyn!' Ruby protested at the same time that Kira interrupted.

'Well, it's not quite like that.'

Ruby reached down to rub the spot that Carolyn had jabbed with her elbow, knowing what Carolyn was hinting at. They had agreed the other week to boost Kira whenever she talked about her work or her training, knowing how her self-confidence had been knocked, and they had agreed to tag-team to help build it back up again.

'Of course, it's like that!' Ruby smiled her widest grin at Kira. 'This place has needed a kick-up-the-ass for a long time now—some fresh new blood bringing our downward dogs and warrior poses into the twenty-first century.'

Carolyn joined in enthusiastically, 'Seriously, girl, we need to get better at being our own champions and the cheerleaders for other women, or some crap like that.' Carolyn continued, 'You know, I was listening to one of those motivational YouTube things again the other day, hoping it would give me some advice about what I'm actually going to do when Josh gets back. I am definitely going to tell him that I want to go back to work, and he can just lump it. I know he won't be happy, but I need something for me, you know?'

'I love being a mum,' she continued 'don't get me wrong, and I love the stuff I do here on the committee, but he can't expect me to just be satisfied with that for the rest of my life. I need to feel fulfilled.'

The wind suddenly seemed to go from Carolyn's sails, and her shoulders slumped a little as she reached for her drink. Ruby, knowing that it wasn't only Kira that needed a boost sometimes, picked up the baton.

'No, you're absolutely right, Carolyn. If we don't champion each other, who else is going to do it? You have every right to be proud of what you have achieved, Kira. Just as you have every right to want to make a career for yourself, Carolyn. And no one—and especially not your husband—should have any right to tell you that you can't.' She reinforced her point by firmly slamming the palm of her hand on the tabletop, causing a mini tidal wave of sickly hot drink to lap over the edge and over Carolyn's phone.

'Oooh, steady on, Rubes. There's you getting carried away again,' she cackled as she grabbed a handful of tissues and wet wipes from her bag. 'I said go back to work, you donut, not run for Prime Minister,' she grinned. 'Look, you gals are the bright ones here—the ones that work hard to get qualifications and all that. I've been there, as you know, but my skills are way out of date. I mean, who wants an old-fashioned PA now?'

'It's all virtual and digital assistants these days. No, I just want something that helps me have a bit of purpose when Josh is away all the time, and when I'm not just being a mum to those pair of reprobates,' she nodded over to where Amber was trying to ram her brother's head into a foam circle in the soft play area, while he, in turn, pelted her with plastic balls from the ball pool.

'Well, anything we can do to help you, then we will, won't we, Kira?' Ruby looked to her friend for affirmation, keen to continue the theme of supporting these two wonderful women wherever she could.

'Absolutely. Anything at all,' Kira smiled back. 'Just talk to us, Carolyn. If we don't know what the problem is, we can't help you. Why doesn't your husband want you to go back to work?'

Ruby looked between her friends, Kira not realising that her probing question was not the direction that Carolyn probably wanted this conversation to go in. Ruby knew that Carolyn was quite comfortable talking about herself a lot of the time, but it always tended to be in jest and a story about one calamity or other.

She certainly didn't seem as comfortable now, talking about something that she was obviously seriously thinking about. Maybe it was a conversation for the sauna another day, when they weren't about to be interrupted by a couple of 10-year-olds fresh out of kids' club.

'That's a good question, Kira,' Ruby spoke before Carolyn could form a comprehensive reply. Catching Carolyn's eye, she could see the look of gratitude for what she was doing in helping to change the subject. 'Let's just say that Josh is an interesting character that I'm sure you will get to meet soon, and things will make sense.'

Ruby checked to her side again to see if Carolyn looked less worried and was pleased when she saw the faint hint of a nod of thanks. 'Speaking of a few weeks' time, why don't you tell us how the plans for the summer pool party are coming along, Carolyn?' Ruby neatly segued into a topic she knew Carolyn could enthuse about and relax again.

'I saw the posters up last week,' Kira confirmed. 'Sue, on reception, was telling me that it's an Aaron Sparks tradition or something, and that all the families look forward to it all year? And that you're leading the events committee to organise it? That must be so much fun!' She smiled at Carolyn and urged her to tell them more.

Carolyn relaxed into the new subject, grateful that Ruby knew her well enough to give her this breathing space. One thing she never needed was encouragement to talk about the Sparks events. She was proud of how she worked with the committee, and talking about the events showed off her exceptional networking and creative skills.

'It is literally the event of the year. Well, apart from, maybe, Halloween and Christmas. We had to cancel it for a couple of years during the pandemic, but it went down a storm last year. The kids loved it, and the parents had a great time. We have so much planned—I've got the kitchen team to set up a big BBQ by the pool, Sarah from spin has decks and actually DJ's at a few local clubs and has agreed to do a couple of sets.'

'There's going to be inflatables in the pool, and Alex from the tennis coaching team has agreed to run a series of pool games for the kids, and then later, some just for the adults. We've got the usual raffle. I think we've even persuaded James—that hot new PT—to set up a tiki bar! You'll have to tell me your favourite cocktail recipes so I can get them on the list!' Carolyn was in her element again now, organising and planning things that didn't relate to her home life, and where she could have a bit of a laugh with her friends.

'Actually, while I think of it, can I put your name down to do pool Pilates? Just a 45-minute session. It will go down a storm,' Carolyn enthused.

'Wow, that sounds great!' Kira smiled. 'Of course, put my name down. I'm happy to help. I know that the management team have said that we still have to run classes as usual if they are scheduled for that morning, but that after 2:30 pm, if we don't have a role to play, I think we can all clock off and join in the fun. I will check though, as I don't want to miss it.'

Kira could just imagine a fun afternoon with her friends around the pool. She was always up for a bit of a competitive pool games, whatever they might be. It had been a while since she had something like that to look forward to. She realised she had zoned out a bit, thinking about where her proper summer gear might be stored in the lock-up. She had still to unpack everything from her move back in January this year; it had all been such a rush at the time.

'What was that?' She looked between Ruby and Carolyn. 'Sorry, I was just thinking about sipping a cocktail by a pool and must have been distracted,' she let out a contented sigh.

'I was just saying, I wondered if you had met James yet—the new PT? You know, the one with the abs of steel and that cute smile?' Carolyn had a mischievous glint in her eye as she continued to objectify Kira's new colleague. 'You must have seen him. Seriously hot.'

'Carolyn, how on earth do you know that he has abs of steel?' Ruby guffawed.

'Well, let's just say that a few weeks ago, he obviously hadn't paid enough attention at his orientation session on his staff induction, and must have got the women's and men's changing rooms mixed up, and well, there he and they were!'

'They?' Ruby looked for clarification, clearly confused.

'Yes, *they*—his abs! Seriously, have you not been listening to anything I've been talking about? They as in plural, as in deserve their own individual names and identities as they are so clearly defined.' She sat back with a shit-eating grin, clearly pleased with herself and her slightly pervy observation.

'Carolyn!' Kira smacked her hand over her mouth, clearly shocked. 'What did you do when you walked in on him? Or rather, what did he do?' Kira herself was never embarrassed by bodies—the amount of events she had competed in where the changing was communal, you just got used to it—but that was very different to having a customer discover you in the women's changing room, on one of your first shifts in a new job. She could feel herself blushing for James.

'Oh, he was completely cool about it. To be fair, he was only naked from the waist up. He just politely apologised, then took his time finding his shirt to pull on,' she continued to grin like the cat that had got the cream. 'I told him not to hurry,' she smirked again as Ruby gave her a gentle shove.

'You are a fucking nightmare! Poor guy probably thought you were going to report him and get him the sack!'

'No risk of that. Don't worry, he wasn't bothered at all. But he has spoken to me a couple of times since then. I guess he thinks he better keep me onside in case I decide to say something—not that I would.' She was a kind person. There was no way she would call someone out like that for a genuine mistake. It's not like he had done it when anyone else was around to be offended, and to be fair, she was anything but. She wouldn't kick him out of bed in a hurry.

'But what he did ask me, that last time I spoke to him, was how I knew you,' she turned her gaze back across the table to where Kira sat, enraptured at the amusing conversation.

'What? What do you mean he asked about me?' Kira looked puzzled—why would this new guy want to know about her?

'Well, it's obvious, isn't it? He fancies you and wants to get to know you, and what better way to do that than by getting to know your friends?' She looked pleased with herself.

'And what did you tell him?' Kira valued her privacy and hoped that Carolyn, in all her friendly capacity, hadn't told him anything about her. The last thing she needed was for a work colleague that she hadn't really met yet to start making advances—even if said guy was, from what she had seen so far, very attractive. She didn't want to give Carolyn the wrong impression, so thought she had better come clean about something she had been holding back from the girls—just as Carolyn said.

'Don't worry, babe. I haven't told him anything! I thought a little mystery was in order while I figured out his intentions, and got some of my spies to find out more about him!' She had been coming to Aaron Sparks for years, and with her position on the events committee—and the amount of time she spent buying coffee and hanging out with the twins—had made a number of good friends on the staff team. Neither Ruby nor Kira were surprised to hear that she was doing her own form of vetting of poor old James.

Despite her wariness about men after what had happened to her last year, Kira was still keen to think about a future with a partner. It was lonely going home every night to her new flat. She knew she had the girls here to talk to, but it wasn't the same as having someone as part of her life—someone she could really be herself with. She was ready to think about that again, but first…

'Actually, ladies, there's something I should probably tell you before you start setting me up with James.' With a faint hint of a smile, she leant forward over the table, hoping that the squeals from soft play would drown out her little announcement. 'Well…'

'Ah, come on, don't leave us in suspense!' Carolyn interrupted.

'Give the girl a chance, jeez,' Ruby looked at her friend, exasperated.

'Sam asked me out!' Kira blurted.

'Sam, as in long-haired lifeguard Sam? Man-bun Sam? Oooh, how exciting! I never thought he would have it in him to make a move—the cheeky little bugger!' As usual, Carolyn knew exactly who Sam was and could probably list his credentials, ex-girlfriends and vital statistics if they let her.

It was time for Ruby to intervene again before her friend put her foot in it.

'Well, that's marvellous. I'm really hoping you said yes. He seems like a really nice guy,' Ruby gave her friend a warm smile.

'Yeah, I did. He's taking me out this weekend—just for coffee, actually. You know, public place, start slow and all that.'

Ruby knew what a big deal this was for Kira, and how even a small step like coffee with a guy was part of her starting to build up her trust again. She was pleased for her, but cautious in how she offered her support.

'Want me to call you after, just so you can let me know when you get home?' she offered gently.

'Yes, please, Rubes. That's really kind,' Kira confirmed.

'Just text me the details, and we will sort it,' she leant over and gently squeezed Kira's hand, just as a pair of 10-year-old whirlwinds came crashing towards the table and interrupted their peace.

'Muuum.' Everything seemed to be done in tandem and at high volume when they were together. 'We need snackkkksssss.'

Carolyn looked between them and sighed as she picked up her mug and drained the contents. 'Come on then, you pair of locusts. Let's hit up Domino's.' She stood and picked up her bag, waving goodbye to the others as she trailed the twins—who were already busy arguing over toppings—towards the door. 'See you in the sauna!'

6

6 Months Ago
July, Ruby

'Ooof, that stings.' Ruby sucked in a sharp breath as the needle dragged its way right down the back of her left arm.

'Seriously, Rubes, I don't know why you act like you've never been tattooed before every time I come at you with a needle!' Paulo sighed with a little laugh under his breath. 'It's not like you're not already covered in them. You're literally a walking advertisement for my masterpieces.'

He wasn't wrong. Despite not liking the initial feeling when the needle hit one of her more sensitive areas, there was always a feeling of relief, a sense of satisfaction and letting go as the ink penetrated her skin. Some might say that Ruby was a little addicted to tattoos. However, she always thought of herself as a connoisseur of self-expression and a very enthusiastic canvas.

'Ok. So, I'm assuming that as we are outlining this arm today, you're gonna want to get the rest of the colours done really soon to fill it in to match the other arm? We need to get it in the diary, Ruby. You know I don't have many 6-hour appointments going at the moment.'

'Well, as soon as you've got this bit down, get your diary out!' she chuckled as she noticed him roll his eyes as he shook his head at her. She knew he would prioritise her appointment over most of his other customers. Not only were they firm friends, and he loved working with her on their unique designs, but he also welcomed the way Ruby was helping his bank balance every time she walked through his door.

As she sat there waiting for the next inevitable sting, Ruby reflected on the time it had taken for her to build up this impressive collection of ink, starting as a legal student when she had hardly any money. She picked small and intricate designs when her pay checks came in, always having them inked in places clients and other attorneys wouldn't spot them.

Everyone knew how judgemental legal professionals could be. It wasn't until she made partner at Mackenzie and Co, specialising in family law, that she started to expand the designs outwards—chest and shoulders first, her sides and torso, and now her arms.

She knew her body art wasn't everyone's cup of tea. She could see the side-eye some people gave her when she was at the pool sometimes—some of the older women looking at her with disdain, or even disgust, while the younger women looked at her in awe and with disbelief. The looks became even more obvious when she was by the pool in the spa area, and toting one of her more outrageous bikinis or swimming costumes.

Well, sod them, Ruby thought, *it's their issue, not mine.* I bet they would never realise that she was the same person when gowned up in the courtroom. Apart from hair dyed to match her name, she looked the same as all the other wigs and could hold her own against any of them. Ink or no ink, she was a damned good lawyer.

There was always one person that she could guarantee would set more tongues wagging about how many tattoos they had and what they looked like—and that was her boyfriend, Kyle. They had met at a tattoo convention at the Hightown Arena just over 2 years ago, when she had stopped to watch one of the live-action stands. One of the world's most acclaimed tattoo artists, Jacob Drakonsson, was performing his magic in person. She had only seen his work online before, so she wanted to get a good view of the genius at work.

It helped that the guy, whose butt he was casually tattooing with a complex geometrical black-and-fade design, was quite frankly the hottest guy she had ever laid eyes on, and that wasn't just because of his perfectly formed behind. He was face down on the artist's couch, with his head turned towards the crowd that had gathered, when all of a sudden, his eyes met hers, and she felt she had been struck down by a bolt of lightning.

His eyes were a piercing shade of blue that looked almost unnatural—a kind of bright topaz that was luminescent, so magnetic that for a second, she couldn't tear her gaze away.

The crowd around her was quite content to keep staring at his perfectly formed glutes, slowly and painstakingly being enhanced by the quill of ink buzzing back and forth across his skin, but she couldn't tear herself away from his stare. It was only when someone in the crowd shouted to him to ask a question about his tattoos that he dropped his gaze away from her and politely addressed the audience member.

Ruby got a hold of herself as her cheeks flamed, feeling as if for the first time in her life that someone had looked into her soul. As she turned to walk away, flustered at what she was feeling and embarrassed to be caught staring so long at a guy that, quite frankly, was probably quite used to all sorts of female attention, he called out, 'Stop.'

She turned back, confused—he couldn't possibly be talking to her?

'Yeah, you, the beautiful one with the bright red hair!'

Their eyes met as she turned back towards the stage, embarrassed to be singled out in front of such a large crowd, and conscious now of people either side of her nudging one another and looking over at her. Ruby blushed even deeper. He gave her a reassuring smile from his place, prone on the table.

'I don't bite, honestly. Come a bit closer, I just want to say hello.' He slowly reached out his left hand to the side as Jacob continued to work.

Ruby edged closer, consciously aware of the onlookers earwigging on their conversation, evidently keen to hear what he wanted to say to her, but too intrigued not to take one more step forward so she was in reaching distance of him.

'I'm Kyle,' he smiled, holding out his hand for her to shake. 'What's your name?'

'Ruby.' She took his hand, that gripped hers gently but firmly, as he continued to look straight up at her.

'So, Ruby,' he continued in his soft Irish accent, 'as you can see, I'm a little incapacitated at the moment, but if you're staying until closing, would you do me the honour of meeting me in the bar for a quick drink?' He continued to hold her hand, gently squeezing to urge on her reply; electric sparks flew up her arm.

'Oh, um, I need to check in with my friend,' she remembered nervously, looking around for Angelica, who had brought her there that morning and who, in the space of 3 minutes, she had completely forgotten existed. 'I'm getting a lift with her, so not sure about the timings.'

She knew in that minute that there was nowhere else she would rather be than agreeing to meet this guy, but that she couldn't let her friend down. But then, as she looked up again to search the crowd, Angelica appeared to her right.

'Of course she can bloody meet you!' she grinned at her mate. 'There is plenty for me to look at here. You take all the time in the world,' she added as she gave Ruby's shoulder a friendly bump.

'Well, that's settled then.' Kyle had looked at her again. 'You've seen mine, so later, you have to show me yours.' And his face split into a huge and stunning grin, and he let out a massive guffaw of laughter. That was when Ruby knew she was hooked.

'What are you grinning about, Rubes?' Paulo's husky Spanish accent brought her back to reality. 'There is no way in the world you are smiling like how you say it, "Cheshire Cat", when I'm dragging a tat gun down that bit on your arm.' He looked at her in mild confusion.

'Well, you're definitely right about that, Paulo!' she exclaimed. 'There is no way any human being would find this amusing, no matter how stunning the results.' She contorted her head back and round to get a glimpse at his handiwork. 'I was just actually thinking back to when Kyle and I met, and my first impression of him.'

Paulo and Kyle had met on a number of occasions now, and the guys had got on well. The fact that they were both covered in intricate designs had helped to cement a burgeoning friendship. They also moved in some of the same circles—on the edge of the biker scene and at tattoo conventions.

'I was going to ask about Kyle,' he hesitated, 'and you, actually.' Paulo stopped the gun for a moment and moved round to face her. 'There's another convention coming up soon, and they're looking for tattoo models to catwalk and also sit and chat to some of the punters. I thought both of you would be fantastic.'

Paulo moved out of her eyeline as he started to replenish the ink well, ready for the next set of lines. He knew that despite Ruby having the most amazing works of art all over her body, she was still fairly private about how and when she showed them off.

She had confided in him about many things over the years. The hours spent sat in his chair in close proximity gave her the security she needed to talk to him about her career, and how she wanted to keep the two halves of her life separate from one another. He knew she was proud of her success as a lawyer, but she didn't want her potential clients or other legal professionals seeing her real self. He moved back round to face her, her head dipped and brow furrowed in concentration. She knew he wouldn't suggest her appearing at the show lightly.

'Ah, I don't know, Paulo. I'm just not sure the wider world is ready for me yet. The last time Kyle did one of those things, it got picked up on social media, and the next thing, he's got a shed load of followers and people interested in his business, booking him in to do their kitchens just to take a gawp at him!' Ruby rushed her answer, then hesitated again as she shook her head.

'No, it's not for me. You know I can't risk any of my clients seeing me like that. You can imagine how that would go down. There's no way my credibility would stand up when I'm in court if they all knew what was underneath all those sensible, boring robes and that fucking wig.

'Kyle can parade up and down in his budgie smugglers and let the ladies drool all over him, and I will stay safely at the back of the crowd, planning my next piece of art.' Ruby gave Paulo a reassuring smile. 'But thanks for asking. It's nice to know that you think I could. That's enough for me.'

'Any time, Ruby,' he patted her gently on the shoulder and inclined his head towards her, before switching to what could only be called a mischievous grin. 'Well, if you're not going to let me show off my handiwork on you at the show, the least you can do is let me take some pics just of your arm for my website?' he asked hopefully, trying to keep the disappointment out of his voice.

He would love Ruby to feel confident enough and empowered to own the two sides of herself and fiercely claim it. He knew Kyle would too, but he didn't want to press the issue. Maybe one day she would feel able to.

'Oh, go on then,' chuckled Ruby. 'Just keep my face out of it!' She laughed as he wandered off to grab his phone, grinning to himself that even this was a little breakthrough, and also that this new post of the delicately entangled vines, flowers and berries he was outlining—clambering up the back of her arm and over her shoulder—was definitely going to get him a few more followers when he posted it later that day.

7
6 Months Ago
July, Carolyn

'Urgh,' Carolyn groaned. It was a typical Sunday—the twins were running riot around the house, getting sticky fingers over everything. She had failed to grab them both with wet wipes after they had finished stuffing their faces with pancakes and maple syrup, and now there were handprints all over the whitewashed walls up the stairs.

Carolyn peered at her tired reflection in the mirror and sighed. Here she was again, alone on the weekend with two unruly 10-year-olds, who needed constant supervision to prevent them from starting World War Three, or smashing each other over the head with whatever latest electronic device their dad had bought them.

Carolyn peered at her sallow skin in the mirror and picked absentmindedly at a spot that had emerged on her bloated face. She really needed some kind of makeover. Her mousy hair was showing streaks of grey again, and it needed cutting back into some resemblance of a bob. She needed a facial and her eyebrows waxing—in fact, scratch that, she needed a full-on facelift!

Opening the medicine cabinet, she reached in. Sticking her head under the tap, she swallowed down a batch of paracetamol and ibuprofen. She had known that the second bottle of Pinot last night was a mistake even as she uncorked it, but what else was there to do? Stuck at home with nowhere to go and a husband working away yet again.

He hadn't even bothered to call last night at his normal time to talk to her and the twins, yet according to his Instagram, he had apparently still found time to play poker with his buddies, so he must have been somewhere with Wi-Fi. Yeah, well, she wasn't stupid. She knew the signs.

He was making it pretty damn obvious that he didn't want to come back from whatever exotic country he was currently working in. He could quite easily come home and use his perfectly good study to catalogue and write up all the specimens he had collected, but the truth was, he clearly didn't want to. To be fair, she couldn't blame him. She was hardly something to come home to. He had made that perfectly clear to her the last time.

She had tried, when he was back for those few months, to be the wife he seemed to want her to be. She had been attentive, had got her hair done, dug out her trainers and signed back up to spin classes, cooked healthy and nutritious meals that the kids complained about incessantly, and even got herself waxed, and yet it still wasn't enough.

It had been years since he had looked at her with any ounce of the lust and desire that used to be the mainstay of their relationship. She remembered how he used to come up behind her when she was cooking and smooth his hands firmly over her hips, before groping her ass as he whispered in her ear what he planned to do to her later, when the kids were in bed.

Sometimes he couldn't even wait, such was his desire for her. There had been that one time when the twins were in their highchairs at the kitchen island, making a mess with spaghetti hoops, when he had dragged her away from the risotto she was stirring into the hallway and pushed her face down across the hall table.

She remembered how shocked and conflicted she had felt, halfway between being so incredibly turned on that this delicious man wanted her so much that he literally couldn't wait a moment longer, and then scared that she couldn't see what the twins were doing. Could they choke on the food she had just put in front of them? Was the dinner burning on the stove? Would the smoke detector go off? Josh clearly didn't have any of this on his mind as he lifted her dress and dragged her panties to the side before furiously expending his desire.

Luckily, that day it turned out that the only damage done was an unsightly mess of half-eaten food on the floor, two beautiful children adorned with orange smiles, sauce spread liberally across both their faces and giggling at one another, and a slight singe to the bottom of what would have been a delicious asparagus risotto.

Yes, she still felt the stirring of desire when she thought about times past, but mostly she felt apathy—that, and extreme tiredness. She looked up at the mirror again. She could fix this; she just had to pull herself together. If her future was going to contain any happiness, she needed first to be happy with herself.

She walked out onto the landing and gingerly picked her way down the wide, curved staircase, wiping the sticky handprints as she went. She walked down the parquet floor of the hallway and into the large open-plan kitchen diner, admiring the bi-folds that opened out onto their 100-foot garden. This beautiful Victorian house hadn't come cheap, and yet here it was, looking like a bomb had hit it.

Plates were piled in the sink, the second wine bottle lolled on its side on the draining board, the last drops dripping across the white marble, a block of dried-up cheddar cheese sat sadly on the cheeseboard, and cracker crumbs dotted the worktop and floor. A pile of laundry spewed half in and half out of a linen basket that hadn't quite made it to the utility room, and there was a pile of kids' boots in a jumbled mess by the back door, crusting the floor with flecks of mud and leaves.

God, she was a slut. She couldn't even keep on top of the house when she didn't even work. Josh was right—she was an utterly shit wife and didn't deserve what was given to her on a plate. Carolyn reached for the orange juice in the fridge, and without bothering to dirty yet another glass, took a huge swig, shuddering as the liquid hit the back of her throat. Replacing the carton, she reached for her marigolds and heard the first screech of the day.

'Muuummm, mummy, Charlie kicked my doggy teddy,' followed by another squeal as Amber retaliated by either kicking or hitting her brother.

'Will you two pack it in?' she yelled as she stomped back up the stairs. Seriously, was there ever any respite with twins?

'Right, that's it. If you want to start this early in the morning with bad behaviour, there is no way on earth I'm taking you to swimming, and then there will be no kids club later!' To which she was rewarded with deathly silence. She already knew there was no way she was keeping up this threat. The only peace she got was while the little monsters were under someone else's charge at the Little Sparks Club. Yet another thing she was bad at as a mum and wife, she berated herself. She was never any good at consistency and discipline.

When it finally went quiet, she went back to her tidying up, waiting for the next crash or yell to punctuate the morning. At least when they were occupied on scooters with Aaron Sparks' "sparkler crew" or on a dinosaur hunt in the kiddies' area of the club, she could meet the ladies for a well-needed catch-up. It must have been at least two weeks since they had had a catch-up in the sauna.

Her body almost physically throbbed in anticipation of a large iced latte in a heatproof cup, the hot slats of cedar warming her body and the relief of 2 hours away from her beautiful but demanding offspring. She also needed an hour or so with the rest of her committee to sort out the last few bits for the family summer fun day.

Why the hell did she think she could hold down a job when she couldn't even get to grips with her home life and volunteering? She let out another deep sigh, letting her head fall forward until her chin rested on her chest, screwing her eyes shut for a few seconds.

'Two minutes, kids. Get your shit together and get in the bloody car!'

8
6 Months Ago
July, Sauna

As was her habit, Carolyn came crashing into the sauna just after 4 pm, slamming the door behind her and plopping down heavily onto the lower slats in her usual spot. She hitched her legs up and swung them round, pointing her feet towards Ruby, who was sat opposite the door.

'You ok, Carolyn? You look a little flustered.' Kira sat up from where she had been reclining above her on the top shelf, frowning down at her friend.

'Josh came home last night,' she grimaced, pushing her fringe back so it stuck up like a cockatoo.

Ruby made a silent "O" with her mouth, which immediately turned into a grimace as she turned to look at her friend.

'Josh?' Kira looked down at Carolyn to Ruby, and back again, clearly puzzled.

'Carolyn's husband,' Ruby confirmed as Kira raised her eyebrows, questioning with her eyes why this would be a problem.

She had obviously heard Carolyn complaining a number of times about how hard it was trying to do everything practically as a single mum, so thought she would be glad to have an extra pair of hands to help. It was only last week Carolyn had poured her heart out again over coffee, saying she was worried about Charlie's behaviour and how much her mum was relying on her now that her dad had been diagnosed with Parkinson's.

She had grown fond of Carolyn's tales of the twins and their cunning antics, like the time Carolyn regaled them with how Amber had convinced her teacher that she had chickenpox, by stealing her mum's old Mac lip liner and strategically dotting her body with "spots", and pretending to be feverish and itchy, having googled the symptoms. It was only when said spots started to wash off in a bath of calamine lotion that Carolyn realised she had been thoroughly duped.

Or the time when Charlie had hidden every pair of his shoes by chucking them down the coal chute, in the pantry of their old Victorian house, so that he had nothing to wear on his feet to trumpet practice. Then, when Carolyn reminded him that as a twin he had the same size feet as his sister, and that a pair of her sparkly ballet pumps would fit him just fine, he eventually came clean. The time it took to retrieve 11 pairs of assorted size 5's meant that he was too late to get to his lesson anyway, so from his point of view, mission accomplished.

However, Kira was still to meet the mysterious Josh. In all the time she had now known Carolyn, she hadn't seen him around Sparks with her. She knew that he worked away, and then when he was back in the UK, he travelled a lot. She remembered Carolyn mentioning that he trained at another gym, so didn't really have a need to venture into Sparks.

But from the way that Carolyn had landed so heavily on the bench, and the look of exhaustion in her friend's eyes, she wondered what kind of person he might be if she wasn't completely thrilled that he had returned home. Surely an extra pair of hands to help with the "little monsters", as she fondly thought of the twins, would be a good thing?

'Where's he been, Carolyn? I know you said he works away, but I wasn't sure what sort of places he travels to,' Kira asked gently, keen to show an interest but also intrigued as to why Carolyn seemed even more flustered than usual.

'Where do I start?' The air seemed to deflate straight out of the normally animated and bubbly Carolyn, as she raked her already sweaty hair back out of her face before blurting in a resigned tone. 'This time was South America; last time was Africa or Asia. He's highly successful,' she said with a hint of scorn as Kira looked on, impressed.

'Yes, my husband is an incredibly handsome, sexy, intelligent, gifted botanist and scientist, who travels all over the world earning a fortune. He keeps me in wine, the kids in shoes and a roof over my head. He wasn't supposed to be back until at least Wednesday, but in his usual way has decided to surprise me and keep me on my toes by coming back early.'

'However, what I don't normally tell many people about this seemingly wonderful husband of mine is that, despite appearances, when you have spent any time in his company, it becomes patently obvious that he is also a misogynistic, arrogant bully.' She pulled an exaggerated smile as she shrugged her shoulders, looking down at her hand resting on her knee, where she was squeezing too hard.

'Oh.' Kira tried to school her face into a neutral place, and not open her eyes too wide as she looked between Carolyn and Ruby in shock, Ruby leaning in gently to squeeze Carolyn's left foot.

'Oh,' Kira said again, at a loss as to what other words would be suitable to answer such a blunt statement.

'Yes, "oh", exactly,' Carolyn sighed again.

Carolyn knew that her revelations would have been a shock to Kira. However, she felt comfortable enough with her now to be brutally honest about the shortcomings in her marriage. If Kira wanted to get close to her and support her as she seemed to, and to grow into a friendship group with these women, then she had to be let into the inner sanctum and let in on a few facts about Carolyn's life.

'Take last night for example. I had no idea when to expect him back. He's been away about 8 weeks, and I've only had sporadic contact with him whenever he's allegedly near some sort of satellite phone. However, I know that they carry those things with them wherever they go, so that's a load of bullshit, and he's been on social media,' Carolyn didn't mince her words.

'So, I wait and wait and think, "Oh, perhaps he's coming back sometime next week and will actually let me know what his plan is", you know, just so I've got time to sort the house out and let the kids know. But as usual, I don't hear anything. Then maybe I think, "Perhaps I've got the date or the month wrong?" He's always a little vague about these things, but I remember him saying no later than the 10th, so it must be this week.'

'So I'm just carrying on as normal, thinking that he will call; and then suddenly, literally as I was just about to leave my parents' house yesterday afternoon, the phone rings and its him saying he's landed at Heathrow and can I come and get him? Like, right now!'

She was indignant now, warming to her subject. 'You would think that after all these years of marriage, he would have the decency to call? I mean, I don't expect regular updates from the jungle, but just a message to at least say when he's coming back. But no, not my selfish bastard of a husband. He just likes to catch me on the hop, so that he can then complain and pick at me about my sloppy ways until he reduces me to a fucking mess.'

Kira looked on in shock, as Carolyn covered her face with both her hands and let out a muffled scream as they waited for her to continue.

'To be fair,' sighed Carolyn, 'once I'd picked him up last night, I didn't even really see him. I'd dropped the kids at Francesca's down the road, so it was late when we got back from the airport. So, by the time I'd got them to bed—after he'd wound them up and got them all excited—he'd gone to sleep in the guest room. I was up and out before he was even awake this morning—thought I'd let him sleep off his jet lag.

'I've been back and tidied up since then, and he was already packing his gym bag to go and meet some of his mates, so didn't seem to mind me coming here to meet you girls. He was even going to pick the kids up from wilderness club and get them McDonald's as a surprise this afternoon.'

'There, see, maybe it will be different this time? Sounds like he's already making an effort.' Ruby looked hopeful, always trying to gee her friend up when she could tell she was spiralling. 'Didn't you say last time he came back from a long trip, he had actually brought you some lovely perfume from Duty Free and presents for the kids? I remember you telling me about those gorgeous bracelets made from cowrie shells from the Gilli islands?'

At the mention of the cowrie shell bracelet, Kira's ears pricked up. Before she could stop herself, her body gave an involuntary shiver as she recalled her ex giving her a bracelet like that, and how she had treasured it so much that she had worn it every day, until the chlorine from the pool had eventually eaten its way through the thin leather strap holding it together.

She remembered how she was going to put it in her memory box until she could work out a way to repair it, knowing that he wouldn't be happy that it wasn't on her wrist anymore. But that had been around the time things had started to get weird. The thought of that time in her life brought Kira's arms out in goosebumps, despite the searing heat of the sauna. It took her a minute to realise that she had tuned out what Carolyn had been saying.

'So, I've made a decision.' Carolyn sat up straighter now, visibly recovered from her outburst and back to her assertive self. 'I'm going give it this summer and then, if we get to October half term and he's upping his game and being a bit nicer to us all, then I'm going to stick with him. If not, he's gone!'

'That's a massive decision, Carolyn,' Ruby interrupted her flow.

'Yeah, I know it is. But I have to be certain that there's some muscle memory of what our relationship once was, and that he's interested in finding it again. It's lonely in my marriage at the moment, and I would prefer to be on my own than with someone who doesn't love me,' she sighed. 'It's not all bad, I guess. He's actually a great dad when he's around, and I know the kids would hate us to leave and then lose the house.'

'He's probably right, you know? I've just got to try harder—you know, get back in the gym, get my lazy ass out of bed earlier in the morning to make sure things at home are under control, give him weekly blowjobs.' She started to smirk; there was no way Carolyn could sustain a depressing narrative for long without either slipping into profanities or smut. 'You know what they say about giving regular blowjobs?' she said with a wink. 'They are the key to world peace!'

Kira let out a gentle guffaw as Ruby sighed and raised her eyebrows—typical of Carolyn to drop a bombshell that she might be considering leaving her husband, then joke about sex. 'Well, Carolyn, if that's true, then perhaps a few more world leaders need to get with the programme for the sake of all humanity,' she smiled down at her friend. 'In the meantime, are there any more updates on the summer family day?'

Carolyn beamed at Ruby. 'It's all perfectly under control! The programme is sorted. The only thing left to see is if your lovely Sam would lifeguard while the others took a break. If he could also help sort out the chill-out music with Sarah, that would be incredible. That is, if the two of you are still a thing? You haven't really dished the dirt on that to us yet.' She leant forward as if trying to urge more information out of Kira.

'Well, there's not much to tell yet,' she blushed lightly as she looked down at her hands, where she was nervously playing with her teaspoon. 'We've had a couple of coffees together, and I'm meeting him at the cinema this Friday, and then we'll see where it goes from there.'

'Christ almighty, Kira!' Carolyn couldn't help herself. 'I thought you younger ones were supposed to be the next liberated generation. You could have jumped his bones by now at least and told us all about it!' She was shocked at her friend's restraint. 'So, has he made any sort of move on you yet?'

'Carolyn!' admonished Ruby. 'Seriously, sorry, Kira. She always gets like this when there's a guy involved. I remember telling her about Kyle, and she proceeded to blow up my WhatsApp for the next 4 hours, until I finally replied to tell her to bugger off and I would fill her in when I next saw her.'

'Well, can you blame me? You sent me a pic of what looked like a muscle-bound walking *etch-a-sketch* with the caption "Would you?" to me, and then went radio silent! What was I supposed to do?' She was affectionate in her indignation, nudging Ruby and then turning her attention back to Kira.

'Well, at least tell us if he kissed you yet?'

'I can confirm that Sam is the perfect gentleman. He knows that I want to take things slowly and that, with everything that happened last year, it takes me some time to trust people. He held my hand over the table last week and then pecked me on the cheek to say goodbye, and that's as much info as you are getting right now!' It was Kira's turn to smirk now.

'You will just have to wait for anything juicier than that, Carolyn. But in the meantime, yes, I'm sure he would be very happy to help on the family fun day. In fact, he's coming on shift shortly, so I'll go and ask him.' Kira bent to pick up her bright green Sparks water bottle. 'Ladies, it has been a pleasure as always, and I will see you Friday in the sauna, if not before.' She stood up to leave.

'Wait!' Carolyn's hand reached out at lightning speed to grab firmly onto her wrist. 'Just one last detail before you go? You never said which cheek he kissed.' As she proceeded to crack up and hold her sides in hysterics, it was Kira's turn to roll her eyes as she left her friend congratulating herself on yet another wisecrack.

9
6 Months Ago
July, Kira

The sun was already warm as it streamed through the Velux window above the bed, as Kira unfurled and stretched out her aching limbs, revelling in the fresh coolness of her white cotton sheets, and the feeling of a really good night's sleep after training hard yesterday. There was nothing better than knowing that you had given your all, and hearing that your coach was proud of you and thought that you really did have a chance to win the Masters this season.

It was utter bliss to have someone believe in her and understand how hard she had worked to get to this point, even with all the setbacks of the pandemic and then the shitshow that was last year. It finally felt as if she was able to give herself over to real pleasure, and not just continue her default position of always trying to please everyone else.

First, it was her sister, who, as her twin, she had felt unwavering loyalty to. Joanna, being older by 10 minutes, had always had the upper hand in their relationship and had always been the more successful. Then it was her parents, trying to fill the void that Joanna left as the favourite when she died. And then, last year, it was him.

Kira had always felt, growing up, that she was lagging behind—happy to let her twin have the limelight and to be the sidekick or best friend instead of being in the lead role. Whatever Joanna wanted to do, then Kira would follow, even if it was something she had no personal interest in, or no natural ability to do.

It was like that time when they were 10 years old and Joanna had decided that they were going to be scientists, insisting that their parents scrape together money to send them to science camp over the summer holidays, and buy them a microscope to share, when all Kira really wanted was the latest My Little Pony, or some more outfits for the Barbies that Joanna felt were already too babyish for them. So, Kira had shut up and put up, always afraid that her beloved twin would find someone more interesting and enthusiastic to play with instead of her.

Kira thought back to the time when Joanna insisted that they have their hair cut short in a pixie style, as it would make them look older, and they were more likely to get served at the bar at Butlins on their family holiday when they were 16.

She calmly pushed Kira down into the hairdresser's seat and explained in great detail to the stylist exactly what look "they" were going for, before seeing the end result on Kira and then calmly announcing that she had changed her mind, and perhaps that style wasn't that much in fashion after all. And, "oh so sorry" Kira, but she was going to keep her long, luscious locks, while Kira had to spend the next few frustrating months growing out a hairstyle she knew really didn't suit her.

It was around that time that Joanna had started going out with Freddie, one of the cool guys in their 6th form college, knowing full well that he had originally been interested in Kira. Joanna shrugged it off when Kira actually had the temerity to mention this quietly one evening, when they were curled up next to each other, reading their coursework books.

Not only did Joanna casually brush off the pain she had caused her sister, but to add insult to injury, told Kira that, 'He just doesn't like your hair, Kira. He has no idea what made you cut it all off.' And then, 'He says my hair is one of my best features.'

She failed to see the look of crestfallen disbelief on the mirror image of her face looking back at her. Despite their unbreakable twinly bond, there was no ignoring Joanna's ability to self-serve at her younger twin's expense.

And yet still, Kira pondered, would she have such a successful career now if it wasn't for Joanna? She had been the one who pushed them both to keep fit and active as a way to attract boys. She had made them take all forms of yoga, Pilates, and then later, running, swimming and cycling to build up to triathlons—which, of course, Joanna excelled at until she became sick. Once Joanna had gone, it felt like the only thing that could still connect them was the drive to achieve something Jo couldn't manage to get over the line in her sadly too-short life.

Kira felt that she had to keep her promise to her sister, made in their last conversation as Joanna faded in front of her eyes on the hospice bed set up in her parents' living room: to be better, to try harder, to push, push, push to get to the top of her game and do something her sister would never be able to do.

Kira had worked hard to get to where she was now. Not only was her coach saying she could finally reach the top of her age group, but she had finally found herself a lovely group of friends to champion her and make her want to prove what she could do. Even her fledgling relationship with Sam was making her feel good and positive for the future.

Sure, there wasn't the instant belly flutter of excitement every time she saw him like she had had with her ex, but he was respectful and kind. Butterflies and palpitations of instant attraction were thrilling, but she was proof of where that kind of cataclysmic attraction could all go horribly wrong.

As she lay back on her bed, contemplating the day ahead, she thought back over the last few years. After 2 years of unsettled times and craziness in the triathlon calendar because of the pandemic, things had finally got back on track. Meets were planned, athletes were prepped and primed and ready to go, and Kira had something to prove.

She had been training hard over the winter in the gym between classes, had been taking the right supplements, getting coaching that nearly bankrupted her and was concentrating on her nutrition. This was her time. She had to get placed for the nationals this season; it was now or never. She remembered it was just at the start of the first meet of the season that it happened. It was almost surreal.

There she was, one minute, checking her gels in her running belt, when she felt the hairs on the back of her neck prick up—an almost sixth sense of someone's eyes on her, drawing her gaze up and across the crowd of athletes limbering up. And there he was.

As soon as her eyes had locked with his, there had been no going back. She had felt the adrenalin in her blood spike immediately—not because she was about to set off for the race, but because of the magnetic pull of their eyes across the crowded car park. It was the way that it seemed like he had always expected to see her there and was just waiting for her to notice, even though they had never met before. And she noticed.

It was hard not to—his bright blue-green eyes, the colour of sea glass, framed by long dark lashes; a cut jaw with a sprinkling of day-old stubble; a white smile—teeth not straight enough to make him pretty, but slightly quirked to one side, as if there was some secret that he knew and that was amusing him; his dark hair cut short and close around the sides, but swept slightly longer on top.

She didn't need to trace her eyes below his neckline to know that he had *that body*—the one that only came with hours and hours of hard, committed discipline in all 3 events of a triathlon. Tall, with pure, toned muscle, but with the broad chest and shoulders and narrow hips from hours spent in the pool.

And that was it. Her race was over before it had even begun. She had spiked too soon, lost her momentum, her mind clouded by this stranger and that intense look. Her mind was distracted all the way round the course, wondering, would she see him again? Would he be at the meet catch-up later around the campfire, when participants actually let their hair down and had a few beers? Would he speak to her?

That alone was enough to get her nearly stumbling into a ditch on the 10k run, as once again her concentration lapsed and she barely placed in the top 10. But she didn't care. This was the one and only time she had felt this uncontrollable attraction, and she hadn't been about to let it go.

She swung her legs out of bed and stood, stretching her arms skywards to ease the tension in her shoulders that always crept back in every time she thought about him. Grabbing her gym bag, she emptied the contents onto the floor, ready to re-pack for the day ahead. Puzzled, she rummaged through both the end pockets again when she couldn't find her headphones or her Sparks water bottle—just typical! She was always losing things at the gym.

She must ask Sue when she saw her if there was any sign of them in lost property. The problem was, everyone had the same bottle. They seemed to give them out right, left and centre. She must remember to buy herself a new, non-branded one. The distraction of her lost items was enough to shake her out of the reverie she was in danger of falling into.

Shaking herself again and then curling over to create a down dog pose, she eased herself through her morning stretches before jumping in the shower. Despite her reservations about working at Sparks, she now loved her life. She just wished she could turn back the clock to the day that she met him, and walk away from him, and prevent the hell that followed.

10
5 Months Ago
August, Carolyn

The day of the summer party dawned, and for the first time ever in the history of summer events in the UK, the sun was actually shining, and so far, everything was running to schedule. Outside, next to the heated pool, hours and hours of preparation had been undertaken: balloons had been inflated, bunting erected, DJ booth installed, ice ordered and BBQ food bought by the ton. It was all going so smoothly that Carolyn had that wary feeling in the pit of her stomach—that she was just waiting for something to go wrong.

She crossed her fingers that the sense of foreboding was more to do with the responsibility she felt towards Sparks, as the head committee member for events, rather than a premonition of anything untoward. She hoped that the sky would remain blue, the staff and volunteers might actually undertake the duties she had carefully assigned them without complaint, and that the day would go by without injury or disaster.

She and the rest of the committee took their duties very seriously. She didn't care that her home life was a veritable car wreck, as long as the events she organised that fell under public scrutiny went smoothly and went down in history as fun-filled but professional.

Over the next week, she wanted to hear at least five stories of hangovers and missed Pilates classes. She wanted an anecdote about yummy mummies getting sunburnt or dodgy tan lines that spoilt their specially curated golden skin, because they had drunk too much "sparky punch" and their "idiot" husbands had failed to wake them from an afternoon nap. She wanted to hear about at least one corporate dad getting caught busting all the moves to the Macarena when they thought no one was looking.

Yes, the day was looking fine. All that was needed now was for her to adorn the waiting crew with Hawaiian leis, and to change into her new tropical print swimsuit and sarong she had treated herself to. She had already bossed Kira, begrudgingly, into upgrading from her usual solid black racerback swimsuit into a bright red string-top bikini and white Daisy Dukes.

The girl had a magnificent figure, and if there was a day and place to show it off, it was today. She looked hot but still managed to look like she wanted to crawl back into the locker room, if anyone so much as looked at her. Ruby, on the other hand, was in her element.

Away from work and from people who may spot her on the legal circuit, she couldn't wait to show off her latest tattoo creations and the world's brightest bikini top, adorned with flowers, palm trees and coconuts—carefully constructed to support her ample assets—and a three-tiered cerise pink party skirt. The Coco Cabana look was topped off with parrot-in-hoop earrings and a magnificent broad-rimmed yellow sun hat with a blue band and a feather. She was a veritable walking rainbow.

It was 12 noon, and the first families had started to arrive, the earliest one claiming their enviable spaces on the sunbeds on the front line of the pool and settling in for the day. There were the "yummys" in their Sea Folly and Hunza G designer bikinis, waiting for husbands to slather their shoulders with Ambre Solair, and looking for an opportunity to top up tans won from days spent relaxing on yachts on the Cote de'Azure.

There were a few of the more mature ladies, showing off their deep brown, crinkly decolletage, from even more years honing their tans from winters in the southern hemisphere.

Then there were the guys—those with the dad bods taking advantage of the bar in their brightly coloured board shorts, paunches straining against ill-matching Hawaiian shirts; then the hot dads, who spent more time looking in mirrors than at their wives and girlfriends, tanned and toned guns covered with tight-fitting T's, sporting short shorts and Ray-Ban aviators with dentist-whitened smiles.

Fewer and far between were what Carolyn thought of as the "normal" people—those families who didn't go to Sparks to brag or pose, those families that saw this place as a refuge, a chance to meet with like-minded people and to possibly lose a few pounds at the same time. The sort of people who sent their kids to Sparks kids club and met in the café bar for a cream-covered hot chocolate on a cold day, or a glass of wine on a hot day.

She really didn't mind which clientele showed up for the family fun day though. It was all about the numbers and raising money for charity. It was also about people having some fun and letting their hair down midway through the summer holidays, which most of them really needed. She chuckled to herself as she thought about the exception to this rule—the yummy set with their live-in nannies, where looking after their own offspring for one day was probably more traumatic than fun.

As she looked around at the patio area, Carolyn reflected again on how lucky she was to have this—that without Josh, there was no way she would be able to afford to bring the kids here and enjoy everything the club had to offer. She had spent so many fun times in this place. She loved being able to walk straight out from the spa area and the heat of the sauna or hot tub, and straight into the crystal-clear, cool water of the 25-metre outdoor pool.

As she buzzed between families, greeting many of them by name, she felt a feeling of contentment at being the one to make this happen. The pool was sparkling in the sunlight, and laughter floated on the warm breeze over the dulcet tones of Jack Johnson. It wouldn't be long until the tranquillity was disturbed when the pool activities started, and those taking advantage of the outdoor poolside bar started to get more into the party spirit.

Well, there was nothing wrong in encouraging a bit more of that. She chuckled to herself as she headed over to where the team were hanging out by the bar—might as well get the party well and truly started!

'Right, James, crank up the rum in that punch. Sam, stick on that '80s mix for now until we get the inflatables in the pool. Nick, if you can start with sausages and burgers first, then chicken kebabs and ribs can go on later.' She issued orders left, right and centre, happy to be in charge.

'Crikey, Carolyn, this looks amazing!' Ruby arrived next to her, cradling a large plastic cocktail glass full of blue and orange liquid, a small parasol balanced in the top skewering a cherry and slice of pineapple.

'What the heck is that? Looks delicious, though.' Carolyn reached her head forward and, without waiting for a reply, nabbed the straw between her teeth and gave a long suck.

'Carolyn!' Rubes shook her head, moving the glass away and out of her friend's reach. 'Go and see James if you want a cocktail. Seriously, he's rocking his best Tom Cruise behind the bar.' Ruby stuck the straw back between her teeth before Carolyn could help herself again.

'Jees Louise! Take a look at him. He does look very Tom Cruise; you're not wrong.' She gave a salacious grin. 'I mean, Christ, have you seen that ass in those tight shorts!' Carolyn, as usual, was unable to take anything seriously. 'What? Rubes, you can't tell me you haven't looked. That white smile, whiter t-shirt and those mixing skills—that's why I got him on cocktails in the first place. If anyone's going to get all the ladies plastered, it's him. We should be raking in the dosh by closing time.'

She rubbed her hands together in glee as she buzzed off in the direction of the bar. Ruby didn't have the heart to moan at her yet again for objectifying the male staff. She knew Carolyn meant no harm and saved her smutty comments purely for the ears of her girlfriends.

She shook her head as she realised, a little too late, that she too was appreciating James' assets and not his skills as a bar tender. It was true that James was pure bliss to look at. However, she really didn't need to ogle him when she had her own gorgeous hunk arriving any minute.

'Ah, there you are.' She jumped as Kyle crept up behind her, sneaking an arm around her waist and leaning in to give her neck a quick smooch. 'You do realise that if we don't get to the sunbeds in the next 3 minutes, they are all going to be claimed, and you're going to be moaning all afternoon about having to sit on a chair in the shade?'

She snuggled back into his arms as she reflected how well he knew her. He took her tote from her spare hand and gently guided her towards the last few remaining loungers. She would get settled, then go and look for Kira. She knew her friend was reluctant to be seen in the bikini Carolyn had insisted she buy, when they went shopping together last week, but they both thought it would do her good, and boost her confidence a bit to show off the body she spent so long honing and training.

She would get Kyle to relinquish his lounger in a bit so they could sit together. He could always go and prop up the bar with his gym buddies anyway. She settled in and sighed with contentment as she took another big slug of the cocktail. She would go look for Kira as soon as she finished this drink.

An hour later, Carolyn came back over for a chat, plate laden with hot dogs and burgers, looking for the twins, who had been joining in with kids' club activities on the outdoor tennis courts, and were due back poolside before the inflatable session started.

'You haven't seen Charlie or Amber, have you, Rubes?' she enquired, plopping the plate down on the side table. 'The little monsters better get back here quick before I'm forced to eat all this brown food, when I'm supposed to be being good.'

'Nope, sorry, haven't seen them. Didn't you say Josh was coming today? Maybe he's found them before you?'

'Yes, he's definitely on his way. He was going to do an hour in the gym first before coming down here, and he knows the kids are with the Sparks crew so he didn't need to rush. He's probably getting a beer at the inside bar—not sure cocktails "a la James" are quite his thing.'

The wind seemed to go out of Carolyn's sails as soon as she started talking about her much-absent husband. She was already thinking to herself that at least if he was having few beers and catching up with the lads that he hadn't seen for months, he would be occupied, and she could carry on doing what she needed to do to keep the party going. No doubt he would join her at some point to put on a husbandly display of affection in front of onlookers, demonstrating his prowess in the pool.

There was nothing Josh liked more than an adoring audience of women admiring his golden body, cultivated through hours of hiking through jungles, up mountains, and, when he was home, running circuits or doing endless spin classes. Yes, he would enjoy today, which, in turn, helped her out really. Maybe tomorrow they would have a lie-in and then go get brunch like they used to do— their first full weekend as a family in 3 months.

'I still haven't seen Kira,' Ruby raised her voice over the first bars of Club Tropicana now blasting out of speakers, as Sarah cranked up the tunes. 'I was meant to go look for her, but just couldn't seem to move my lazy ass once I sat down and had drunk this.' She waved the now-empty glass in front of Carolyn's face.

'Is that your second?' Carolyn questioned.

'Fourth, I think!' Ruby's grin was a little lopsided. 'Kyle kept me topped up, but now he's gone for a wander.' She manoeuvred herself into a sitting position, a little wobblier than usual. 'Cripes, Carolyn, what the hell did he put in that drink? My head's already spinning.'

Before her friend had a chance to answer, the music changed to the hard beats of club music, and 50 inflatables were chucked into the pool by the Sparks kids' team, closely followed by a bunch of dive-bombing kids—all eager to claim a giant inflatable flamingo or crocodile.

Ruby swung her legs around next to the lounger.

'Do you think one of us should go look for her?' she shouted over the loud music. 'You know how nervous she gets around big crowds, and she really didn't want to wear that bikini!'

'It's ok. I'll go in a minute.'

'Well, if you're going anyways,' she handed her empty glass to Carolyn, 'be a babe and go and get me a refill, and get yourself one?'

'What about all this food?' Carolyn looked wistfully at the slowly cooling grilled meat wilting on the plate. She glanced at the pool, finally spotting the twins unsuccessfully trying to drown each other. 'And what do I do about the twins? What if they actually do kill each other?'

'Isn't that why you organised all those lifeguards?' She glanced at the yellow-and-red-clad figures dotted around the pool. 'You did that so that you and the other parents could have a laugh today and let your hair down. You need to lead by example!'

She was decisive as she stood up. Putting her hands on the other woman's hips, she turned Carolyn in the direction of James and his multi-coloured delights. 'Refill please. Get one for Kira too. I'm going to get her out of that locker room if it kills me.' Ruby slipped her feet into her pink wedges and headed inside.

11
5 Months Ago
August, Ruby

'Kira? Kira? Come on, babe, where are you?' Ruby weaved her way through bikini-clad bodies and kids chasing each other across the patio to get inside to the café bar.

There didn't seem to be many people around, and definitely no sign of Kira. She turned down the corridor and pushed through into the ladies' locker room, working her way round the changing area to see if she could spot where her friend was hiding, but there really wasn't any sign of her. Unless she'd contorted herself to actually hide inside a locker, she definitely wasn't there, which meant she had to be in the staff room, or worse, she had bottled it and had gone home.

There was nothing for it but to go grab a staff member and see if they would take a peek in the staff room for her. She set off back towards the bar at a quick trot, her pink wedges slapping against the anti-slip floor of the corridor. She had just turned the corner to go and grab Sue from reception, when she collided with a solid wall of man, who immediately put his hands out to steady her.

'Ruth?' The man looked at her with shock, as she took a step back. He removed his hands as she stepped back and straightened her kaftan, she looked up and met his eyes.

It took her a second to focus in the brightness of the hall after being in the dark locker room, and at first, she thought she must be mistaken, but there was no way that those distinctive wide almond eyes, lined with dark lashes, could belong to anyone else. The instinct to run, to flee, to get in her car and drive and not stop was almost overwhelming.

She couldn't quite comprehend what she was seeing—years and years after she had put that chapter of her life behind her, changed her name, changed her appearance in a way in which she thought made her unrecognisable to anyone who knew her as Ruth—and yet, here he was, a vivid reminder of everything about her past that she had left behind, and with good reason.

'Todd? What the fuck?' She instinctively put her hands up to push him further away, back towards the wall, as he started to talk.

'It is you!' His words were inflected with amazement. 'I thought I saw you by the pool earlier, but I couldn't be sure. You look so different. In fact, you look amazing,' he gushed, grinning, clearly pleased to see her after all these years. 'What are you doing here? Do you live locally?'

His South African accent still strong after all these years, the questions rolling off his tongue. He obviously hadn't noticed her instant discomfort.

'Like I said, what the fuck?' Ruby repeated. 'Why, what, um, I mean, why are you here?' She stumbled to form a basic sentence. What the hell was wrong with her? She didn't need to speak to this guy, and she certainly didn't owe him any explanation.

'Actually, forget that. I don't care why you're here, and I really don't want to fucking talk to you, so move.' She shoved the bulk in front of her to one side as she started down the corridor towards the staff room, all thoughts of finding Sue forgotten, as she attempted to get away from the one person she associated with a terrible time in her life. 'Don't even think about following me, and if I were you, I would find myself another sports club as soon as you can, since you are 100% not welcome here,' she spat over her shoulder as Todd kept pace.

'Ruth, seriously, what's wrong? I only wanted to say hi. Christ, I don't know what you think I've done, but I haven't seen you for years. Just talk to me!'

'My name is Ruby!' She spun round to face him, her finger aimed at his broad chest. 'Ok? Ruby!' she hissed. 'So don't be calling me Ruth. I don't know who she is, and I suggest you forget who she was.' She turned again, picking up speed on her march away from him, leaving him standing stock-still and in shock, genuinely bewildered by her reaction.

Ruby was surprised but relieved to find the front desk unmanned as she made her way through the bar and behind the front counter, so that she could hammer on the staff room. 'Kira? Kira!' she hammered again. 'I know you're in there. Let me in!' She was panting, her breath coming in short bursts as she felt her hot face flushed with panic. She just needed Kira to open this door so she could escape before he caught her up.

The door flung open, and there was Kira, staring at her indignantly.

'Ruby, seriously, what's the matter?' Kira shook her head, clearly confused by her friend's flustered appearance and aggressive hammering. 'Is the building on fire or something? I was about to come out and find you all.' She stepped back to let Ruby into the room. Turning, she looked at her friend again and noticed Ruby's flustered appearance and that she was out of breath.

'I was just trying to sort out the playlist on my phone for the water Pilates session later, but the Wi-Fi has been playing up,' she paused. 'Are you ok? You look like you've seen a ghost?' She reached out a tentative hand and smoothed down a tendril of Ruby's hair that had escaped from her banana clip.

Ruby took a steadying gulp of air, calmly composing herself before answering. 'Um, we were worried about you, that's all'

'But why are you so flustered? What's happened?' Kira couldn't help but show her concern. She had never seen Ruby lose her cool like this before. There had to be more to it than the fact than Ruby searching for her.

'No, nothing's wrong, honestly. I've just been all round this club now, looking for you for ages, and I'm a bit out of breath after a few cocktails.' She took another deep breath and plastered on her broadest smile—this was the Ruby they all expected, in control.

'Anyway, now I've found you—and you look amazing—and everyone's waiting for you by the pool, so I've come to get you!' Her words rushed out, hoping that Kira bought into her running round the club searching for her, and didn't ask her too many other questions.

The real explanation and truth was something no one needed to know. She could only hope that Todd had got the message and wouldn't bother her again when she went back out poolside. She needed to find a way to find out if he was a member, or was just tagging along for the family fun day. There was no way she could cope with seeing him here every time she wanted a sauna or a coffee; no way.

'Right, missy, unplug your phone now. Yes, that's it. No, we don't need more tunes; Sarah can sort that. Yes, you look lovely. No, you don't need a t-shirt; the bikini looks stunning.' She linked her friend's arm as Kira took one last look longingly at the safety of the staff room, before allowing Ruby to pull her through the door, letting it slam behind her.

'Twit twoo,' a slow wolf whistle hailed Kira's entrance into the bar, Ruby firmly linking her elbow to stop her wriggling away, colour already rising in Kira's cheeks as they both looked around and saw Sarah, the hench spin instructor, giving Kira the once up and down. 'Well, who would have guessed, hey?' She aimed a wink approvingly at Kira, who she smiled back shyly as they continued walking towards the outdoor patio.

'Better get used to that, my love,' Ruby enthused, patting her arm. 'They won't be able to take their eyes off you by the pool.'

They fought their way through the crowd mingling on the patio in front of the tiki bar, Ruby still holding firm to Kira, her eyes scanning for any sign of Todd and secretly praying he had got the message and left. Ruby led Kira through a sea of people dancing along to *Living on a Prayer*, colourful Hawaiian leis swinging from the necks of the uncool dads playing air guitar, beers held high, until they made it back to the loungers next to the pool.

Kira, seemingly oblivious to the admiring looks she was getting from many of the guys—but also the envious stares from their wives—walked beside her. Ruby shook her head in wonder. If she looked like Kira, she would be flaunting her toned midriff and endless tanned legs for all to see! Her friend really did need to see herself as others saw her.

Ruby continued to scan the pool area anxiously, looking for Todd and hoping to hell that she didn't see him. She swept her eyes over the queue for the BBQ, and then back over to the giant Jenga and Chess sets that had been set up on the kids' lawn tennis area. Nope, not a sign. Thank God, it didn't seem like he was still here.

Perhaps her message had sunk in—that she didn't want to see him, or for him to acknowledge her. However, she still didn't feel like she could relax. She would just have to hope that the alcohol in her Long Island Iced Tea was enough to drown out the anxious feeling creeping up her neck.

'Kira!' Carolyn looked delighted as she spotted them approaching—so much so that she ran forward and reached her arms out to envelope her friend in a tight hug, before drawing her back to take a look at her. 'Yep, she scrubs up just fine!' she beamed. 'What you need now is a cocktail to loosen you up a bit. We'll have you relaxing in no time.' She proffered a fruity-looking pink concoction to Kira's outstretched hand. 'Go on, get your lips around that!'

'Well, maybe just the one,' Kira was hesitant. 'I've got to do the poolside Pilates in a bit, don't forget. I'm already feeling self-conscious. The last thing I need is to mess it up and end up nose-diving into the pool or something, while doing a stretch.' Kira loved a cocktail or two but knew her limits. She didn't want to make an idiot of herself.

'Come on then, Carolyn, hand over the goods!' Ruby reached out her hand to take delivery of the other deliciously strong cocktail, balanced precariously on the table next to Carolyn's lounger, before taking a long suck on the pink straw, her red lipstick leaving its signature red mark as she leant back, smacking her lips.

'Ah, that's better.' She flipped her huge cat's-eye sunglasses back down from her forehead as she sank back down onto the lounger. 'This is the life,' she grinned up at her friends and patted the space next to her.

'Come on, Kira, you can squeeze in next to me,' she said, before turning back to Carolyn. 'Where did Kyle go, babe?'

'I think he said he was grabbing you some of those chicken skewers you like, and a serving of that chocolate gateaux before the kids demolish it. He looks after you, you know,' she smiled indulgently at her friend. 'Unlike my bloody fella,' she grimaced, and pulled her sunglasses out from the front of her tank top, and plunked them firmly back on her face. 'He promised me he would be here today.' Spreading her arms out in front of her, she gestured across the expanse of moving bodies. 'And yet, where is he?' She scanned across the party.

'Well, fuck him! I'm going to enjoy myself, and he can just look after the twins when he arrives, can't he?' she finished, pleased when her friends quietly nodded in agreement. Well, she might as well soak up the rays and have a good time with the girls, if Josh couldn't be bothered to put in an appearance.

12

5 Months Ago
August, Kira

It was funny—Kira reflected as she crouched in the dark at the back of the sauna—that she truly believed that she could run away and he would never find her. She used the breathing techniques her therapist had talked her through to try and slow her heart rate somewhere near back to normal. As she wiped the palms of her hands, that were dripping in sweat, down her drying bikini top, she willed the goosebumps on the back of her neck to go away.

She knew all along that there was inevitably a time in the future where she may bump into him, perhaps at a Tri meet—after all, that was where they had first met—or perhaps in a supermarket or even a bar, but what she hadn't accounted for was seeing him right there today, in her club, her workplace, the place where, with the help of her lovely friends, she had put her life back together and had felt safe.

Kira had known, deep in her bones, that wearing a red bikini was a mistake, that it drew too much attention to her, and in wearing it, she couldn't hide like she usually did at the back of a room or behind her co-workers. She had felt so out of place not wearing her usual sporty leggings and baggy tee—even in her completely unflattering fluorescent running jacket, she often felt invisible.

The bikini basically shouted "look at me". Maybe she should have just got a poster printed and paraded up and down poolside with a loud haler. A shudder ran along her body as she thought back to what had just happened and the sequence of events.

If only she hadn't let Kyle and Ruby persuade her to jump in the pool with them when Sarah had ramped up "Walking on Sunshine". If only she hadn't had that one strong cocktail that had given her instant bravado and a sense that "yes", she could be that girl—the one who jumps around in a swimming pool with 50 other adults splashing each other and laughing, trying to remember and do all the moves to "Saturday Night" as the DJ set reached a messy, watery crescendo. The girl who actually knew how to have fun.

All it had taken was one glance, half a second between the spray of water from Kyle's hand as he swooshed a wave across the pool towards her and Ruby to soak them, a tiny slither of light between the seething bodies, and she caught the magnetic draw of his stare piercing her, as if it was a stake right through her heart.

The world had seemed to slow, the music faded to a muffle in the background, and the blood had started pumping in her head until the only sound she could hear was her own deafening heartbeat. She stood stock-still, the water around her frothing and boiling as the rest of the mob continued to rock out, jumping high, arms waving, thrashing and splashing all around her.

She felt herself moving backwards, bumping unsteadily into bodies behind her, trying to get to the side of the pool as quickly as possible—the water and writhing bodies hindering her progress, forcing her to look up again to steady herself, and there he was again—hard, toned body leaning up against the bar, bottle of beer held between finger and thumb, staring, just staring right at her.

Fear had threatened to envelop her then, to drag her down, down into the water, to smother her senses, to drown her. She couldn't tear her gaze away; it was as if he still had a hold over her, and she was powerless to move until he let her. After everything he had put her through, she thought that she had moved on, that she finally had her life back, and yet, there he was. The crippling realisation that she was never getting away or going to be free of him had overwhelmed her.

Just as she managed to steady herself long enough to grip the edge of the pool to pull herself up so she could get away, he had half turned away, dropping his stare for just a second as someone had called him. He had reached over to set his beer back on the bar then and crouched a little, opening his arms wide as a 10-year-old blonde whirlwind jumped into his arms.

'Daddy! You came!' she said, closely followed by a second 10-year-old voice—this time from an identical little boy.

It was then that the shock hit her for real—not only had Jay found her, but "Jay" was Josh, and Josh was married to Carolyn.

The shivers continued to roll down her spine as it had registered with her, in that instant, that every time Carolyn had talked about Josh, she was actually talking about her "Jay". She knew that it was probably short for something, but she had never really stopped to think about what his full name was, just assuming it was short for Jason. But there he was—Josh, Carolyn's husband! At first, she hadn't believed what she was seeing.

In the split second, that she had processed that he had finally tracked her down and was coming to finish what he had started, she now realised that not only was he married (yet another thing he had lied about when they were together), but that he was the husband of one of her best friends. She had hauled herself out of the pool then, in a blind panic, wanting to get as far away from him as possible, while he was distracted by the twins grabbing him.

She had set off at a slippery sprint through the double fire doors that had been propped open into the spa area. It was quiet and dark inside after the chaos of the outdoor pool.

She had known that Josh had seen her get out. She also knew that now that he had found her, there was no way in the world that he was going to let her go. She took stock for a few seconds. He was guaranteed to think that she had headed for the changing room or maybe the car park, so she had doubled back at the last second, retracing her steps, and slid into the pitch blackness of the sauna, which had been switched off for the day.

She had sent up a silent prayer that it was impossible to see inside from the outside, especially with the bright afternoon sun streaming in through the spa windows, and glinting off the bubbles in the large hot tub right in front of the sauna. She had clambered up to the top slats on shaking legs, struggling to get her breathing under control as she squashed as far as she could into a dark corner, wrapping her hands around her legs and bringing her knees up to her chin as she made herself as small as possible.

She had been in here for at least 10 minutes now and could hear voices outside coming closer. From what she could hear, it sounded like Ruby and Sue shouting for her and making their way through the spa towards the changing rooms.

'Kira?' Sue's worried voice sounded right outside the sauna.

'Sue, you go out towards reception, and I'll take the changing room,' Ruby reasoned.

'But why did she run off like that? Is she ok?'

'I don't know, love, but what I do know is she didn't look great. Maybe she swallowed some pool water or something and felt sick. I just want to check on her and make sure she's ok. Meet me back out by the pool in a bit. If you find her before I do, then call my mobile.'

Kira could hear her friend trying to keep the panic out of her voice, followed by what she assumed were Sue's retreating footsteps heading back outside, to take the circuitous route back to reception, that didn't involve going through the changing rooms.

'Kira?' she heard the heavy sauna door being pushed gently open as her friend whispered her name. 'Are you in there?'

'Rubes,' she whispered. 'Quick, shut the door. I don't want him to find me!' she hissed back.

'What's going on, love?' Ruby pushed the door closed silently and crept closer to the figure cowering on the top bench. 'Why did you run off? And why are we whispering? I'm worried about you.'

Kira had let out a more audible sob then, before she felt the strong arms of her friend wrapping around her shivering body.

'Shhh, its ok. I've got you.' Ruby rocked her gently. 'Come on, love, tell me what's going on.'

'Oh, Ruby, he's here! Jay! I can't believe it. It was him, but then it was Josh, and then they're the same person, and then I saw him with the kids. How can he be the same, and how did he know I would be here? Has he come for me?' she blurted, her words tangling and tripping over themselves in her rush to get them out.

'Slow down. Come on, take a breath. You're not making any sense. Who's here?'

'Jay,' Kira squeaked.

'Jay? As in your ex-Jay? As in the Jay you have a restraining order against, Jay?' Ruby's shock was palpable. 'What did you mean when you said he was Josh? I don't understand.' She eased her arm out from around Kira's back and put her hand under Kira's chin, gently getting the younger woman to raise her head from her knees, and look at her in the soft red glow of the LED light on the emergency alarm button next to her.

'All that time I was with him, Rubes, and I remember thinking that maybe he's married or hiding something from me,' she sniffed, 'when he'd disappear for weeks on end, and then turn up again saying he had been away travelling for work. But then I'd almost catch him in a lie, but then he'd get scary again and I'd shut up. At that point, I didn't know how bad it would get, so I just put up with it. But I swear I didn't actually know he was married or that he had kids,' she started babbling again.

'If I had known, there was no way I would have got involved! No way! And then I would never have got myself into that situation with him, never had to put up with what he put me through. I've got my future back now—this place, this job, you and Carolyn—oh fuck, Carolyn.' Kira buried her head back in her hands. 'What the hell do I tell her?'

'Oh shit!' Ruby's eyes went wide with shock as the realisation of what Kira was telling her dawned for the first time. There was no going back from this for any of them.

'I get it now, Kira. Josh is Jay, isn't he?' Ruby started to shake her head in disbelief as a new wave of tears poured down Kira's face. 'Oh, girl, this is bad, bad news.' She put her arm back around her friend and pulled her in for another hug. 'What the hell are we going to do?'

13
5 Months Ago
August, Carolyn

Carolyn couldn't believe Kira had flounced off out of the pool like that. Sometimes, she thought, that girl was just a bit flaky. She didn't seem to understand the responsibility she had taken on when she agreed to do the pool Pilates session, that everyone was excited and waiting for. She thought she had seen a different side to Kira today.

She had actually braved the red bikini Carolyn had helped her pick out the week before, and she had certainly looked like she was enjoying the cocktail she was drinking earlier. She had even spotted her flirting with Sam at one point, before they had all started splashing in the pool. Why the hell couldn't people just be reliable and do what they said they would do? She bet that drink had gone to her head or something.

Kira always said she didn't drink much, because her body wasn't used to it. Maybe she was in the bathroom now puking up, or maybe she and Sam had run off for a quickie. She hadn't spotted him around for ages. For fuck's sake! She was going to have to go and ask Alex, the yoga guy, if he wouldn't mind stepping in for an hour to just help them stick to the programme, unless she could find Kira in the next 5 minutes.

She continued to be incensed as she marched around the pool. Not only could she not find Kira, but now it also seemed that Ruby had gone AWOL too. She had asked Kyle a minute ago where she was, but it seemed the last he had seen of her was when she was heading towards the spa with Sue, so he assumed she was getting out of the sun for a few minutes or heading back to change.

He seemed to be enjoying himself too much with a bottle of beer swinging between his fingers, and the other hand dipping in and out of the peanut dish on the bar, just like all the other guys. She could bet that Josh was around here somewhere too. He had finally shown up half an hour ago and hadn't even bothered to come over to her to say hello. She had spotted him ensconced at the bar, quite obviously already a few beers deep, and he had vaguely nodded in her direction.

He never did need an excuse to make the most of any situation where there was a bar, sunshine, and pretty girls clad in next to nothing to ignore her and the kids. It was hard to try and spot him now with the waft of BBQ smoke, disco lights and the hordes of kids running back and forth. She knew that she was being irrational really, that she should be more concerned about where her friend had got to instead of being mightily pissed off that everyone seemed to be having fun apart from her, that she was being left with a load of shit to sort out as usual.

After yet another lap of the outdoor pool, and a quick check to see that the twins were happily joining in with the Little Sparks Club craft activities and being supervised by the Sparkies crew, she wove her way back through to the spa and indoor pool. She thought that if she could just rule out the changing room and maybe check if the normal locker Kira used was still padlocked, she could at least establish if she was still on the premises or if she had done a bunk.

That way, when she went to drum up Alex to help with the Pilates session, she could at least legitimately say that she had exhausted all avenues of trying to find Kira and begging for his help when he wasn't really working. She could tell when she last saw him, he was definitely looking forward to another Tequila Sunrise or three after she saw him chatting to Brian, the PT, earlier. She knew he had been waiting to get enough Dutch courage on board, before trying to establish if Brian was single and did he seem interested.

Distracted for a moment with the thought of doing yet some more matchmaking, she smiled to herself for a second. She would have to promise to do some extra snooping herself to make up for this. She pushed open the door and stepped into the quiet tiled area, relishing the comparative calm for a second before a faint noise caught her attention, coming from the sauna.

She knew instantly that something was off. They had agreed with the staff that the sauna and steam room would be turned off today, so that the emergency alarms could remain deactivated and unmanned for the afternoon. They had even put signs up on each of the doors saying that they were "temporarily unavailable".

But there it was again—she could hear crying and another voice soothing whoever was in quite obvious distress. Her motherly instincts kicked in, and she moved closer to the door. She gently edged it open just an inch, so that the occupants didn't realise that she could hear their conversation.

'I know he hurt you, and I don't just mean that your heart was broken and you hated yourself for loving a man like that, but I know what he did to you physically. I was there that night at A&E. I remember what a mess he made of your face, and how much pain you were in when he broke your fingers. It's not something I can ever forget,' Ruby sighed before continuing.

'Kira, I promise you, honey, there is no way on this earth that Kyle or I will let anything happen to you. We have the restraining order in place—he knows that. He now knows that I know you. You were standing right by me in the pool. There is no way on earth he would expect you not to tell me once he spotted us together. He has everything to lose,' Ruby spat, her distaste clear.

Carolyn shrank back in shock. She couldn't see who Ruby was speaking to, but whoever it was, was clearly upset enough to be hiding and crying in the sauna, and whoever it was had clearly had a shock. But who could it be? She had only really seen Ruby with Kira today in the pool. There was a loud sniff and then she got her answer.

'I know, Ruby,' Kira's voice was wobbly. 'I know logically that he can't come after me again. Last time, he got arrested, didn't he? I'm not sure how he would explain that today if I called the police right now and said he was here harassing me. I'm pretty sure you're right that he didn't expect to see me here, but it's still such a massive shock. I just want to get away from here until I can process what to do next. I need to find out if he's going to be a regular here or if it's just a one-off.'

It was clearly Kira that was upset, Kira who had had a shock, and Kira who was hiding in the sauna from some mystery guy, who, it sounded like, had really hurt her in the past. Carolyn knew that Kira had had a really hard relationship break-up late last year, but she hadn't realised the extent of what had happened to her—that it had been violent. No wonder she was always so timid and reluctant to pursue a relationship with anyone or to trust people.

It had taken what seemed like months for her to let her guard down with Carolyn and actually start to share things with her. She must have had such a terrible time. Oh, she felt like crap now. What was she thinking, getting annoyed at Kira for disappearing when she needed her?

There was no way she could expect her to put on a brave face now and go back out, especially as Carolyn didn't know who this creep was. If she could at least get a name from Kira, she could get Sue to find out more about this guy. Maybe even get him banned so that Kira felt safe. She was just about to push the door open and see if she could offer her help and support, when Ruby started to talk again, and she pulled back.

'Kira, I'm going to share something with you that happened to me today. It's something I have literally never told anyone, not even Kyle, but I'm hoping that by sharing my situation, you will understand how I am going to help you and protect you. This is fucking personal for me.' She could hear the intensity in Ruby's voice. 'I also want you to know that if he comes near you again, I will fucking kill him!'

'Ruby, you don't have to share if you don't want, honestly. I'm just glad that you're here looking out for me.' It was Kira's turn to sound concerned. 'But I want you to know, I'm here for you too, you know.'

Carolyn leant closer, waiting for Ruby to speak. Just at that moment, her foot slipped on the wet floor, and her elbow gently nudged the door, her elbow giving a resounding clunk.

'Hello?' Ruby's anxious voice was muffled behind the partially closed door. 'Who's there?'

'Shit!' Carolyn muttered under her breath. She had two choices now—slink away before the door opened and hope they didn't spot her, or open the door and join in the conversation, but without giving away that she had been earwigging outside and had heard what had been going on. In that split second, she made a decision and grabbed the door with force, swinging it open with her usual gusto.

'There you girls are!' She forced a smile to the front of her face, almost grimacing as she faked that she had literally just found them. 'I wondered where you were hiding. Don't blame, you both. To be honest, the little brats around the pool are just getting a bit too much, aren't they!' She looked between them, hoping her fakery wasn't too obvious, then pretending to notice Kira's tear-streaked face in the gloom of the sauna for the first time.

'Oh, Kira love, whatever's the matter?' She looked between them for an answer. 'Is it the bikini? Are you upset that I made you wear it? Or is it the Pilates? Seriously, I can get someone else to help out if you don't want to be up there in front of everyone,' she waffled on, hoping that her cover-up wasn't too obvious. It was Ruby who spoke first.

'Look, Carolyn, it's not a good time, sorry. Kira here has had a bit of a shock. Well, so have I, actually. We've both seen people here today that we weren't expecting to see and, well, to be quite honest, we both need a bit of time to process it and, you know, just work out what to do.'

Carolyn could see Kira looking nervously and expectantly at Ruby, as if waiting to see what she would say next.

'How about I take Kira home or back to mine for the night, and then we regroup in the sauna on Monday night as planned, and I explain a bit more about what's going on?'

'But is there anything I can help with? You know I know most people and their families that come here—maybe I can help you understand who these mystery people are that you were shocked to see?' Carolyn was eager to find out more. 'I mean, me and Sue on reception are like this.' Carolyn held up crossed fingers on her right hand to demonstrate. 'There aren't many people here that we don't know between us.' She looked questioningly between her friends.

'Believe me, Carolyn, this is something we both need some time to think about, before we talk to anyone about it. I'm not shutting you out, I promise. You know you're my best friend, but just for today, I need to ask for you to just understand. We don't want to put a downer on your day. You've done so much to arrange all this, and I'm sure all those people out there are looking forward to the rest of the activities. Why don't you head on back out, and once I've sorted Kira out, I'll give you a call, ok?'

Carolyn could tell she was being placated, that Ruby just wanted her to go and leave her and Kira to their private conversation. She forced down a wave of disappointment and irritation, as she took a step back from the bench where the others were sitting, Ruby's arm still draped around Kira's shoulder.

'Well sure, I wouldn't want to get in the way of your cosy little chat, would I?' she snapped, taking another step back towards the door. 'Well, you know where I am when you get a chance to fill me in on what the hell's been going on.' She spun on her heels, pulling the door forcefully as she strode out. She knew that she probably sounded completely unreasonable and unsupportive, but couldn't help feeling rejected.

Well, sod them. She would go find Alex, get him to do the best fucking poolside Pilates anyone had ever experienced. She would ask Sarah to crank up the volume even more, and play the best party songs, and ply everyone with more alcohol. It would be the best summer party in Aaron Sparks history, and they would be talking about it for years to come. Who cared if her two very best friends in the world were hiding secrets from her? She didn't. She had a load of people that needed her! She strode back out poolside, barking orders as she went.

'James, grab that large plastic tub that had the first lot of ice in, and mix up a huge bowl of punch and get those plastic cups full. It's free punch happy hour. Alex, put that cocktail down and stop flirting with Brian. I need you in 30 minutes, ready and waiting to deliver the best Pilates session of your life. You're covering for Kira.'

'Sam, get your lifeguards together and round up everyone for a 30-minute mega mix disco. And Sarah,' she turned round and gave the spin instructor a grin, 'you're so good at spinning on a bike, but now I need you to spin some seriously good tunes! Crank up Blur Song 2 to the max, and follow it up with Don't Stop Me Now!' Well, if that didn't say summer party vibe, then what did?

14
4 Months Ago
September, Carolyn

It hadn't always been like this, Carolyn thought, as she bent down to pick up yet another carelessly discarded crayon, unhooked a charger cable that was being used to tether a Barbie to the bottom rung of the stair banister, and shoved yet another half-deflated football in the toy trunk inside the lounge door. There was a time in her life, not even that long ago, where she wasn't just a wife and a mother—running round after kids and elderly parents, supporting an unappreciative and critical husband.

The summer party had been a huge success and people had been stopping her to congratulate her at the club ever since, they had raised a huge amount for charity and the bar had been drunk almost dry. So why did she still feel so deflated and unfulfilled?

She turned the dial on the washing machine for the 3rd time that day, and leant back against the utility room unit. What had happened to her? The girl who had all that ambition and zest for life must still be in there somewhere. She knew that she wasn't the only one who felt like this. There must be thousands of women out there in the same situation, waiting for the day to come when they could finally reclaim their identity.

Carolyn sighed again. It wasn't even that long ago since she thought she actually loved her life and was still in love with her husband. But now?

Josh used to tell her how beautiful she was, how adorable, and how he found her so sexy. Huh, that felt like an age ago. She knew that she shouldn't put up with the constant criticisms every time he came home from a trip—that he could at least pull his weight around the house a little more, and understand how hard the twins could be at times. But even as she was inwardly berating herself for putting up with it, she did feel like he had a point.

He worked hard to provide for them all. The house hadn't come cheap, and it was her that wanted to stop working full-time to have children. The least she could do was to be grateful that he didn't question what she spent on the credit card. But did he have to constantly point out every tiny little thing that she hadn't done well? Who cared if Charlie had a stain on his rugby shorts—they were only going to get covered in mud. And did it really matter that the pasta sauce came out of a jar that night instead of being carefully home-made?

The thought of Italian food made her think back to their honeymoon—only 12 short years ago, but it felt like a lifetime. The feeling of the warm evening sun and the smooth terracotta tiles under her feet, the scent of rosemary and hot garlic and oregano on the breeze as they sipped crisp white wine on the balcony of their hotel, looking down at the sparkling sea below and the Italians taking their evening constitutional. She could still feel Josh's hands on her hips, then them tracing up her spine, before he took her glass from her hand as he led her to their sumptuous four-poster bed.

Back then, he really couldn't get enough of her. He was constantly touching her, suggesting things that she should wear, encouraging her to let go, be wild, and do things she couldn't have imagined doing with anyone in the bedroom before. It had been such a long time since he had looked at her like that—like he could devour her, that he wanted to savour her. Now, it just felt like he couldn't wait to get away from her.

She knew she had changed. She wasn't the person she was back 15 years ago when they first met. She was ambitious, a few years out of university and chomping at the bit for adventure, while temping at an events marketing company the summer that they met at a friend's BBQ. She had been instantly impressed by this tall, strong guy, who had helped her to open the lid of a jar of pickles, and then laughed with her as they both fought over the last hot dog, telling her how much he loved a woman who loved food.

She had known then that he was the one for her—just 15 minutes in his charming company and he had won her over. So she hadn't hesitated when he asked for her number; and then here they were, nearly forty and miserable. She appreciated that the twins had all but wrecked her body, but there was more she could—or probably should—do. Weekly spin and a bit of yoga was about as much as she could stomach.

Josh, however, looked better than ever—his body toned and firm from hours of hard-core training, honing his body to compete on the Tri circuit, but also getting fit and strong so that he could parachute into tropical, dangerous locations for his work as a botanist. She would just have to accept that genetically, she was destined to be softer around the edges—nurturing and homely. If only Josh could see that there was much to appreciate about that, and that the hard muscle and sculpted features of those women she saw at the gym were not for everyone.

Carolyn pushed open the door of the pantry with a disgruntled shove. She needed a little excitement in her life—something that would give her something to focus on and stop feeling sorry for herself. Last week, Sarah had told her about a job going at an events management company that needed a new events coordinator. She knew that Josh didn't want her going out to work, but she was fed up with being his doormat and wanted to get her teeth stuck into something.

She wanted to talk it through with the girls, but they had been strangely evasive over the last few weeks. And with the start of school and getting the twins organised—uniforms bought, shoes fitted, new stationery, and them both signed up to all their after-school commitments—she hadn't really had a chance to catch up with them about what had happened at the summer party.

Sure, she had had a few texts from Ruby, and they had seen each other briefly in the café bar the other week, but were interrupted as soon as they got there by Sue, wanting to gossip about the new tennis coach who used to be a professional and on the circuit back in the day. They then got to arranging Sue to babysit for the kids that weekend at Carolyn's house, while Carolyn had Sparks committee meetings—something Sue was always happy to do.

By the time she'd finished wittering on, it had been kicking out time at Little Sparks, and Amber had had yet another argument with one of her little friends, Isabella, over whether Bigfoot was real, and insisting that her dad had seen a Sasquatch when he was on an adventure in Canada. Not surprisingly, Issy had ended up in tears.

She knew Ruby felt bad for not telling her yet what had been going on, after she had caught her and Kira in their secret conflab in the sauna at the summer party. She had made a point of saying to Ruby that they needed to get back in their routine, and that she would see her the first Monday at 5 pm in the sauna, as soon as the kids were back at school.

So here she was today, getting her stuff ready, making sure she had playtime snacks for the twins in her bag and their playing-out clothes—complete with Little Sparks ball caps—ready for them to change into as soon as she collected them from school.

Josh had left 10 days ago for another work trip. Admittedly, he was only in London and had been home a few times for the night, but he was still going to effectively be "working away" for the next couple of weeks, before his next big trip in November. It would be four weeks this time, taking him to Papua to collect some specific nut for the national collection. It was a big deal, and he was already in planning mode, making him even more unreasonable and rude to her than usual.

He had hit the roof the other night when he had popped back to collect a load of samples he needed to take to the Natural History Museum in Oxford, when he had found Amber and Charlie poking around in the drawers of his specimen cabinet in his office. He had screamed at them so loudly that Amber had promptly dropped to the floor and rolled into a protective ball, while Charlie had fled in tears to hide up in his treehouse, refusing to come down until he heard the sound of his dad's car leaving the driveway.

Carolyn had borne the brunt of his rage and fury. It was "her fault the door was unlocked", even though she didn't even have a spare key to his office, and she was a "stupid fucking bitch for not being able to control her nosy brats".

When he had calmed for a couple of seconds, he had explained that some of the samples in the drawers were of a type of fungi only found in remote Central African jungle, that the toxins could go untraced in bloodstreams and it could be deadly, he quietly admitted that he wasn't supposed to have them. Carolyn had shaken her head at him then (a mistake, as she should have known), as he had proceeded to fly of the handle and pin her against the wall, grabbing her throat as he whispered a threat close to her face.

'If no one knows I have it, then who's to say it couldn't be used and I wouldn't be found out?' His cold blue-green eyes had bored into hers, the threat clear. 'Now take those fucking kids out of here, I'm warning you.'

He had released her then and, letting her scoop Amber from the floor, pushed them out of the room. She had taken her shivering daughter upstairs to her bedroom in the attic, out of the way, and soothed her as Josh proceeded to stomp around the house packing his suitcase. As he drove away, gravel spinning under his tyres, and Charlie had made his way cautiously back into the house, she had dried their tears and put a shiny front on as she always did.

'I'm sorry about Daddy. He gets angry when he worries about you both, and there are things in his study that you shouldn't be touching, ok?'

They had both given her a tentative nod as they huddled closer to each other on the sofa, small feet swinging in unison.

'So, how about we forget fish fingers tonight and go grab pizza at Sloppy Joe's?' She smiled at them as they nodded back enthusiastically at her, their woes forgotten. How many times had she had to use this strategy now?

As she walked around the house now, finishing tidying before she headed out to meet the girls, she allowed herself a few minutes of reprieve. Slumping back against the sagging cushions of the sofa, she rested her head back as the tears poured silently down her face. She needed a way out. It was only because Josh had to be somewhere else the other night that the situation hadn't escalated further.

Thank goodness he was away so much, as it gave her more time to ponder what she wanted to do with her life. She would talk to the girls about it and get them to help her think up a strategy. This was what Ruby was best at—thinking through choices and options, but also being a kind and listening ear—something she had sorely missed since that afternoon at the party.

15

4 Months Ago
September, Kira

Kira was going through her own cool-down after teaching her afternoon class, before getting her swimwear on and heading to the sauna. It would be the second time today that she was back at the pool, having completed a series of time-trialled laps back and forth in the early morning quiet, before the Silver Squad turned up at 7 am—a lovely bunch of retirees who loved to swim and have a chat three mornings a week.

It made Kira smile to see that. Even though these were people who were in the later years of their lives, they not only had time for one another, but also made time to exercise, never losing their love of the water. She hoped that she would be like that when she was older—that she would keep her mobility and flexibility, and be able to glide up for as long as was possible.

It had taken her a few days to get her confidence to go back to Aaron Sparks after the summer party. All she had felt was a deep feeling of pure dread in the pit of her stomach, making her go hot one minute with the shame of what had happened to her last year, and then cold and shivery as she remembered the fear of that final night when she had finally had the courage to seek help.

She had called in sick the day after Ruby had taken her back to her house and sat with her, while she had talked her way through all of her concerns again about Jay—or Josh, as she now knew him as. Ruby had been nothing but an angel that night, telling Kyle that an ex of Kira's had shown up at Aaron Sparks and that it had upset her. Kyle had left them to it, but had kindly ordered in Chinese later that evening, subtly leaving them in the kitchen to talk, while he hung out in his man cave, playing on his Xbox.

Ruby had called in sick for Kira the next morning, telling Sue that Kira was too poorly to call in herself with sunstroke—that she had been vomiting all night and was sure she would be right as rain by the Wednesday. She had let Kira stay another day at her house, knowing full well that Kira was afraid to return home to an empty flat, when she didn't know Josh's whereabouts.

Ruby had reassured her on the Monday that he wasn't going to be around, as she had spoken briefly to Carolyn, and asked a few tentative questions to establish that Josh had gone back to London for the week—meaning it was fine for Kira to go home, and that, more importantly, she was okay to go back to work.

It still didn't stop her feeling jumpy. Every corner she walked round in the building, she expected to run into him, but she knew that she couldn't let this stop her moving forward. She had the injunction in place and the backup of her friend.

She knew at some point she would have to tell Carolyn the truth, but for now, she and Ruby had agreed that they needed to see the lay of the land. Carolyn had talked openly over the last few months about wanting to leave Josh and make a fresh start—about how his bullying was wearing her down, and how she wanted to work, but couldn't do it if she was married to him.

Ruby had reassured her that she would get Carolyn alone soon for a proper chat, and to provide her with some legal advice about what would happen if she did want to leave Josh. That way, hopefully the decision would be made before Kira had to come clean about what had freaked her out, and, more importantly, who had hurt her.

Just the thought of telling her friend that she had been sleeping with her husband for the better part of 18 months, and that he was the one that she had a restraining order against, was enough to bring her out in hives. A shiver cascaded down her back, and she pulled her brightly coloured beach towel tighter around her.

She was hoping that it would just be her and Ruby for the first 10 minutes at least. She knew that Carolyn had to get the kids settled in Little Sparks before she could meet them. It would at least give them a little time to compose themselves before the inevitable questioning began. She knew that Carolyn knew that she had been avoiding her over the last few weeks, but she hadn't been able to face her before now.

Sure enough, as she pushed the door open, she could see Ruby in a bright orange and pink one-shouldered swimsuit sitting on the lower shelf on the back left of the sauna. She was impatiently tapping her long, bright red nails against the bench, obviously as anxious as Kira to agree tactics before Carolyn joined them.

'Ah, there you are! Thought you were going to be a bit earlier than this. I managed to get away from chambers well early today. I guess that's what happens when you spend all Sunday with your head in case files and planning a defence,' Ruby grinned and patted the bench next to her as Kira walked over, folded her towel in two, and sat down on it, one leg pulled up close to her chest so she could wrap her arms around it.

'Hi, Ruby,' she smiled faintly. 'Sorry, it just took me a bit of time to get myself together in the changing room. I'm kind of dreading this. I don't know what to say to her.'

They both knew that she was referring to Carolyn. Kira turned to look expectantly at her friend, hoping that Ruby would provide guidance and help with the flow of the conversation—something that Kira always struggled with.

'It's fine, honestly. I'm going to talk to both of you about what happened with me on that day. I assure you that it's enough tonight to take Carolyn's mind off what was going on for you. If she does ask, then I can just say that you were a bit overwhelmed with all the attention in that sexy bikini and that it freaked you out—all those guys ogling you after what had happened before. Does that work?'

Kira nodded gently. 'Thanks, Rubes. I feel like such an idiot not even being able to explain myself, but I think you're right—that this isn't the time to tell her about Josh.'

Ruby nodded back at her.

'It just wouldn't be fair for her to know what happened when we don't know if she's going to stay with him. She has to make her mind up herself. There is no way in the world I want to be part of that decision-making process for her.' Kira shivered despite the heat. 'Actually, I have another idea—and one that's actually nearer the truth and might make Carolyn understand a little more about why I ran off.'

'Go on,' Ruby nodded encouragingly.

'I split up with Sam.' Kira's lips pursed out into a rueful pout. 'Before you say anything—it's fine, it's honestly fine. It didn't exactly happen that day, as you know I was in no fit state to talk to anyone, but I did call him a week or so ago to call it off.' She gently shook her head.

'He is such a nice guy, Rubes. I was really starting to think we could go somewhere, but everything that happened with Josh just made me realise all over again that I'm just not ready yet to trust someone and let them get close to me.' She smiled as Ruby patted her hand.

'Well, that may be a better option today, love. Sad as it is that you've broken up with Sam, I think Carolyn will be…' Before she had a chance to finish her sentence, the door to the sauna swung open with Carolyn's usual force behind it.

'What will I be?' Carolyn looked expectantly between her friends before shutting the door firmly and taking her place between them. 'Come on, spit it out—"Carolyn will be"?'

'Understanding,' Ruby finished. 'I was saying that once Kira told you about breaking up with Sam at the summer party, that you would be understanding.' She raised her eyebrows, urging Carolyn to come back with an appropriate and measured response.

'Ah, yes, so this is when I say "sorry to hear that, Kira", and how sorry I am. Yeah, I can do that.' She turned to look at Kira. 'Kira, I'm very sorry to hear about Sam. I thought the two of you made a really lovely couple. I'm sure that you have good reasons for it ending.' Her lack of sincerity was palpable. 'However, I'm still pissed off that you left me in the lurch with that bloody Pilates session!'

'Carolyn!' Ruby shook her head in disbelief. 'She's just told you her relationship ended and all you do is think about yourself? The day was a massive success, wasn't it? At least Kira had the guts to come and meet you here today to tell you what was going on.' She cringed inwardly at her own lie by omission. 'The least you can do is try and be supportive.'

Kira, yet to say a word, watched her friends talk about her as if she wasn't there.

'Well, she could have at least have sent me a text to apologise or say something, couldn't she?' She looked directly at Kira now. 'Couldn't you? Look, I'm not one to stay mad for long, but if we are true friends—which I really hope we are—then you need to be able to be honest with me and say what's on your mind. I don't mind covering for you or helping you out, as long as you're honest. Fair enough?'

'Sure, Carolyn. I'll be honest from now on, and I am truly sorry. I didn't mean to cause any problems on the day or leave you in the lurch. It was just that something unexpected happened, and I didn't know how to deal with it.' She didn't feel that this was dishonest again as such—Carolyn wanted the truth between friends, so what she didn't know wasn't a lie; it was just a secret.

'Fine, whatever. Apology accepted, and I am genuinely sorry it didn't work out. I still think there's something between the two of you though—I see the way he looks at you. I know you have a shitload of stuff you're still working through with your last relationship, but I can tell a good guy when I see one. Believe me, I know.'

Kira was just grateful the sauna was dark enough that Carolyn couldn't see the look on her face as she talked about good guys, and Ruby breathed a small sigh of relief as Carolyn hijacked the conversation—that her revelation would now have to wait for another day.

'Now, can we get on with talking about all the other gossip from that day, please? Did you know, for example, that nice, old, and very-much-married Mr Kennedy from Seniors' Spin was caught by Sarah at the back of the BBQ tent, applying suncream to recently-widowed Mrs O'Neil, in a very interesting place on her body that was not ever likely to see the sun?' She waggled her eyebrows suggestively at them.

'And then there's what happened with the Lewis' 18-year-old daughter and that visiting tennis coach. seriously, he's her sports coach, I think Sue reported him!' It didn't take long for Carolyn to get back to her old self.

16
4 Months Ago
September, Ruby

Despite the make-up in the sauna earlier that week, Ruby still felt uneasy about hiding the truth about Josh from Carolyn, and the subterfuge she had used to elicit information about him and his whereabouts over the last month or so. She had been gathering information covertly and passing it onto Kira whenever she could, waiting for the right time for Kira to tell Carolyn the truth.

She had hoped Kira would feel strong enough by now, with her support, to talk things through with Carolyn, but as soon as she had met her in the sauna, she knew from the look on her face that she wasn't ready. She knew better than anyone what it was like to have a secret. She had promised the girls that she was going to share with them what had happened to her at the summer party, but even she had bottled the opportunity to talk to them about something that she'd been holding onto for the last 20 years.

She knew that sooner or later she would have to tell Kyle, and that having her friends by her side—ready to catch her if she fell, if Kyle didn't want to be with her after she told him the bitter truth that she had been holding back from him since they met—was essential. Maybe today was the time to do it. She just had to be brave.

She had never really thought about telling anyone about her past before she was ready to share with Kyle. She had imagined the scenario many times, talking to him late at night after a few beers, and they were having a deep and meaningful conversation. They talked about so much, but for some reason, the time had just never felt right. She knew that hiding these things from him was pointless.

The more they discussed their future, the baby that he was desperate to have with her, and the longer they failed to conceive, the more and more difficult it became to confront her fears and to come clean about how she was a failure. So, here she was, about to share her secrets with her best friends, in the hope that it gave Kira the courage to tell her story, and gave Carolyn the nudge she needed to make her mind up once and for all, about leaving the husband who not only treated her like shit, but was holding her back from everything that she could be.

She genuinely didn't know what reaction she was looking for, but she did know deep down that she needed to talk to someone soon. Every month that passed without Kyle's dreams coming true, the more the bitter truth ate away at her. She finally had to reveal herself.

As she sat on her own for a few minutes more in the dark, womb-like environment, nursing a large frozen coffee, she contemplated what her future might hold. Would the girls reject her when they realised that she wasn't who she pretended to be? Would they understand how she had to give up her whole identity to escape the stranglehold of her strict upper-class family, who wanted nothing more than a daughter who married money and kept house?

Would they think, as she had done for so many years, that she had made a mistake in the choices that she had made back then, when the choices seemed so few—that she was evil, a terrible person for doing what she did? That the problems she and Kyle were having conceiving were something she deserved, because she had brought this fate on herself?

Before she could contemplate more about what may be, the door edged open, and Kira's lithe form appeared silhouetted in the doorframe as she held it wider to let Carolyn pass.

'Come on then, Rubes, spill the beans. I've rushed getting the twins ready and to Sparks club to get here. We've been putting this off for what seems like ages now! Seriously, you should have heard Charlie moaning when I forgot to pack his snack box and told him he'd have to share with Amber. The grief he's going to give me when I pick them up—better make this worth it!' Carolyn said, as she slung her towel over the lower slats and plonked herself down next to Ruby.

'Are you ok, Ruby?' Kira asked sensitively, as she climbed up and over her friends to reach the upper layer of the sauna. 'I was worried when I got your text. Is there something wrong with you and Kyle?'

'Ah, thanks, Kira, for caring as usual, unlike this one,' said Ruby, as she prodded Carolyn's toe with the end of her straw. 'There is something I need to talk to you both about.' She hesitated before drawing in a stuttered breath, still not quite knowing where to start.

'Look, I meant to tell you this the other day, and I'm sorry it's taken me until now to get round to it, but I just need you to listen, if that's ok? I promise that you will have questions, and I'm very willing to answer them, but I just need to tell you what's going on first. It's not pretty, and you might be angry at me, but I needed someone to talk to. This is something I've been holding onto for so many years, and you're the first people I've told.'

She looked between her friends, who were clearly confused and intrigued about what she was going to say next.

'Go on,' said Carolyn gently, realising now that perhaps her earlier tone wasn't quite so appropriate, for whatever it was that Ruby was going to share with them.

'Well, you remember the summer party?' she rushed to continue, not wanting Kira to think that she was going to out her about that day. 'Well, I bumped into someone there, who I wasn't expecting to see. Someone from my past—basically, someone I had spent 20 years trying to forget.' Ruby's mouth was a grim line, as she tried to work out how to explain why this had impacted her so much.

'This guy, Todd, was someone I sort of grew up with. I think he might be a member here now, and I guess I might bump into him again—which is why I'm telling you this stuff.' She looked at them both again, the confusion still etched on both of their faces.

'What I'm trying to say, inarticulately, I had to change my life to escape my family and all that they stood for. I had to run away to escape something terrible and violent that happened to me. What I need to tell you is that my name isn't Ruby—it's actually Ruth. And I'm not who you think I am.'

17

4 Months Ago
September, Sauna

The women sat in stunned silence as Ruby spoke and started to tell them about her family and her past. The only sound interrupting the quiet reverence was the occasional sound of a drinks' bottle opening and the drip of condensation.

Ruby explained to them how she came from a monied background and grew up with a life of privilege. Her father worked in law. He was very well respected and had built the family's reputation around the family name—that they had money and all the privileges that came with it: private education, country club membership, and summers spent at holiday homes in Barbados and Salcombe. Her mother was stuck-up but weak.

Having come from money, she wanted a husband who could keep her in the lifestyle she was accustomed to, and that meant having a daughter that she could manipulate and groom to be a clone of her. Her mother had spent years drilling into her the etiquette of what rich and entitled men wanted, and what they didn't, and how it was up to her to do everything society expected of a young, privileged lady, following the example set by her mother and grandmother before her.

Ruby explained that these monied families didn't want an educated woman in the family—one with a career and independent prospects or opinions. They wanted a pretty daughter who understood that her primary role in life was to marry into a good family, keep a nice house, look after herself, stay slim, get her hair done at least once a fortnight, instruct the help to cook delicious meals for her husband's tennis partners and the boys from the club, and bear him sons to carry on the family name.

'Basically, my father treated me like a pretty toy or an ornament—someone he could wheel out in front of his tennis buddies on a weekend at the country club and show off for my good manners,' Ruby sighed. 'It was an absolute joke.

I used to just go along with it until I was about 13 or 14, when I finally started to question women's rights and liberalism from things we were learning at school, and I looked at my mother and just thought, "you're pathetic". And she was!'

The women shook their heads in support, and Ruby continued her story.

'So, my birth name is actually Ruth,' she looked between them, 'and I'm sorry I never told you about this before, but I changed it such a long time ago that that girl was dead to me. She was nothing like I am now—almost unrecognisable. The only thing that we had in common, I guess, was our ambition. I always knew I wanted to study law or politics. I had the grades and my teachers were really supportive, but living in the world I lived in, it was just never going to happen,' she sighed again.

'I tried talking to my father one day after my form tutor suggested I sit the entrance exams for Oxford and Cambridge. I wanted to get his approval, but you should have heard him. Honestly, it was straight out of the book of patriarchy.' Ruby shook her head as she relayed the conversation.

'I went into his study one night after he had had some work associates over for dinner. He always took a whiskey after dinner while he finished off any paperwork. He seemed in a good mood, so I thought "this is my chance" to talk to him seriously. I knocked and went in, telling him firmly that I wanted to be a lawyer and go to university, that the teachers at school thought I had a good chance, and would he support me?' Ruby's face contorted into a frown. 'You know what he did?' she looked at them both.

'He patted me on the head and turned me away, telling me I had been reading too many books, and that they were putting funny thoughts into my head,' she scoffed before continuing.

'I tried again a month later. I needed him to sign a form for a field trip to the High Court as part of moving to the A-level politics course, and he refused. He was so angry that I had even asked—that I had dared to come to him again and ask to follow my dreams—that he blew smoke from his disgusting cigar in my face before telling me that I wasn't to go against his wishes, that I had always been a disappointment to him, and that if only he had had a son.' A slow tear tracked its way down Ruby's face as she continued.

'And this was what it was always like. Any time I wanted to do anything that didn't fit with their convention, any time I wanted to pursue my own life, he took me down, made me feel like shit, reminded me what a disappointment I was to him,' she took a steadying breath.

'But what he didn't bank on was my determination. There was no way I was going to give up on my dreams. My best friend at school, Serena, agreed to help me. We didn't know how we were going to do it, but between us, we were going to cook up a plan for me to get into university and run away from my parents. Once I was 18, there was nothing that they could do to stop me doing whatever I wanted.'

A rueful smile crept along Ruby's lips. 'Serena was great. She helped me siphon off bits of my allowance, helped me buy the books I needed, and gave me a place to study while telling my parents we were at deportment class!' she chuckled. 'What a fucking joke!'

'So, what happened next, Ruby? You must have made the plan work, otherwise you wouldn't be here today, I'm guessing?' enquired Kira.

'Well, I did get to uni, yeah. But my parents holding me back and trying to prevent me from having my dreams is only part of my story—only one of the reasons I changed my name and everything about my appearance. Seriously, you wouldn't have recognised me back then. I was skinny with these long blonde ringlets, always dressed conservatively.'

'Who would have known,' muttered Carolyn, shaking her head.

'Yeah, I know. I had to undergo a bit of a dramatic transformation, but that wasn't just to separate myself from them, from that world. It was to escape something else—something terrible.' Her body gave an involuntary shudder.

'You don't have to tell us, Rubes, if it's too painful. We're here for you,' Kira spoke gently into the gloom of the sauna.

'No, I need to do this. I need to tell you my story, so that you can both see for yourselves why sometimes the only course of action to get through or over something is the most dramatic.' She slammed her green water bottle down onto the slats to reinforce her point. 'I was raped at 16 and that rape got me pregnant.'

18
3 Months Ago
October, Halloween

Ruby clocked Josh leaning on the bar as soon as she walked into Sparks, his Scream mask propped up on top of his hair, with the elastic stretching round the back of his head, while he swigged a bottle of beer. Silently, she cursed herself for not checking his whereabouts tonight—stupidly thinking that this wouldn't be his scene. A shiver crept down her back as it dawned on her that she needed to warn Kira.

Before he could make eye contact and accost her, she dipped behind one of the decorated pillars and bent down to rummage in her bag, hoping if she could text Kira in good time, she could change her mind about coming along tonight and stay home and safe.

'Fuck,' she muttered to herself, as she grabbed out handfuls of sweets for the kids later, tissues, lipsticks, her work diary and house keys. Where the hell was her phone?

Just as she was about to dump the contents of her bag out on the floor, she had a sudden vision of plugging it in to charge earlier by the mirror, as she had watched a make-up tutorial—determined as she was to perfect her "day-of-the-dead" face ready for the "best dressed" competition later. She knew in her heart that there was no point looking for her phone in her bag—she wasn't going to find it there.

Well, she would just have to go and grab Kyle when he arrived and borrow his phone. She had to let Kira know before it was too late, but Kyle wasn't due to get there for another 45 minutes, so all Ruby could hope was that this would give her enough time to get the message to Kira before she turned up.

Resigning herself to waiting for Kyle, there was nothing for it but to do the rounds and have a chat with a few people, while still avoiding Josh. Carolyn had been slaving away with the Sparks committee to put on this event for the last 6 weeks, and admittedly, the place looked incredible this evening. Swathes of black and orange material cascaded down in shredded curtains, from the balcony above the bar area. Reams of stretchy cobweb material clung to the bar, pillars and backs of chairs.

Fake spiders, bats and worms hung around the bar, and sheets of coloured decals covered all the lights, casting a red, orange and green glow over the whole area, creating a Hammer House of Horrors atmosphere. James was already at the DJ decks spinning out Monster Mash, lights flashing as a gaggle of 6-year-olds spun and whirled in their bright-coloured, highly flammable nylon outfits.

Ruby spotted a couple of mini pumpkins in their bright orange matching suits, pushing each other and arguing whose outfit was the best, a tiny witch whacking a Harry Potter with her mini broomstick, and a skeleton and ghost dancing under the glitter ball, and smiled to herself.

Ruby thought back to her childhood, and how incredibly snobby and stuck-up her parents were about Halloween, forbidding her to attend any of the neighbouring kids' parties and making sure any trick-or-treaters were firmly discouraged, by the gate being firmly closed at the end of their long driveway. Just the thought of what she had escaped from—and the life she had now, despite the secret she was still keeping from Kyle—made her break out into a huge grin, and to congratulate herself on what she thought was her best Halloween look yet.

She had been practising her intricate "day-of-the-dead" design for the last 3 weeks, using gems and facial glue to decorate the incredible pattern that covered the whole of her face, right down her neck to the hideous slit throat she had enhanced with putty and fake blood, drawing on each individual stitch in the mirror this afternoon. It had taken her at least 2 hours, and she couldn't wait for more of her friends to arrive to admire her effort.

Her outfit was another masterpiece—a seamstress friend had designed the dress, covered in skulls and dead roses, with a full-netted retro vintage 1950s-style skirt, leading up to a halter-neck which showed off her impressive cleavage, dripping with fake blood. There was no way anyone else was winning the adults' outfit prize tonight!

She grabbed one of the free cocktails from the bar—a blood-red concoction, sickly sweet but very strong—as she went in search of Carolyn. The least she could do was congratulate her on a great night, and she wanted to show off her make-up to someone who appreciated it before she went in search of Kyle. But first, she needed a quick pee.

The queue for the toilets in the bar area was already building up, with sticky-fingered children and parents eager to get back to the bar, so Ruby took a left down the dark corridor towards the changing rooms, in the hope that these ones would be quieter. She hadn't gone far before she heard what seemed to be Carolyn's muffled tones coming from near the staff supply cupboard.

'Honestly, Sarah, I don't know what he's doing here.'

Ruby crept closer to hear the reply.

'Carolyn, you don't have to tell me anything. You know I'm here for you if you need me. You can talk or not talk, I just want you to know you can rely on me, ok?'

'You don't know how much that means to me at the moment. Honestly, things just haven't been the same with the girls since the summer, so having you there is a real help.'

Ruby hung back. Despite it being hard to hear what Carolyn was saying, it was nice to know that she was getting on well with Sarah and had someone else to talk to about things at home. She knew that she had been spending a lot of time with Kira recently, and that her friendship with Carolyn had been a little rocky, but she had thought they were on the mend.

She just needed to have an honest conversation with Carolyn about Josh, and she still didn't know how she was going to do that without breaking Kira's confidence, or making Carolyn despise her for keeping things from her, or for calling Josh out. She startled a little as she listened to the rest of the conversation.

'Babe, sometimes I think what you need is someone to just hold you. When was the last time anyone put their arms around you or gave you what you really needed, physically?' Sarah's voice had dropped an octave as she talked soothingly to Carolyn.

'I...I really don't know,' she stuttered. 'Honestly, it's been so long since he's even looked at me, let alone held me. I can't even think like that anymore. I feel like a husk, like a shell,' Carolyn's voice hitched, as if she was struggling to hold back tears.

'Well, come here then, let me hold you.'

Ruby held back her breath as the muffled sound of people moving together came to her ears. Was that all that was happening? She knew that Carolyn had spent a bit of time with Sarah recently, but she had also seen the way Sarah had started to look at her friend. Maybe there was more to this than she had heard, and maybe this would be just what Carolyn needed to get her to believe in herself again and make a decision about her marriage.

Ruby shifted her position, turning to creep away back to the bar. The last thing she wanted was for Carolyn to know that she was eavesdropping. She really hoped that her friend got what she needed tonight—everyone deserved to feel that closeness of being held. And if it was Sarah that could give this to her friend, then that was great; it was no less than Carolyn deserved.

19

3 Months Ago
October, Kira

Kira had spent the better part of an hour fussing over her Halloween outfit. Carolyn had dragged her shopping last week, after her Wednesday morning class, after hearing that Kira definitely wasn't coming along to the Halloween do: (a) she hated Halloween and (b) she didn't have anything to wear. As usual, Carolyn had seen this as the ultimate challenge—an opportunity to ambush Kira after class in the presence of her colleagues, so that she couldn't say no, and then treating Kira like her own personal mannequin.

After an hour of making her try on one outrageous outfit after another, they both agreed and settled on Bat Woman—slightly less revealing and sexy than the Catwoman outfit, but still revealing enough to make Kira feel uncomfortable without a few drinks inside her. One thing she hadn't really been able to establish when she was with Carolyn was where Josh was. There was only so much she could ask without looking nosy, and the last thing she really wanted was a heart-to-heart with Carolyn about the state of her marriage.

She had tried to skirt around it by asking questions about the twins and their outfits for the party. Carolyn's answers had given her some reassurance that it was just the three of them coming along, and she had mentioned feeling "like a single parent as Josh is away again". That was only last week, so she guessed that Josh wouldn't be there tonight, and anyway, she knew Ruby would let her know if she had heard any different.

Kira had still felt a sense of uneasiness when it was just her and Carolyn alone together, without Ruby as a buffer. In the back of her mind, she couldn't escape the fact that Carolyn still didn't know that her Josh was Kira's "Jay", and that she didn't know what had happened between them. She had talked it through extensively with Ruby after the summer party to try and work through what to do, and her fear that she was going to see him again at the gym.

It was only Ruby's constant and pragmatic counsel that stopped Kira from instantly quitting Aaron Sparks, and basically jumping on the next flight out to Outer Mongolia, or somewhere she could disappear once and for all, where he couldn't track her down.

Ruby had convinced her that Josh was not a full member of the club, that he spent most of the year abroad and rarely came to any of the functions Carolyn organised, as he was either off with his buddies at another gym, or training with a triathlon team that Kira knew were based at least an hour's drive away. Ruby was happy to grill Carolyn about Josh's whereabouts, to find out if there was any risk that he would show up at the club when they were not expecting it.

It had all come down to what Kira had to lose. She had spent the better part of the last year building back her confidence and building up her training to serious competition level. She had a lovely flat, a good job and the respect of her colleagues. She never thought that she would be confident enough to face Josh down, but now, she was starting to think that if he did ever come near her or confront her, then maybe she would.

She also had the restraining order that Ruby had helped her with. She never wanted to have to use it but, if necessary, she would. There was no way she was giving up her life now just because some nasty guy wanted to make her fear him, and to trap and control her. She was stronger than she had ever been, and she owed it to Joanna and to herself to prove that no man was going to hold her back.

Then there was Sam. Their acquaintance earlier in the year had only been fleeting, but it made her see that a relationship in the future was absolutely possible, and that there were actually some good guys out there that would be patient, and kind and loving. He had been so incredibly understanding when, after their 4th date, she had broken down in tears as he had gently asked if he could kiss her, and she had frozen like a rabbit in the headlights as soon as he had placed his hand on her cheek to draw her close.

Instead of going on the defensive and getting annoyed at her for leading him on, he removed his hand and gently asked her if she was ok, and would she maybe like a hug instead? She had felt herself trembling in his arms as the tears came in gulping waves, and he smoothed his hand down over her hair, waiting patiently until she was ready to talk. His kindness and understanding had let her feel that she could tell him part of her story.

She could tell him that she wasn't rejecting him, but that someone in her not-too-distant past had really hurt her—not just her heart, but physically. That now, when she felt his hand on her face, her body had an almost instinctive reaction, as it felt that the gentle touch was going to be followed by a backhander that led to her being violated and left shaking on the floor.

She had felt Sam tense with fury as he held her. Men like him, who were true and good—it went against all of their values and instincts to do anything to hurt people. Sam was a lifeguard; he was in a profession that literally saved lives. He had then been more than understanding when, a week later, she had sat him down and explained that she just wasn't ready for a relationship yet.

She explained that she had been for some counselling previously to help her recover from the trauma and to process what had happened to her, but that maybe she needed a bit more time before she was really ready to be with someone. She didn't tell him that she had recently seen "him" up close again, or that she even knew who he really was now, and that Sam would also know him. She couldn't face that level of reaction from anyone yet, with the exception of Ruby.

She hoped that maybe Sam was around tonight. The more resilience she had started to build over the last couple of months, by being around Ruby, had made her start to think perhaps the time had come to give him another chance and see where things went.

Kira smiled at the thought of seeing him, as she gathered up her leather jacket and cute orange felt bag in the shape of a pumpkin, that Carolyn had insisted she had to accessorise her outfit with. She double-checked her lipstick and phone, along with the handful of sweets that she could hand out to the kids.

She peered at her reflection again in the mirror in her hallway, stifling a laugh as she saw how funny she looked with her face contoured with black and grey make-up, and her long dark hair crimped and backcombed into an outrageous mess—so different to her usual neat and tidy look. The Bat Woman logo stood proudly on a vest top tucked into black leather shorts over thick black tights, her cape swirling out behind her. If only Joanna could see her now.

Kira was always the sensible sister, who never really had a wild side, or if she did, she certainly hadn't explored it. She was always waiting to take Joanna's lead. Tonight, this was a part of her personality she was happy to explore, now that she had the safety net of her friends and lovely colleagues. For the first time in a long time, Kira felt a bubble of excitement building in her belly as she walked out into the dark night to her car.

20

3 Months Ago
October, Carolyn

The place looked fucking awesome! Carolyn grinned as she surveyed the lobby and café bar area of Sparks. The events committee had worked so hard to make the meagre entertainment budget, that was fundraised from all the previous events stretch as far as they could this year, and the results spoke for themselves. After her five minutes of frustration, her chat with Sarah had really buoyed her up, and she could appreciate how good the place looked.

She knew that some of the decorations were a little cheap and tacky, but with the lighting and the music, and most people embracing the option of dressing up, she couldn't help but feel really happy and pleased with herself. Everyone had played their part in getting the room ready, but it had been Sarah who had really made most of the effort in the days leading up to the event.

Despite being one of the busiest PTs, and running spin classes at both Sparks and a gym on the other side of town, she had been more than willing to run around collecting deliveries, calling up local businesses that had promised raffle prizes, and keeping Carolyn caffeinated.

It had taken them an age to hang all of the garish decorations, and she was grateful that Sarah could reach much higher than she could. She wasn't sure that the amount of blue tack and sticky tape they had used met their current fire regulations, but it was too late to worry about that now.

They had spent a lot more time together since the summer. It had been Sarah that had helped her when Josh was away, when she got a flat tyre in the Sparks car park. She had used her tyre repair spray, and then insisted on coming with her to the local repair shop to get a good deal on the replacement, where she knew the guys on the sales counter. It was Sarah she had sat with, enjoying a cold beer after a committee meeting a few weeks ago, when the kids were at their grandparents' for the night.

There had been the odd moment when Carolyn had felt a fleeting stir of something deep in the pit of her stomach as Sarah's hand had brushed her arm, as she had sat next to her on the sofa. Or maybe it was just that she had been so devoid of Josh's, or anyone's, attention for so long that she was getting ahead of herself. Carolyn berated herself. Just because Sarah was gay and single, and also incredibly kind and attentive to Carolyn, didn't mean she fancied her.

She had nipped home after finishing up the decorating earlier in the day, and it had taken her longer than usual to get the kids organised and faces painted, after Charlie had flat out refused to wear the mini Frankenstein outfit he had chosen himself off eBay just last week—now saying that the green face paint was going to ruin his street cred and his chance of a dance with Lilly, a girl from his swimming class.

He had decided last minute that he now wanted to be Dracula, with the minimum of paint on his face, but with fangs that he could pretend to bite people with. Carolyn had then had to abandon her plans of getting ready early, to dash out to hunt down a last-minute mini cape and pair of fangs, before Charlie had a full-on meltdown.

She was about to bundle both kids out the door to run to the supermarket to see what she could find, when the front door had slammed shut, and Josh had suddenly appeared in the hall, dragging his holdall behind him. Just the sight of him had made her jump. She wasn't expecting him for at least another couple of days. As usual, he had turned up without calling, just to keep her on the hop.

He had tapped her on the shoulder gently as she had her back to him and had proceeded to pretend to bite her neck, causing the twins to giggle uncontrollably, as he then slid his arm around her side.

'Where are you all dashing off to, eh?' He released her as he bent down to give first Amber, then Charlie, a quick hug. 'Trying to avoid being my welcoming committee?'

Amber replied first, the distain for her brother clear in her tone.

'Charlie is being fussy; he doesn't want his face all green as he wants Lilly to kiss him, and now my make-up isn't going to be done on time 'cos Mum's got to go buy him a stupid Dracula cape!' said Amber, which had promptly earnt her a kick on the shins from Charlie.

'I always wanted to be Dracula. Tell him, Mum!' He had tried to launch himself at Amber again, as Josh had grabbed the hood of his coat.

'Ok, enough of that, you two! How about Mum pops out and gets the outfit, and I stay here and sort your make-up out?' he placated. 'And while she's out—Mummy, can pick me up something to wear for tonight?' He had looked up and met Carolyn's eyes then.

She knew that she had looked confused. Josh never wanted to do fancy dress, nor did he actively want to participate in events at Sparks when he didn't have to. The fact that he was back early was one thing, but having him tag along to her event, when she had made so much effort and wanted to let her hair down, was another.

Before she could say anything that would have inevitably started a fight and set the tone for the evening, he came up to her and gently slid his arm around her side again. 'It will be fun! Do I need to feed them too, or will there be snacks at Sparks?'

She had been so astounded at his soft and helpful tone that for a second, she couldn't answer, before shaking herself out of it.

'Well, that would be great, thanks. I'm sure they will love you helping them get ready,' she smiled back at him, still unsure about this supportive exchange. 'They definitely do not need feeding. There will be a kids' buffet and a shed load of sweets that they are no doubt going to eat far too much of, so they should be fine.' She put her hand over his, where it was still wrapped lightly around her waist.

'Cool. Right, well just pick me up some kind of mask and cape thing. You know I can't stand all that face paint stuff, but might as well make an effort!' He gave her waist a quick squeeze before pecking her lightly on the cheek and releasing her.

As Carolyn had bent to pick up her shopping bags from the stand in the hall, she had paused briefly, still uncertain about this sudden change in attitude, but just grateful that Josh seemed in a great mood and wanted to join in with the kids for a change. There had to be a reason for this change of heart, but she couldn't put her finger on what it was.

She heard him rounding the kids up as she opened the front door. 'Come on, kiddos, get your butts upstairs, you little monsters. Let's see if we can get your faces done before Mum gets home!' Followed by screeching and giggling as he herded them from the sunroom and through the kitchen, roaring at them like an out-of-control monster.

Now, as she looked at the effort everyone had put into making the event amazing, if Josh actually carried on behaving himself, then perhaps tonight could be like old times—fun, relaxing, and with them together as a family and happy again. Perhaps Josh would let Amber stand on his feet as he whirled her round to the Time Warp, or maybe he would pull silly faces and do a zombie walk to make Charlie laugh.

Maybe they would go home, and even though it would be late, dial up a pizza and sit and dissect the evening together over a nice glass of red. As she watched her husband down another double whisky, as he leant over the bar to chat to James, she shuddered—perhaps not.

21
3 Months Ago
October, Kira

The absolute terror that shook her came in waves and waves, physically wracking her body with almost uncontrollable convulsions. Her mouth was so dry, her chest heaved and her heart pounded, sweat dripped from her palms, and she could see she had smears of red and black all down her forearm, where she had wiped her face.

She had no idea if it was from her face paint, which she assumed was now smeared across her face, or if it was actually her blood—or maybe his blood? Her head was swimming, and she couldn't focus as she scrambled back against the hard plastic side of the cross trainer, where she had landed when Kyle had dragged him off her.

She couldn't quite process what had just happened, and now she realised that Kyle had left her on her own. She had no idea where Kyle was, what was happening, where Josh was, or if he was going to come back. She couldn't seem to get purchase on the floor to push herself up, her legs felt bereft of any feeling, her body starting to numb as shock set in and the adrenaline wore off.

She could still feel him now, one hand grabbing and yanking her hair as the other wrapped around her throat, forcing her up against the wall, somewhere between the kettlebell station and the free weights. She could feel herself clawing at the hand around her throat, her eyes bulging as she tried to plead with him through her restricted airway to stop, and that she would do what he wanted.

His hands had gripped tighter as she forced herself to stay upright, as he had moved his hand from her throat to squeeze her face, either side of her mouth, his hot breath pungent with whiskey fumes, his spittle flecking her cheeks as he spat venomous words into her face.

'You fucking prick tease, coming here tonight all dressed up like a tart. Did you think I wouldn't notice all the other guys staring at your cunt in those tight little shorts, that I wouldn't notice that soft prick Sam pawing at you like a piece of meat?' He had squeezed her face harder and then brought his mouth crashing down hard onto hers, as she continued to squirm and try and get out of his grip, as he had continued to spit into her face.

'Don't even try and answer, you bitch. You want to show off to all the men and show them your tight pussy, then you're going to get what you asked for.' His bloodshot eyes had bored into her as he had moved the grip from her face to the back of her shorts, grasping for the zip as he started to rub his crotch against her.

'You know you love me giving you a good fucking. Have you missed me? You know I was the best you could get. You shouldn't have pushed me away. You're always going to be mine.' He was breathing heavier by then, as he had pushed a knee roughly between her legs. 'You're fucking hot for me, admit it.'

She had felt the tears slipping down her face, her eyes stinging from the mascara, her hands moving to push the knee away. All of her instincts had told her to do something, but the paralysis of complete abject fear prevented her from doing anything but silently sobbing as he forced her down, clawing at the thin fabric between their bodies and tearing his way in.

A sudden crash and a roar, and all of a sudden, he hadn't been on top of her any longer, but sprawled sideways across the gym mat with what looked like the Joker from Batman, landing a heavy punch straight into his face, sending him slithering further across the gym floor.

'Get the fuck off her! What the hell are you doing, man?' the Joker had screamed. 'Don't fucking bother to speak; just fucking stay there, away from her!'

It had taken Kira a moment to register that the voice under the face of white make-up had been Kyle, as he had landed a swift kick into Josh's body before moving over to help her up.

'Come on, it's ok. I've got you. I won't let him hurt you again, its ok. Let's sit you somewhere you can get your breath back, before I drag this scumbag outside and beat seven bales of shit out of him. That's it, come on.' He had gently lifted her up and started walking her back towards the machines on the other side of the gym, away from where Josh had been attempting to right himself. He had lowered her down in a spot against the cross trainer and had gently smoothed back her hair, and told her something about getting rid of Josh and finding Ruby.

She startled now as she heard the gym door opening and hurried footsteps approaching.

'Oh fuck, Kira. Oh my poor love, come here, let me see you. Let's get you down to the changing rooms where I can look at you properly, and we can figure this out. It's ok, it's ok, he won't be coming back; Kyle's seeing to that.'

Kira looked up gratefully at the shock of wild red hair and the crazily painted face, as her friend enveloped her in a soft embrace. She leant her weight into Ruby's soft frame, grateful for the support, knowing that there was no way she could hold herself up properly as Ruby carefully lifted her, sliding her arm under her and started to semi-lift her towards the main stairs back down towards the café.

'Rubes, wait.' Kira could hear her voice slurred and uncertain, as she squeezed her friend's arm to get her attention. 'We can't go down those stairs. Everyone will see. I've got my staff pass in my bag. We can go down the back way to the changing rooms.'

'Will you be ok if I lean you here and go back to grab your bag?' Ruby gently propped her against the doorframe to the spin room, seeking assurance that Kira would be fine for the seconds it took her to run back.

'Just go, Rubes. Hurry though; the bag's shaped like a pumpkin, so it should be easy to spot somewhere over by the treadmills.' She groaned as she transferred her weight to her other leg, realising that she probably had a deep tissue bruise forming that would set her back in her training for next year.

She pushed that thought to the back of her mind. All she needed to do now was get cleaned up and get the hell out of here, before Josh came back from wherever Kyle had dragged him off to. She put a tentative hand up to her forehead, feeling the sticky mess of a cut oozing blood mingled with black and white face paint. She couldn't even begin to imagine what the hell she looked like—it was a good job it was Halloween.

Why on earth had she decided to go and look for her lost headphones up in the gym this evening? There was no reason why she couldn't have waited until the next day. It wasn't like she needed them there and then; she was always misplacing things. People tended to be pretty honest, in her experience, and handed stuff into lost property all the time. She had been so determined to have a good time tonight, and then look how it had turned out.

She had arrived late after talking herself into the costume, grateful that Carolyn had convinced her that it was a good idea. She had let Sue, on reception, know she would be leaving her car and grabbing a cab later, as after one glass of wine she thought it would be good to have a laugh with her friends and let her hair down a little. She hadn't even had a chance for a sip out of her second glass, before she had stupidly come upstairs to look for her bloody headphones—and this had happened.

She hadn't even had a chance to speak to Ruby, before she had gone upstairs to the gym. She had spotted her frantically waving at her across the bar area, but had managed to get herself waylaid first by Sue and Bonny from reception, who admired her outfit. Then there was Taylor, steering her off to the side of the kids' play area to ask her if she would help judge the best thriller dance competition later, to which she had agreed—but only if Taylor agreed to join in the dancing herself.

She could have spent two more minutes watching and laughing at the kids joining in apple bobbing, and trying to eat a ring donut off a washing line that had been strung up across the kids' play area. She could have made time to see what Ruby was waving to her about. But no—she had to go and look.

She let out a low moan as Ruby appeared back at her side, torn pumpkin bag hanging limply from her hand. She held it out for Kira to dip her hand in and to thankfully grab her staff pass. As she looked up at Ruby, she could see the concern and pain reflected in her eyes.

'You tried to warn me, didn't you?' she asked sadly. 'I told you I wasn't going sure if I was going to come tonight, and you knew that you had to try and tell me in case I changed my mind. I saw you waving but thought it was because of what I was wearing, that you were going to have a joke with me about it. I should have paid more attention, Ruby. I'm so sorry to put you through this.' She started to sob as Ruby pulled her close, gently nudging her towards the staff stairs.

'Kira, if I could have done anything to prevent this happening, I would. I'm just so sorry I left my phone at home by accident and couldn't get hold of you. I feel so responsible,' she whispered as her eyes pooled with unshed tears.

'And Kyle? I've dragged him into it too. He didn't even know about Josh, did he?' Kira asked.

'No, he didn't. But Kyle is a good guy. There is no way on this planet that he would stand for a bloke hitting a woman. He had to do something; you see that, don't you? He would do anything to protect me, and that means protecting my friends too,' she continued as they moved slowly down the stairs.

They both started at the sudden noise of the door to the gym above them being pushed open and the sound of footsteps.

'Rubes?'

Ruby let out a relieved breath as Kyle caught them up, taking more of Kira's weight as he helped them both through the door into the locker room, walking Kira down towards the benches where he helped lower her gently—already sensing her discomfort, but also her gratitude for his patience and kindness.

'Kyle?' She looked up at him now, grateful for everything he had done. 'I think you just saved my life; I actually think he was going to kill me.'

22

3 Months Ago
October, Carolyn

At first Carolyn couldn't work out what she was seeing and hearing as she crept forward through the locker room. She had been heading back towards the bar from the storeroom, after picking up more paper plates, and had spotted what looked like Kira being half-carried by Ruby and then Kyle, the three of them hustling into the women's changing area from the back stairs.

She quietly set down the armful of plates on the bench and moved forward to listen. She knew that from this angle they couldn't see her, as the changing areas were arranged in a staggered formation. Each area had its own set of benches and lockers off a central walkway leading to the hairdryers and make-up mirrors.

She could hear what sounded like someone crying and another person making soothing sounds, and wondered if Kira had fallen and hurt herself or something. It wouldn't be out of character for Kira to want privacy if something had happened instead of any embarrassment in front of the party crowd, and Ruby was her go-to person. But then Kyle came into view.

She could see him reflected in the mirror on the wall opposite at the hair-drying station. She ducked lower so he couldn't spot her. She could see he was visibly worked up, clenching his fists and shaking his head, a bruise visibly blooming on his lower jaw and blood by the left of his lip.

'I should have fucking ended him. Seriously, Kira, if you just say the word, I'll go right now and put his fucking head through a fucking window. I can't believe that nasty fucker did this to you. No one should lay a hand on a woman. I mean, what was he thinking? Why would he think that was acceptable?' he continued, pacing back and forth, scowling across at where Carolyn assumed Kira and Ruby were sat in one of the changing areas.

'We should call the police,' Ruby spoke up now. 'Kira, they already know about the history and what he had been doing to you.'

'No, no police; not tonight,' Kira's voice was ragged and breathy, as if getting the words out was taking all of her effort.

'But you've got the restraining order. They can arrest him now,' Ruby insisted.

'Not with all these people here, Rubes. They're all having such a nice time, and Carolyn has worked so hard to make it nice and raise some more money for the kids' clubs. I don't want to ruin it and for everyone to know what's been going on.'

Carolyn physically recoiled at the sound of her name, and that whatever had happened to Kira, she didn't want help because she didn't want to spoil it for her? This wasn't right. Why wouldn't she want help if someone had hurt her friend? Just as Carolyn was about to step round the corner to make her presence known and to offer her help, she stopped in her tracks as Kyle said loud and clear.

'Josh needs punishing.'

The world swayed beneath her feet; her head started to swim as she staggered backwards towards the changing bench. What the hell? They were talking about a Josh—it had to be hers. They didn't know anyone else called Josh at the club. Her calves hit the bench, and she shakily let herself slump down, not sure if she could listen to whatever came next.

'Ruby's already told me, Kira, that someone had been stalking you for months? That she had to help you move flats, that you took this job here to get away from him. I just didn't realise it was him,' Kyle sounded bewildered. 'I can't believe something like this can just happen and then he gets away with it,' he sighed. 'You don't deserve this, Kira. No one does.'

She could hear Kira audibly sobbing again, and Ruby hushing and soothing her.

'But it's my fault,' Kira hiccupped. 'I should have worked out he was married and no good. It was obvious, really. I just didn't want to see it, and then by the time I tried to end it, he had already started hurting me. I was just so scared.'

'There is no way on earth this is your fault,' Ruby's voice was stern, as she berated Kira for even suggesting that she was to blame for Josh's behaviour. 'Married or not, what he has done to you is assault. He has intimidated you, stalked you and made you feel in threat for your life. I don't care who he's married to or how great a dad he is. He has to pay, and you need to feel safe.'

'But what about Carolyn and the twins?' Kira sniffed.

'Let me talk to her. Let's just get through tonight, and we can make a plan.' Ruby was firm.

'I thought all this was behind me,' Kira muttered.

Carolyn had to lean forward to try and hear what she was saying. It was like all the energy had gone out of Kira, her voice resigned and defeated. Carolyn's heart felt like it was going to break as she listened.

'I thought that once I had moved flats, changed my job, that he would stop, that he wouldn't be able to find me. You know I cancelled all my social media, which hasn't helped my PT stuff at all. I got you to help with that restraining order, Rubes, and I hadn't seen him for months. But then there he was at the summer party, charming everyone like he hadn't a care in the world. And all I could think of when he spotted me across the pool was, this guy is going to kill me! I was so frightened,' Kira paused.

'But then once I knew who he was and that he travelled for work a lot, I thought maybe it will be ok, maybe I won't see him. Now that he know that I am friends with his wife that will be it. But then tonight,' she exhaled a long, slow breath. 'Then tonight he tried to rape me, and I swear, Kyle, if you hadn't found me, he would have done even worse.'

Carolyn felt her chest constrict. The strain on her felt like heavy, hot weight bearing down, making her feel faint and woozy. How could she ever look Kira in the eye again? How the hell could she go home tonight to Josh, knowing what he had done to her friend? It was all well and good him treating her like shit, demeaning her, getting rough with her, but she was his wife; she could handle it. Not poor, lovely Kira.

She had to get some fresh air, get out of here to make a plan. She scrabbled behind her to get purchase on the bench with her sweaty hands, and then watched in horror as she pushed herself upright—and her stupid, ridiculous witch's hat, that she had thought was so jaunty and fun earlier in the night, slid off her head and, before she could grab it with a shaky hand, gusted out of the locker cubby and into the walkway, into the view of the next changing area.

'What the fuck! Who's there?' Kyle started.

Before Carolyn had chance to gather herself, he appeared round the corner. Carolyn gave him a weak, watery smile, tears starting to fill her eyes as he reached out his hand to steady her.

'Kyle, what's going on?'

She could hear the fear and anxiety in Ruby's voice, and then the sudden intake of breath as Kyle led Carolyn gently round the corner.

'Oh shit, Carolyn!' Ruby gasped, as Kira looked up at her trembling friend in disbelief. 'How much of that did you hear?'

Carolyn could feel the blood draining from her face as the realisation hit her—that things could never, ever be the same again. That the family life she had built and the security the twins had with Josh's money—the lovely house, the club membership—was about to implode all around her.

There was no going back now. This was it. This was the time she confronted what she had known for a very long time—that Josh, once a loving husband who had held her so gently when they danced at their wedding, was in fact a nasty, cruel, misogynistic, abusive bully.

'How much did I hear?' Carolyn repeated back to them quietly. 'All of it,' she muttered as she turned and fled.

23
3 Months Ago
October, Ruby

Ruby knew she was supposed to be relaxing after last night's Halloween party nightmare, but she couldn't switch off the thoughts whirling around her brain. It had taken all her energy to gently coerce Kira into letting her take pictures of her injuries, and then email them to herself at work. She'd then cleaned her friend's face carefully with make-up wipes, and helped her into a pair of Kyle's Pyjamas, before holding her until she finally fell into a fitful sleep in their spare bedroom.

Kira had spent the day recuperating, eating small mouthfuls of soup through her bruised lips and dozing through daytime TV shows. Ruby had left her to sleep now before dinner, knowing that they needed to pick up the conversation about what they needed to do about Josh and Carolyn, but dreading it all the same.

She ran the hot tap again, sinking deeper into the bubbles. She still couldn't shake the feelings that this incident had stirred up for her. The more she thought about it, the more she started to tremble, despite the scalding water pouring in around her. It was no surprise that she was so affected by what had happened last night.

She had told the girls the story about what happened to her when she was 16 just the other week, so it was still raw in her mind. Seeing what Josh had done, had just resurfaced it all again—feelings she thought she had dealt with and locked away firmly in the past, bubbling back up to the surface all over again.

She knew the time was getting nearer when she would have to come clean to Kyle and tell him about her history. It was still so hard to contemplate, but since seeing Todd at Aaron Sparks, everything had become more fraught, more real. The truth and the time when she had to talk to Kyle were drawing closer like a net around her.

Last night, she felt that she couldn't let her guard down in front of Kyle or Kira. She felt she had to be the brave and strong one. She had pulled on her sternest and angriest face, determined not to let the mask slip. But now, in the sanctuary of her bathroom, she allowed herself to let go as she encircled her legs with her arms, pulling them up to her chest, letting noiseless sobs catch in her throat. She was just grateful that Kyle was listening to the football on the radio downstairs, so that he couldn't hear her.

How could she explain to him about that one terrifying night in her past that changed the course of her life? That one night had led to her doing something she had regretted for the last 20 years, and now meant that she couldn't give him the one thing that he desperately wanted—the chance to be a father. She couldn't contemplate what it would do to their relationship if he found out that she was dirty, soiled, that she was damaged beyond all hope.

She closed her eyes again as she thought back to that night. No 16-year-old deserved to go through what she had been through. Years before Everyone's Invited or Me Too, she had had no one to speak out to, no one to share the most horrendous night of her life with.

Todd had seemed such a nice guy when he joined their high school as the new boy at 15, moving back from life overseas in South Africa, where his dad was working. His tanned skin, floppy blonde hair and piercing dark eyes were so different to the normal guys in her class, with their mousey buzz cuts and pink-and-white complexions. He was a curiosity and intriguing. He seemed so worldly and well-travelled from his years spent at international school.

It was no wonder everyone flocked to him—he was a far cry from the usual skinny runts the girls at St Jude's were used to. Like most of her peers, he was rich and had parents who spoilt him, but unlike the others, he didn't show off when his parents bought him the latest phone or cool video game. He was so cool that, even though all the guys were jealous of him, they still wanted to hang out with him, as if it gave them street cred by association.

There had been so many girls to choose from that he was spoilt for choice. They had fawned and swooned, eyelashes fluttering, applying lip gloss and fluttering mascaraed lashes in his direction. Ruby knew he was the kind of boy her parents would push her towards—a family with money and a house in South Africa, someone she could look pretty for, stay thin for and have sons for. But she had no interest in boys.

Even when she turned 16, and he started to show more of an interest in her, she brushed him off. She had her studies to get on with, and there was no way she was going to play into her parents' hands and make it easy for them to palm her off on the first rich kid to show her attention.

Then came the day that she looked back on with so much regret. As she sat here now in the bath, listening to the remote sounds of Kyle's radio from downstairs, and breathing in the scent of her delicious rose candle she had lit to try and calm her thoughts, she still couldn't believe how stupidly naïve she had been back then.

She had tried everything to resist Todd—ignoring him, blatantly walking away from him when he talked to her, dismissing him in class when he tried to engage her in conversation. The other girls jealously sneered at her, convinced he was only hitting on Ruby as a dare when she made it so obvious she was more interested in books and studying than boys.

He had continued to seek her out in the library each lunchtime, slowly chipping away at her until she finally talked to him, secretly thrilled—despite herself—when he asked her to be his study partner. He talked to her respectfully, breaking down her barriers until she felt safe enough with him, to tell him all about her plans to secretly study to get into university to do law behind her parents' back.

So, when the final exam days were nearly upon them, she finally accepted his invitation to an after-prom party at his house. Her parents were thrilled, of course—having got to know his parents at the country club, her mother gushed over the opportunities this date between their two children could bring for their family.

Ruby knew that the fact that Todd was interested in her would be a massive distraction for her parents, and that the more time they spent "getting in" with his family, the less time they would spend scrutinising what she was actually doing. Ruby almost smiled ruefully to herself then, as she thought back about how she fooled her mother into giving her the cash to go and buy accessories for a prom dress.

Little did she know that the money paid for books for next year instead, and that Serena lent her shoes and a bag for prom. Her parents had agreed she could stay at Serena's the night of the party. Getting ready together, they gossiped about the boys in their class—who was inevitably going to get off with who—but also how they just wanted to go for a dance and to have a laugh.

Ruby shook herself out of her thoughts as she realised that the water had cooled around her. She shivered as she levered herself out of the bath and grabbed a towel off the heated rail. She knew better than anyone that dragging up the past and dwelling on it never changed anything for the better, so there was no point reliving that night over and over again, and thinking about all of the "what ifs". She was where she was now, and even though it wasn't by the original route she had planned. By changing her name, her identity, her style over the last 20 years, she had been confident that her past could remain just that—something that happened to Ruth, not to her, Ruby.

Angrily, she swiped at the steamy mirror and stared at her reflection. How dare one person's actions impact another person's life so viciously? Ruby was so fucking angry. How dare Josh get away with this?

24
3 Months Ago
October, Carolyn

Carolyn had let herself into her car last night with shaking hands. The adrenaline coursing through her body had yet to subside, and she had sat taking a few deep breaths, knowing that when it wore off and the inevitable crash came, it would exhaust her. It was the same every time Josh had raised his hand to her or shouted in her face over the past years; her heart would feel like it was beating out of her chest, and her brain felt like it would explode into a thousand pieces.

She had rummaged in the glove box, grateful for the tub of sweets she kept there for long car journeys. She had chosen a chocolate bar to give herself a sugar spike to combat the adrenaline dip that was inevitable.

Looking back on everything that had led up to this, she knew that there was no way that she was going to stay with Josh now. All the doubts that had been crystallising in her mind over the last few months had come to a head. She just had to plan carefully how to end it with the least amount of collateral damage. The fact that he had been having yet another affair didn't actually bother her in the slightest.

It also didn't surprise her, as she had known there was something going on back last summer, when she had found a secret credit card and receipts hidden in the lining of his overnight bag. The nights in hotels, the florist and lingerie bills, the one for jewellery were nothing to her, but the fact that this time she knew the victim was Kira had sucked the air out of her and shocked her to her core.

Carolyn had known early on in their relationship that Josh had a certain way with women. Not only could he charm them and wrap them round his little finger, but that pretty much any woman who happened to encounter the depths of his crystal blue eyes often felt unable to tear themselves away from his transfixing gaze and his easy charm.

But then, there was the other side, the one that had grown more and more dominant over the years—the one that mimicked his father, who thought nothing of treating his multiple wives like shit, who used his looks and charm to reel them in and then spit them out.

Yes, Josh was a chip off the old block, but looking back now, she realised that she had always been too scared to admit what he really was or, to see that he was making a fool out of her. She felt stupid and weak. She knew that people must pity her—she had overheard people gossiping. Just the other year, she had heard Sue at the gym talking about how Josh had put the moves on Melanie, who ran the health spa down the road, and had been spotted verbally berating her in the car park late one night when she turned down his advances.

She had told herself that Josh rarely came to Sparks, so it probably wasn't him. Sue couldn't have met him more than once before that alleged incident, so how would she recognise him in the dark? She had denied, denied, denied, but now here it was—she couldn't be an ostrich any longer. She had to look the truth hard in the face, and own up to the state of her marriage, and the reality about the monster that was her husband.

There was no way she could have faced going home last night. She knew that Josh had been drinking, and from what she heard in the changing room, she guessed he might possibly bear the marks of the altercation, and she had had no desire to ask him about what had happened or to listen to any more of his lies. Any confrontation would have only ended one way, and she had had enough shock for one night. She had decided she would go to a friend's house, lay low for the night, and plan what to do next.

She knew it was only a matter of days until Josh would be heading back to the airport for his next trip, to study some long-lost plant or something. The twins had already planned to have a sleepover at a friend's house after the Halloween party, so she had had no need to sort them out. The problem had been, who to call? Her two closest friends were still inside Sparks. It had taken her a second or two to think through her options, but really, there was only one. She had picked up the phone and called Sarah.

The next thing she did was text Josh—the only way she could bear to communicate with him.

'Dad has had a fall, left the party early and will stay at my parents. Kids are at a sleepover. Hopefully see you tomorrow before you leave for the airport.' She wasn't expecting a reply.

Josh wouldn't bother to check in to make sure her dad was ok. He had made it clear over the last couple of years that he had no interest in maintaining any meaningful relationship with her family, after her dad had openly called him a bully a few years ago at a family wedding.

No, Josh just cared that the more time she spent at her parents, the less time she spent keeping up appearances at home, and keeping the house clean and tidy for when he came home. He didn't give a toss that her father had Parkinson's and was quite poorly most of the time—he was so fucking selfish.

She was so glad that she could rely on Sarah. She knew that after she had helped with the decorations earlier that day, and had made sure that Carolyn had everything she needed at the start of the party, Sarah had snuck out, headed home. Fancy dress wasn't really her scene, but she had gone out of her way to make sure that Carolyn got the help she needed to make the place look great, and for that, Carolyn was grateful.

She was even more grateful when, on reaching Sarah's flat, she had opened the door and, without asking for any explanation, had taken a shaking Carolyn in her arms before leading her through to the kitchen.

25

2 Months Ago
November, Carolyn

The morning after the Halloween party, Carolyn had had to make a tough decision. Sarah had been good as her word on the night and hadn't asked any questions. She had simply shown her into the kitchen and then, without any preamble, pulled two beers out of the fridge, twisting the caps off before handing one to Carolyn. Carolyn had taken it with a still-shaking hand and followed Sarah's lead by pulling out the bar stool opposite the one she had perched on, at the small breakfast bar, and taking a large, much-needed swallow.

Sarah had reached out and gently put her hand over Carolyn's hand. This simple act of kindness was enough to open the floodgates—first the tears came, then the rage came, as Carolyn had paced up and down Sarah's cramped kitchen.

She had talked to the girls a little about her life with Josh before, but this was the first time she was completely honest about her experience. She finally had the courage to hold a mirror up to her life and to let it all out. The years of belittling, the emotional abuse, the gas lighting, the way he made her feel like she was less than nothing, the cheating, the lying, the criticism of her as a wife, a mother, a partner—using this as a justification as to why he looked elsewhere.

How he was self-made, he was famous in his field and deserved a wife who was more than she was, that she should make more effort, lose weight, get her hair sorted, entertain his work colleagues and not be a fat, lazy, uneducated slob.

And then came the story of Kira. How Carolyn had known last year that Josh was up to something again, and that this time, she thought it might be more serious. How Josh had not been away as much as usual, even though the offer of field trips were still coming in frequently, but she had heard him declining these—instead, taking trips to visit other universities and projects in London. She had seen the pattern before.

When the twins were 6 years old, there had been a woman he met at a conference. He had said it was a one-time thing when she had caught him out in a lie about who was texting him. Now he never let his phone out of his sight. Before that, there was a woman who had turned up at the house when the twins were 2 years old, shouting about how he had promised to leave Carolyn for her and that she was pregnant.

The pregnancy had been a lie—a pathetic ploy of a woman desperate to have Josh's attention after what he swore again was a one-night thing, maybe two nights at the most. That time, Josh had spent months wooing her again and winning back her trust.

This was before he travelled so much for work. He had arranged babysitters, bought her new underwear, new dresses, taken her out to her favourite restaurants and on dates to the theatre, which she knew he hated. He had done everything obvious to win her back, and on the surface, it looked like he was trying really hard, that there was sincerity in his actions. But even back then, Carolyn could still feel the undercurrent of duplicity and manipulation.

He still didn't want her working, discouraged her taking on additional commitments and responsibilities, didn't want her to have any level of independence. Stupidly, back then, she had loved that he wanted to take care of her, to be the provider, and to spend his hard-earned money on her and their family.

He bought them their beautiful house, paid for the twins to attend the best private nursery and later the best prep school, and he gave her an allowance, making her completely dependent on him. He encouraged her to spend time with her parents, to go to the gym and to accompany him to his work functions. Apart from that, she didn't really have much of a life to speak of. It was only when he started to travel more that she had joined the Sparks committee and started to meet the girls, but he had still always wanted to know where she was going and what she was doing.

She remembered the way he used to say to her:

'Aren't you so lucky that I love you so much to buy you chocolates even though they're going to make you fat?'

And when she couldn't find a vase big enough for the bouquet he brought home:

'You know how much I've spent on these flowers? I just want you to feel special, but if you don't appreciate them, then shall I just chuck them straight in the bin?'

The times when he put her down, eroding her confidence:

'You used to be so much fun, Carolyn. Now all you seem to do is moan and be a misery. Haven't I given you and the kids everything? I mean, look at this beautiful house—so many people have nothing in the world, and you have everything. Would you rather go back to how you were when we first met? Poor and living off your parents' pity?'

And how she had known it was more than just a one-night thing with the woman last year. Josh had been even more cautious about locking his office and taking the key with him when he went away to stop her prying. Then there had been the time when he said he was in London, but Sue had spotted his car in the next town, parked outside a restaurant, and had texted Carolyn to ask if she was enjoying her fancy dinner at Le Bistrot.

She had been too embarrassed to reply that she wasn't at Le Bistrot, that she was currently wiping up a squidgy pile of spaghetti bolognese from the hall carpet, after Charlie had launched his dish in a tantrum. He had been sent to bed to think about his temper, while Amber calmly sat and twirled her pasta between fork and spoon, eyes not leaving the TV as her brother raged and ranted before stomping up the stairs.

As she had scrubbed the orange stain, looking again at the message, she remembered a chill rolling over her again as she guessed that it was happening yet again—she was being treated like a fucking idiot.

'Yes, it was delicious, thanks!' she had replied to Sue, while wiping her eyes on the sleeve of her ratty old cardigan.

Then there had been less money in their joint account month on month, a new standing order of £1k a month being moved into what Josh had said was a savings account, to build a garden gym sometime in the next couple of years. She had been sure then that it was a load of crap, but she didn't want to rock the boat until she had more proof and until she had a plan. She had to be able to stand on her own two feet, and back then, she hadn't quite worked out how she was going to do that.

With Sarah's gentle patience, the whole story had come tumbling out. How Carolyn had known that Kira had been in an abusive relationship last year, and that the guy had turned really nasty—stalking her and physically harming her.

That she and Ruby had known the guy was called "Jay" and lived a few towns away from Sparks. That Kira had had to move house, change jobs and get a restraining order against this guy, before the message had sunk in, and he had finally left her alone from around January this year.

But that tonight, this Jay guy had run into Kira again and attacked her, and then the shocker—as she blurted it out finally to Sarah—that "Jay" was just the guy's initial, and that his real name was Josh, her Josh!

Sarah had taken her in her arms then and smoothed her hair, as Carolyn had sunk down to the floor in a pool of emotional exhaustion, and acceptance of the fact that she was married to a terrible man—a man that hurt women. She knew then that she couldn't do it anymore. She couldn't pretend that she wanted to save her marriage, that she loved him anymore, when the truth was that Josh actually scared her.

She knew that her decision was made for her. She just needed time to put a plan together, but also to let Ruby and Kira know what she was thinking of doing, and to reassure Kira that there was no way in the world she was letting Josh get away with what he had done. It was only a couple of days until the annual bonfire night and fireworks—a time when she would have got all her family and friends together to watch the massive display that the local high school always hosted.

She knew the kids would be disappointed if they didn't get to go this year, and she knew that Josh would be suspicious if she suddenly didn't want to attend. But she didn't want to have any opportunity for him to run into Kyle and Ruby, or God forbid even Kira, before she had had a chance to talk to them all.

She had to call an emergency meeting with Ruby and get a plan together in the next couple of days, and during that time, she had to stay as far away from her husband as possible. She unplugged her phone from Sarah's charger and flipped it over in her hand, fully expecting a number of messages from Ruby or even Kira, but surprisingly there was nothing from them. The only message was a simple thumbs-up emoji from Josh in reply to her message last night.

She breathed a sigh of relief as she then opened WhatsApp. There was no need for any explanation or preamble as she messaged Ruby: 'Sauna, Tuesday 5 pm.'

26

2 Months Ago
November, Ruby

In the days since the Halloween party, Ruby had been reflecting on the night years ago that changed her life. She knew from years of therapy that sometimes, the only way to move on from something was to confront it head-on, and to be honest with those around you. She knew she wasn't quite there yet. There would be a time when she could open up to Kyle and show her true self, but the thought of him not being able to handle the truth, about who she really was and where she really came from, scared her much more than she cared to admit.

She had been lonely for so long before she had met Kyle, and now, she had the security of a guy who loved her and made her feel safe. She didn't want to risk losing this just because she had failed to tell the truth when they first met.

If only she hadn't had that swig of vodka from Serena's parents' drinks cabinet before they left for prom, if only she hadn't drunk the glass of fizz offered to her in the back of the limo, if she hadn't taken a sip from a hip flask here, a shot of tequila there, a gulp of sickly sweet punch, then maybe the world wouldn't have spun out of control. The surge of bodies on the dance floor in the school gym, the DJ picking the tempo up, pushing the fader up on the treble and the bass, the roaring of electronic music in her ears, had carried her away.

She had seen Todd watching her with his posse of mates, his sycophantic hangers-on always trying to get his attention, wanting to be the ones to be invited back to his parents' huge white mansion on the hill, and to hang with him in his fabled rec room, complete with pool table and incredible sound system.

They had all been sucking up to him since the start of the term, wanting to be the ones he picked to come to his 16th birthday party at his house after prom, showing off to girls at school that they were his mates and could also get them an invite just to get themselves dates. The two most obnoxious, attention-grabbing boys that hung around Todd like a bad smell had already been bragging at the end of term how they had scored with Melissa and Bella, the two "hot girls" in her English class.

They, in turn, had bragged about being the first to lose their virginity, and it was common knowledge they were willing to put out again to secure an invite to Todd's party. It was going to be the place to be, and Ruth couldn't believe that she and Serena had been invited.

When Todd approached her near the end of the night, as the lights were being dimmed for the slow dance, she didn't pull away. She basked in the thrill that, of all the girls he could have picked, he had picked her. When the lights had come up and they all piled out into the car park, it seemed natural for Todd to take hers and Serena's hands, ushering them towards his limo and driver, as the other guys piled into their chauffeur-driven cars and followed the entourage back to Todd's house.

Ruby remembered that she had already felt woozy in the back of the limo, as Serena wittered on about how she was going to try and make out with Troy if Melissa had to leave early, and that she had always thought he was hot. She remembered giggling and nodding along as they piled out of the limo and into Todd's rec room. She remembered plastic cups of beer being poured and a bottle of frozen vodka being passed around, loud music, dimmed lights, dares.

In her fuzzy memory, she remembered people pairing off into dark corners, more people crowded round the pool table for a game of beer pong, the floor getting sticky where the beer had been spilt, then hands on her waist as she moved to the music. She had been very drunk by then. The room had started to spin as reality became distorted, and then, when she had tripped and staggered a little, she remembered Todd and some guy called Damien propping her up, one of them pushing his body against hers.

Her memory grew hazy then as she tried to process what had happened next, as she had felt her hand being taken, a hot, hard body moving in rhythm to the music, pushing up against her, holding her as she swayed, eyes glassy and blurring, him leading her away down the dark corridor, leading towards some storage rooms, things moving faster and then slower as her head span, his hands moving more and more urgently over her body. And then the pushing became harder, the room spun faster.

She remembered the feeling of terror, and she heard herself crying out, 'No, stop.'

Her voice sounding slurred to her own ears, and then trying and failing to move herself away from him. Him pulling at her dress, pushing it up, telling her how much she wanted this, how he was hard for her, how she was going to take it and fucking like it. Her face being pushed down into a pile of cushions. The suffocating feeling of being crushed, the ripping of sound of her underwear, the raggedness of her breath as he forced her harder and harder into the sofa, as he pushed himself on top of her.

The feeling of his hot breath on her neck as he grabbed a handful of her hair to control her, and to push himself harder between her thighs, into her, over and over again. Then spit trickling down her cheek as he salivated, telling her again and again that she was fucking loving it, that she fucking wanted it, that all the girls wanted him—so wasn't she lucky that he picked her? And then the weight was gone. She had slid limply down to the hard concrete floor, the pain deep into her muscles as she turned her head and vomited all over the floor.

The hours after that had been a complete blur. Serena had found her in the bathroom, trying to clean herself up—wiping the essence of him from between her legs, washing away the make-up that was streaking her face, plugging her bloody nose with toilet paper. Then, even worse, her friend's complete lack of compassion or comprehension as to what she had just been through.

'Really, Ruth? The one fucking time I get to have a chance with a hot guy, and you go and drink too much!' Serena had sighed as she dragged Ruth back outside, calling a cab as they went, before sneaking them both in the back door of her house, so her mum didn't see Ruth with vomit stains down her dress and them both reeking of booze. Her friend shoving her in the shower, telling her to 'clean the fuck up and get to bed,' without bothering to ask what had happened.

The morning after was almost worse, as the hangover had kicked in and the shame had hit her full force in the gut, as she had realised that nothing would ever be the same again. That she was dirty, used, soiled. Every month now, when her period came, she knew that she was disappointing Kyle, over and over again. That he desperately wanted them to go and talk to a specialist about fertility treatment, or at least get tested to see what the issue was.

She knew that this latest drama with Kira would take his mind of having a baby for another month, while they worked out together how to handle it, but the truth was that it wasn't going away. She needed to tell him.

Her phone buzzed then, shaking her out of her reverie. She wasn't at all surprised to see Carolyn's text: 'Sauna, Tuesday 5 pm.' And then she instantly replied with a thumbs-up emoji. At this present time, no more needed to be said—her friends needed her. Kyle would have to wait for the truth.

27

2 Months Ago
November, Kira

Kira looked down at the water pouring over her body, across the ugly bruises blooming on her inner thighs, the edges already starting to turn green. As she lathered up her hand with yet more soap, she caught a glimpse of the fingerprint bruises and the violent red streaks of nail marks down the inside of her arms. This had to be the last time. She couldn't imagine ever, ever, going through that again. She knew that Ruby wanted her to call the police, but just the thought of what that could do to her made her sick to her stomach.

Everyone knew that the CPS hardly ever prosecuted rape cases, let alone attempted rape. She had been in a relationship with Josh, she had dressed up for him in the past, he had those pictures of her. Yes, there was the restraining order, but what did that really mean these days? There would be eyewitness accounts of her in her sexy Halloween outfit—who wears thigh-high boots like that if they weren't trying to attract attention?

She cringed, a hot flush of shame pouring over her, shivering despite the heat of the shower. No, there was no way in the world that any court would believe her, if it even got that far.

She had let Ruby and Kyle gather her up the other night, and walk her out through the staff exit at the back of the building to the alley by the tennis courts. She hadn't even wondered about whether either of them were safe to drive or where they were taking her. All she knew was that Ruby would keep her safe, and if needs be, Kyle would do all he could to protect both of them.

She remembered Ruby comforting her in the back of Kyle's car, asking her gently if they could call the police or take her to the police station. Asking if she could call her parents, was there anyone else that she was rather there? Then asking about the police again as she shook her head, slowly at first, then faster and more urgent. No, she didn't want the police. No, please no, just could Ruby stay with her? Hold her?

When they had arrived at their house, Kyle had parked up and then gone inside to turn the lights on, before coming back to the car to get them, helping Ruby to hold her up as she leant her weight on her, her limbs soft and boneless as adrenaline wore off and shock set in. Then the shivering had started. Ruby had helped her undress and had insisted on taking photos of her injuries, before pulling back the duvet in the guest bedroom and letting her slide in, before she climbed on top of the covers next to her, making her feel safe.

Ruby must have left after she fell asleep. Surprisingly, it was probably one of the best and deepest sleeps she had experienced in the last 3 or 4 months—certainly since that day in the summer when she finally discovered who Josh really was.

The next morning, Ruby had brought her a hot, strong cup of tea:

'With real sugar, hope you don't hold it against me!' which had drawn a small smile from her.

Ruby knew how strict she normally was with herself. And then the small pleas had resumed, the gentle, soft asks for Kira to consider calling the police, before she hopped in the shower and destroyed any evidence. Kira had pushed herself up to sitting, gently moving Ruby's hand from her arm and looking her straight in the eyes.

'I can't. You know that, Ruby, don't you?' she fixed her with her best firm stare, well aware that Ruby could see right through her and know that she was still terrified. 'It would kill my parents, Rubes. After everything with Joanna, my mum's depression, Dad feeling like he failed her, this would be the last straw. I finally feel like they're moving on, that they can see a future without her, where they can fully support me now.'

'There is no way I want to drag this into a court room and have to have them support me through that! There has to be another way, surely?' she had looked up to search her friend's eyes, hoping beyond hope that Ruby would understand and agree.

'Sure, there can be another way,' and Kira had felt the relief wash over her then; she knew that Ruby would help make it right.

It had been a few days now, and Kira knew she couldn't outstay her welcome. As she climbed out of the shower, she had contemplated her options. She didn't have the money to squander on a hotel and wasn't really close enough to any of her other friends, to just turn up without a decent explanation as to why she needed to stay for a few days. Her best bet, even though it pained her to think about it, was that she was to go to her parents.

They had always said that she was welcome home any time, but she—since Joanna died—wasn't sure she could stand it. Her parents were so quiet and introverted these days, living out their suburban lives in a time warp. She knew it wasn't their fault, that what had happened to her sister had irretrievably scarred them, and that they were shadows of their old selves, but she didn't want to spend any more time with them than was strictly necessary.

The odd Sunday lunch, family birthdays and Christmas were about all she could muster the energy for these days. She didn't want to be alone, but she could hardly tell them the truth about what had happened, could she? But what choice did she really have?

In the car, as Ruby was driving her to her flat to grab her stuff, she had tentatively called her mum, catching Ruby's eye and her raised eyebrow as she explained that her flat had a water leak and could she stay for a few days, and no, it was all fine, the landlord was dealing with it, and, "no, no, it's fine", she would drive over shortly, she just needed to grab a few things.

'So that's settled then?' Ruby asked kindly. 'Your mum will look after you? You know you could stay with us a few more nights, Kira. It's really not a problem.'

'Honestly, Rubes, you have been amazing, but I don't want to put you out anymore. Carolyn is your friend, and she's also going to need you,' she emphasised. 'You have done more than enough for now. I need some time to get my head straight and then we can talk, ok?'

Ruby gave a curt nod in response as she pulled up outside the block of flats, and Kira let herself out of the car.

'Want me to come with you?' All Ruby wanted for her friend now was for her to be safe and well. She knew that Kira was grateful for her concern, but she also knew that she had to let her friend get on with it.

'No, it's fine. I'll keep my phone in my hand and scream if I need to. I don't want you to get a parking ticket,' she smiled reassuringly as she used her fob to access the entrance door.

'Ok, but I'm just right here if you need me!'

Ruby opened her car door and stepped onto the pavement, cautiously standing sentinel outside the flat, while Kira had legged it in to pack a bag with a few days' worth of clothes and grab her car keys. Ruby had breathed a sigh of relief as her friend reappeared and opened the boot to swing in her holdall, before she asked Ruby to do her one more favour.

'Rubes, I hate to ask, but can you call Aaron Sparks and leave a message for Michael, the duty manager, to apologise—say that I'm sick? I just know that if Sue answers, she's going to know something is wrong, and I can't bear the Spanish Inquisition right now. Can you just say I've got laryngitis and lost my voice, and that I hope to be back in time to teach my Friday class?' She knew she was asking a lot, but she also knew that, of course, Ruby would do it.

'Say no more. As soon as I've dropped you at your car, I'll make the call.'

'Rubes, you're the best, you know that?' She breathed a sigh of relief; she had never been more grateful to her friend.

And now, here she was, sitting on the edge of the avocado green bathtub in the family bathroom at her parents' house, just trying to process and make sense of it all. Her mum had been fantastic—it seemed that having someone to care for again had finally brought back all her nurturing emotions. She had commented on how pale Kira was, not yet noticing the bruises around her mouth she had artfully concealed with make-up that morning, or the fingerprints covered with a fluffy scarf.

She knew it was only a matter of time until one of her parents noticed. Living at close quarters in their suburban semi meant she was right under their noses and wouldn't be able to escape telling them the truth. With that thought in mind, she pulled on her old pink dressing gown that was still hanging on the back of the bathroom door after all these years. She took a deep breath and went to find her mum in the kitchen.

As soon as she caught her mum's eye, she could see the penny drop—her bruised face was no longer hidden with make-up, and with her hair caught up in a towel on her head, the blue and green marks on her throat stood out against her pale skin. Her mum walked slowly over to her, confusion and fear clear in her eyes as she reached out, questioning.

'Kira?' Her fingers gently turned her face to the other side; her voice was soft and filled with emotion. 'Who did this to you? Love, what's going on?'

It broke Kira's heart to see her mum's eyes fill with tears as she pulled her into a cautious embrace.

'It's a long story, Mum. I will tell you, but right now, I just need you to look after me,' her voice weakened to a whisper as she leant then into her mum's arms, and let herself cry and let herself be held.

Her mum hadn't tried to get her to talk right then. Instead, she had led her back up the stairs to her childhood bedroom, pulled back the covers on her old single bed, and helped Kira climb in. She had sat with her for a while, her soothing presence lulling Kira back into a deep sleep.

This time, when she awoke, she had found a jug of Robinsons barley water on her bedside table, and later, her mum had had prepared her childhood favourites of Heinz Tomato soup and toast with lashings of butter and marmite—not taking no for an answer when Kira started to complain about her carb intake.

'Kira, love, I know you are making a name for yourself with the triathlons, but even I know this is the off-season. A little bit of comfort food this week will not make a massive difference to your training now, will it?' Her mum had looked deep into her eyes and gently squeezed her arm to reinforce the point—tender but firm, a side she hadn't seen to her mum in years—and she had easily conceded defeat.

What was a few slices of toast really, in the grand scheme of things, after what she had been through? And so, she had sat up against the headboard and accepted the tray.

'Kira, there are a few things in this world you have to realise. You may be a grown woman, and you may have all these routines and disciplines that I cannot fathom—heaven knows it was the same with your sister—but I will never stop being your mum, and that means I will never not look after you. Do you understand?' She stood over the bed, and Kira knew she was waiting for her reaction; she met her mum's eyes and gave a tiny nod.

'I know that we don't talk about what happened with Joanna. I have never forgiven myself for not seeing that she was in pain and needed to see a doctor sooner than we took her. We just thought that by pushing her and encouraging her to keep going, keep training, that she could break through the wall. It's my biggest ever regret, love. And if I could go back in time and do it differently, I would. We didn't know she was sick,' her mum's voice broke a little as she sucked in a deep breath to continue.

'I know that over the years we have hurt you by not being there to support you, that maybe you didn't think we were as proud of you as we were of her, but it wasn't that all. We couldn't be more proud of everything that you have done,

Kira, but it was just so, so hard for me to be there at those events, when all I could see for years was Joanna in those racing colours. It had been our routine for so long—me plaiting Joanna's hair, making sure she had all her nutrition, and your dad making sure her tyres were pumped up.'

'I just didn't know if I could stand it, being there again to watch you—and that was wrong, and I'm so sorry. I didn't know how to move on, but now I think I can. I want you to know that you can rely on me, and that if you ever need someone to take care of you, I will be that person. So you can stop trying to hide whatever it is that has happened from me, love. I'm here when you want to talk.'

Kira met her mum's eyes and nodded slowly, realising it was time they turned a corner—that she could forgive her mum for all the times it had felt like she had forgotten who Kira was, for the times when she had no one there to support her at her events, knowing now from the look in her mum's eyes that it would have been too soon and too painful for her after Joanna had gone.

That they both had to let go of the past now to move forwards, and that her mum was right—she could love and protect and support Kira as she had done with Joanna in the past. It just needed Kira to let her back in. Maybe in a sick sort of way, this was the world's way of intervening, of making her see that her parents did love her, and that by pushing them away all of these years after feeling rejected—by not talking about Joanna and hiding their feelings—they were stuck in a cycle.

It had been later that evening, when she had had time to process what had happened that afternoon, that she felt like years' worth of weight had been lifted from her shoulders.

After her mum had left her to eat her soup, and Kira had washed her face and pulled on a pair of jeans and an old sweater of Joanna's she had found in the wardrobe, she had found her parents pottering around in the kitchen—her mum making pastry for tomorrow's dinner, and her dad attempting a Sudoku in the paper. They had met each other's eyes briefly, as if talking in secret parent code.

'Right, love, sit your butt down here and give your dad a hand with this flippin' Sudoku thing.' Her dad had pulled out the seat next to him, while her mum asked, 'Cuppa?'

And she knew then that everything was going to be ok. That whatever happened now, things with Josh would be brought to an end, and that she could look forward rather than back. That she could stop living in Joanna's shadow and be her own person.

'Mum, Dad, I've been having a think,' she looked at both of them, hoping that they would support what she was about to say. 'You know that when Joanna died, the funds for her training and sponsorship got put into a trust for me?'

Her mum moved closer then, pulling out the seat on the other side of her.

'Well, you know some of it helped me put a deposit on my flat? Well, there was money left over that I thought could help with my training—you know, travel, help me buy a new bike and stuff. Well, I've been thinking, and I don't know if I want to train for Tri's anymore.' She could see the look of confusion crossing both of their faces.

'But this is your life, pet. You've worked so hard for this. Why would you stop now?' Her dad's concern was touching.

'It was Joanna's life, Dad. Really and truly, she was the one that was supposed to win races and go on to be an Olympian and all that. That time has passed me by now. Yes, I can still win on a good day, but to be really honest, I don't think I really enjoy it anymore.'

'But all the hours of work, all the time you put into your diet and your training?' Her mum frowned.

'Yes, all of that was great when I thought that a win was what I really wanted from life. I thought I owed it to Joanna—that because she would never have a chance to reach the finals of the World Championship, I needed to do it for her. That I needed to prove that one of us could make it.'

Their silence encouraged her to continue. 'But what I really want, and what would make me so much happier, is to quit while I'm ahead, and to put that legacy money towards something that I'm really passionate about—to help people who are struggling, and those that need extra support and coaching to make the most of themselves.

'What I really want to do is open my own fitness studio,' she finished quietly, certain that they would feel betrayed—that she had always promised to finish what Joanna had started, and that the only way that they could be truly proud of her would be to see her finally up on the podium at the World Championships.

What she didn't expect was her dad to break into a huge grin and reach out across the table to cover her hand in his. 'Pet, that's a wonderful idea. Isn't it, Margie?' He smiled across at her mum.

'Absolutely. I can't think of a better way for you to spend that money.' She reached over and added her hand to the pile on the table, giving a firm squeeze. 'We are so proud of you, love.'

28
2 Months Ago
November, Sauna

They had managed to time their meeting to perfection—the oldies from water aerobics had just finished pouring out of the spa area and back into the changing rooms, and the parents of the kids in swimming lessons were still sat poolside for the next 45 minutes, cheering on their little lovelies as they doggy paddled and splashed their way across the pool, after a multi-coloured cloud of rubber ducks.

They could have met elsewhere, but the comfort and familiarity of the sauna after years of meeting here felt safe and cocooning, when they both knew that this was going to be a really tough conversation.

Carolyn had arrived first, her hand clutching an insulated cup of iced coffee. She had laid her turquoise towel across the lower slats on the far side of the sauna, and sat with her back propped against one of the cedar-planked walls, legs stretched out in front of her. To anyone walking by, she would look perfectly relaxed, and yet she had never felt so tense in her life. As Ruby gently nudged open the door, and dumped her bright pink and orange fluffy towel on the bench nearest the door, she could see what a façade it was.

As Carolyn looked up and met her eyes, she saw the hurt and the truth reflected in them, and they both crumbled. Carolyn had stood up to allow herself to be drawn into Ruby's decorated arms, the embrace warming her heart as she knew that she had her friend's full support, but also chilling her as she realised the road ahead of her was long and had only just begun. There was very little for them to say to one another.

Ruby just asked a few simple questions. 'Are you going to leave him?'

And Carolyn, who had sat back down opposite her on the other bench, gave a faint nod. 'Yes.'

'Do you need my help?'

'Yes.'

'When are you going to do it? Just so I can help you plan and make sure you're safe.'

'After Christmas. I need to get a plan in order before then.'

'Are you scared he will hurt you?' Their eyes met across the dim red of the sauna interior, Ruby seeking reassurance from her best friend that she had this under control and that she didn't have to worry about her.

'I'm not sure. After what he did to Kira, I don't think I know him at all now. He's volatile. I mean, there have been times before when he has hurt me, so I just don't know. He's about to go away for 5 weeks, but will be back just before Christmas, so I'm hoping that will give me chance to work stuff out before he comes home.

'I just need to get through the next few days and avoid him as much as possible. He thinks I'm at my mum's because Dad had a fall, so I can say that's where I am again tonight.' She spoke more confidently as she outlined her plans.

'Sarah has offered to take us in if things get scary before I have my plan together.'

Ruby raised her eyebrows slightly and tried to hide her interest in this statement, being patient and listening as Carolyn went on.

'When this is over, I want to go to the police, Ruby. I want to report him for all the years of abuse and trauma he's put me through. I want him to pay for what he did to me,' she paused, 'and to Kira.'

'He'll pay, Carolyn. Don't you worry about that,' Ruby smiled sadly at her friend, as they reached out and grasped hands in the dark. 'We'll bring him down, together.'

29
2 Months Ago
November, Kira

Kira knew after a few days that people would start to notice her absence from work and start to worry about her. She had thought that a few days at her parents would give her enough time to sort her head out, and for some of the bruises to heal and fade, so that they wouldn't be noticeable in her gym wear, but as the days had worn on, she realised that she just wasn't ready yet.

Ruby had called in sick for her at first on the pretence of laryngitis, so she knew that if she called Michael or Davina, one of the duty managers, she would have to at least come up with some kind of croaky voice to play the sickness card for a few more days. She hated lying to them, but knew that she needed a little more time in the safety of her parents' home, to process her feelings and to think about what she would do next.

There was no way she felt safe enough to return to her flat yet, and even though her parents' house was only in the next town, it felt a safe distance away from Carolyn and Josh. She also needed a few more days to work through her ideas with her dad about her plans to set up her own studio. Once they had started the conversation the other night, the floodgates had opened, and she had seen with her own eyes her parents take on a new lease of life. Their enthusiasm and support were infectious, and she had felt emboldened by their support.

Who knew her dad would have so many good ideas? Or be a real whiz when it came to looking at properties in which to set up the business, and then creating spreadsheets to track all the possible expenditure for setting up this venture? She owed it to them, and herself now, to invest a bit more time in this fledgling relationship and let it blossom.

She had just gone upstairs to her room and was searching through her old chest of drawers, hunting out the old travel hairdryer she knew she had left in there many years ago, when she heard her phone ping. Even though there was no way that Josh could have found out her number, and she knew that she was perfectly safe here, there was still a split second where fear crept up her spine. Shaking herself, she hurried back down the stairs to where she had left her phone plugged in. A message had appeared on the notification screen from an unknown number. Her heart started to beat harder as she tentatively reached over to pick it up.

Hey, Kira, sorry to message while you're feeling crook. Just wanted to say the women from your 2 pm class today were not impressed with me as their sub (laughing face emoji), and we can't wait to have you back! And then another ping. *P.S. This is Sam; I got a new number.*

She smiled at the texts, her stomach doing a little dip of joy when she realised who it was from. It was just like Sam to not only make her laugh when she was feeling a bit down, but to also time the text just right. She knew that it was hard on him when she had broken it off a couple of months ago, and that he didn't know the full story behind her rationale, but he had been so kind and gentle, not pushing for more of an explanation or pressuring her.

They hadn't really kept in touch much after. Obviously she had seen him at work when their paths had crossed, but they had kept a polite distance from one another. So it was lovely to see that there was no ill feeling on his part, and that he obviously still thought about her.

She jumped into the text conversation, grateful for the distraction.

I'm much better, thanks. Would have loved to have been a fly on the wall to watch your downward dog! (grinning emoji) she replied.

Well, you should have seen my warrior pose—seriously shit-hot. Might even give you half-price off a private lesson before I get booked up! (winking emoji) Seriously though, it's good to hear you're on the mend. I always get so bored when I'm laid up, so shout if you want any company.

Her heart fluttered a little at the mention of his company. There was something so reliable and strong about Sam that made her just want to be near him, like he really could protect her—one of life's genuine good guys.

No funny business though. Sorry, Kira, that last text may have come out a little wrong!

She laughed, poor Sam thinking that he could possibly offend her when all he had done so far was given her a boost and made her feel a bit normal again.

I am actually going a little stir crazy now, to be honest. I've been at my parents' in Hallstown, and despite their good intentions, we might be starting to get under each other's feet a little.

There was a slight pause before he replied.

Well, that's a coincidence. I'm literally dropping my grandmother off at the church on Parkway over at Hallstown today at 4 pm. How about I swing by and take you out to get some fresh air for an hour?

Before she could stop herself, she tapped out a short reply and hit send.

Sure. Would be good to see you.
Great. Send me the address and I will see you in bit. 😊

As she hit reply with a pin to her parents' address, she stopped short for a second. What the hell was she thinking? The marks on her arms and throat were still visible, and she still couldn't stop the palpitations in her heart every time she thought about stepping outside the front door of her parents' house.

How could she possibly see Sam? And what did he know? Was there gossip going round Sparks about what had happened a mere few days ago? What if it wasn't really him, and it was a trick, and she had just given out her parents' address to Josh by mistake?

She started to breathe heavily, panic seeping through her body as she started to catastrophise all the terrible scenarios, slumping down onto the bottom step, hand covering her face as she started to hyperventilate, her breaths ragged and shallow, consumed with her own stupidity—that she had probably just invited a psycho to her parents' house—that she didn't hear her dad's key turn in the lock.

'Hey, pet,' her dad's cheery greeting—failing to rouse her—suddenly became one of concern. 'Kira, love, what's happened?' And then her dad was crouching before her, pulling her hands from her face before putting them firmly on her shoulders. 'It's ok, love. Just breathe. That's it—in and out, in and out.'

She let the weight of his hands work their magic in calming her, and his hypnotic voice soothe her panic.

'Oh, Dad, I've been such an idiot!' Kira poured out the story of the text message, and how she didn't even know it really was Sam, and what the hell had she been thinking? It might be Josh, and what if he was on his way over here now, and she had led him straight to her parents?

Her dad, as always, was the voice of reason. 'Ok, so you don't know that this person who texted you wasn't this Sam you think it was? So, it could genuinely be him?'

'Yes.'

'And you gave him our address but didn't say you were going to be alone in the house, so for all he knows, not only could your tough old dad be here, but so could your 5 tough uncles?' He started to smirk a little, pleased that Kira's breathing was now back to normal and that she was starting to listen to him.

'So, let's say I call up a few of the old boys from the rugby club and get them to pop over shortly, with the promise of a beer or two and a catch-up, so that "if", and that is a big "if", this guy isn't who he says he is, then he'll have a little surprise waiting for him?'

'You would do that for me, Dad?' she asked expectantly.

'Of course I would! You're my baby girl. No matter how old you get, I'm never going to stop wanting to protect you.' He ruffled her hair. 'Right, let your old man find his phone and get this ball rolling. You go get yourself together and looking nice, 'cos if this Sam is the real deal, then he's going to be wondering what on earth he bothered to come over for, if you're just going to be sitting here in your old PJs with a moping face on you.'

Kira smirked as her dad gave her a knowing smile as she realised he was right—she was no longer fighting battles on her own. Her family was there for her, all the way, and they wanted to protect her. She knew many of her dad's friends from the rugby club, and they were tough old guys. There was no way that anyone was going to mess with her on her home turf.

The next hour proceeded to drag as she anticipated what might happen next. She had managed to pull herself together enough to rummage through the limited items of clothing she had brought with her from home the other day to find something half-decent. She slid her slim, muscular legs into soft, worn skinny black jeans that made her endless legs look even longer. She pulled on a plain white vest top and topped it off with her favourite pale grey cashmere sweater, that she knew complimented her long dark hair and her blue eyes.

She wasn't sure what to make of the effort she seemed to be putting into this makeover. However, it felt good to feel normal again after the last few shaky days, and to try and put her fears behind her.

She sat on her bed and contemplated what she had learnt about her parents over the last few days. She hadn't realised how much of her parents' lives she had failed to appreciate, or realise, that the times she had seen them, that maybe they were holding back on her—not wanting to make her feel like they were prying into her life or pushing her, like they maybe felt they pushed Joanna all those years ago.

She hadn't realised that her dad now had a more active role at the rugby club, helping out behind the bar and supporting the under-15s coach by organising transport, sponsorship and kit washing for the more junior team. She also hadn't known that, since last Christmas, her mum was now administrator for the local athletics team that she and Joanna had been with since they were tiny.

Admittedly, it was a long time since Kira had been involved in the little league junior athletics circuit—now that she trained with the senior clubs at the upper range of the support, governed by the professional body—so how could she know? Her mum had seemed almost embarrassed to admit to Kira that she loved her volunteer role, and that she got a kick out of knowing which young athletes were being picked up to go to county trials.

That sending their parents the letter to inform them gave her such a thrill—that she was involved in these young people's future from such an early stage of their potential career.

When her dad had appeared back at her door, Kira had looked up at him with hope. For the first time in a long time, she wanted to hear what he had to say—to heed his advice and take his support.

'Love, we are all sorted. Steve and Brian are on their way over. We've got a bit of club business to sort out tonight anyway, so they didn't mind starting a bit early.' He leant against the doorframe, suddenly seeming larger and more dad-like than he had in years. And it made her think, for a brief second, that this seemingly quiet and brooding man, that she was used to, was now suddenly finding his voice and expressing things he seemed to have held back for years.

'You do know that we want the best for you, don't you? We may be getting on a bit now, but all we've tried to do over the years is make sure that you know that you don't have to look out for us. We can do that for ourselves, and hopefully, we can look out for you now too.' He seemed almost surprised at his own candidness. 'I don't know quite what happened to you with that idiot who hurt you, but what I do know is that I would do anything to see him pay for what he did to you.'

Before Kira could interrupt, he held up his hand to finish. He continued, 'I know that's not what you want right now. You want to deal with this in your own way, and I respect that. All I ask for is that you let me look after you, but also, that you start to do more things in your life that make you happy. We've already talked about the studio, and you know that I think it's a brilliant idea, but I want you to also be happy—maybe find someone?'

'It doesn't have to be this Sam or anyone soon, but please don't think all guys are bad, Kira. There will be someone out there that treats you with the love and respect that you deserve.' Her dad's eyes grew damp as he spoke his words softly, aware that she was on the edge of tears too.

'Oh, Dad.' She couldn't say anymore.

She just smiled and held his eyes for a moment longer, and with a swift nod of his head, he turned and headed back downstairs. Kira let out a long breath she didn't even realise that she was holding, overwhelmed with feelings of love and support, but also knowing that he was right. All these years, she had devoted herself to her training, to moving up to the top of her game, trying to please her parents and prove to herself, and to Joanna's memory, that she was worthy.

The time she tried to do something for herself by having some fun with Josh had severely backfired, and she had been burnt. She guessed she had to apply the same resilience that she always seemed to find in her training to her personal life. If she got injured on the track, then what did she do? She got help to fix it, she built herself back up, she fought back, she took control.

This was something she could do now; it was sink or swim, and she had everything to swim for. When the doorbell sounded an hour later, she had felt even more positive about the future when, instead of her worst fears coming true, the lovely Sam was there—good as his word—ready to take her out for the afternoon. She had put her arms around her dad and given him the most genuine hug she had handed out in years, to reassure him that, yes, this was Sam, and yes, he would look after her.

Sam had given her a small series of puzzled looks as he then also sought to reassure her dad, and had received a handshake as he promised to return her no later than 10 pm. She had tentatively put her hand on his arm as he opened the passenger door for her and said, 'Honestly, I will explain everything.'

And, as with his usual good grace, Sam hadn't pushed her for any answers—just nodded and softly closed the door behind her.

30

2 Months Ago
November, Ruby

Ruby knew from her catch-up with Carolyn that Josh was due to travel again on bonfire night. She had been stewing over what had happened in the last few days, and had worked herself into a frenzy of anger about what Josh had done, and how he was likely to get away with it, as Kira still flat out refused to press charges.

She knew that Carolyn had said that she was going to do something about it, after she had her plan to leave Josh all wrapped up, but Ruby felt deep in her bones that if they had to wait until then, it might be too late. Carolyn hadn't seen how Josh had attacked Kira first-hand.

Ruby had absolutely no doubt in her mind that Josh was going to come for Kira—if not immediately, then as soon as he had a plan for how he could track her down and get her alone. Men like that didn't take kindly to rejection, and the ways in which he had already hurt her had escalated.

She had seen it so many times in her profession—the way men like him started with low-level coercive control, working up to full-blown violence. She was lucky that the women she supported, had had the strength and the means to be able to escape before it had gone so far as to harm them irreparably or heaven forbid, kill them.

Ruby wanted to take back some level of control of the situation. She knew Josh's flight was early afternoon, so more than likely he would be at home packing this morning, and Carolyn was still at her parents. She made her way to the office and flipped the switch on her printer. If the only way she was able to fight this at the moment was to use what they already had to hand, then she was going to do that. She would go and tell him what she thought of him, and give him a copy of the restraining order she had helped Kira with back in January.

They had served the notice to his place of work last time—an anonymous office in London that neither of them had visited, as Kira didn't have his home address. Despite all the time she was seeing him, he had never once—not surprisingly now—taken her home. She knew that Kira had never really questioned him—first, because she was in awe of this supposedly perfect guy taking an interest in her, and then when she was too scared to say anything, after he became increasingly controlling and violent.

She knew Kyle would blow a fuse if he knew what she was going to do. He had already made it clear to her that he was just biding his time to work out what he could do about Josh. In his world, you didn't hurt women, and he needed to teach Josh a lesson. Ruby wasn't even sure she knew if Kyle would act on his rage. She really didn't think that he would, knowing the effort he had put into his own anger issues stemming from his messed-up childhood.

He had spent some time in juvenile detention, but had finally got the help he needed when he went to live with an ancient aunt. Maud had paid for him to see a psychologist, and Kyle had turned his life around. The only legacy of his misspent youth being some of the earlier tattoos he still had etched onto the knuckles on each hand; the others had long since been covered covered-up.

She knew that if people really knew Kyle's story, they would seem like an odd couple—his criminal past almost a juxtaposition to Ruby's pursuit of the law—but she had utmost respect for the way in which he had started over. And although he didn't like to talk about the things he had been involved in earlier in his life before his time with her, she knew that he still had contacts, still had people on the periphery of their lives together that could be called on, to cause harm.

She didn't think he would do anything about Josh, but she couldn't be entirely sure. As she still hadn't had the courage to talk to Kyle about her own past, and the changes she made to her identity, she knew that people could still have secrets and still hang onto traits they thought they had ditched years ago.

She slowed down a gear as she pulled onto Carolyn's street. The detached Victorian houses set back from the road each had driveways for at least 3 cars, with neat gardens and established magnolia or cherry blossom trees growing neatly on the front lawns. She thought to herself that it was amazing what went on behind closed doors—even in the more upmarket neighbourhoods—that no one truly ever knew their neighbours. As she pulled up by Carolyn's house, she kept her eyes open for a parking space.

She didn't want to risk getting stuck on the driveway when this needed to be a quick confrontation. She slid the car into neutral as she found the perfect space right at the end of the driveway. She knew that she shouldn't feel nervous—years in court rooms confronting bullying husbands in front of strict judges should have helped her keep her pulse rate somewhere near resting. However, there was no denying that there was serious adrenaline coursing through her veins as she walked up and rapped on the shiny red door with the bronze lion's head knocker.

She had been to the house many times, but it was almost sad to see evidence of the twins' lives right in front of her: an NHS rainbow picture left over from Covid still pinned up in one of the sash windows, a pink bike carelessly strewn into one of the flower beds next to the driveway, a monster truck minus a wheel leaning up against the side of the front porch. It was a timebomb—all of this was about to come crashing down.

She knew that there was no way that Carolyn could afford to buy Josh out of the house, and with his history, there was every chance she would get full custody of the kids when it came to it. Amber and Charlie would have to live a very different life when it was just Carolyn supporting them. She knew Carolyn wanted to go back to work, and that, with her independence, she would be able to do whatever she liked, but there was no way it could afford her this same lifestyle.

There was still no answer as Ruby pounded the knocker once more. She couldn't see any lights on, but then she knew Josh's office was round the back of the house, looking out onto the beautiful back garden. She started to creep around the left side of the house. Josh's Tesla was in the driveway, but there were still no signs of life. She carried on past the window to the downstairs cloakroom until she reached the small waist-high gate. She leant over to unlock the latch and pushed into the back garden.

Even in winter, she had to admit, the garden looked stunning—the dew still shining on the lawn, vibrant Japanese Japonicas glowing red and lighting up the gloomy day, holly berries gleaming. Carolyn was going to miss this, but she certainly wasn't going to miss the trouble that came with it.

Ruby hesitated a couple of seconds before she pressed on to the back of the house, where Josh's office window was located, stepping back to look up at the Virginia creeper winding its way up to the second floor. She was about to go and peer through the back window when suddenly there was a smash, and she felt a roar of pain as she hit the floor face first. Before she had time to respond, she was being roughly flipped over onto her back, the wet grass soaking into her dress as the full weight of Josh landed on top of her, pinioning her to the floor.

He grabbed both her arms up over her head, using his forearm to push them together and hold them tight, while kneeling across her legs and holding her mouth shut with his other hand.

'What the fuck do you want, Ruby?' he spat at her, so close she could feel the vapour from his hot breath in the cold morning air pooling on her cheek. 'Let me guess—you're coming to my house to tell me to stay away from your slut of a friend?'

Ruby wriggled from beneath him, trying to get any sound out, as his hand stayed firmly clamped on her mouth.

'Don't even fucking try and speak, you stupid bitch! You think I'm scared of you and your tattooed dick of a boyfriend? I could finish all of you off in no time. You know the sorts of plants I deal with, Rubes? Poisons. I could fucking take you all down. Or perhaps I'll get you struck off from the bar by raising suspicion about Kyle's links back to his criminal past, and how you've been helping him? Doesn't take a lot to dig up dirt on people—you should know that.'

Ruby continued to wriggle underneath him, feeling the wet garden soaking her clothes.

'Or maybe I'll tell Kyle about that dirty little secret you were telling Carolyn about. Didn't you know that it's rude to keep secrets about your fertility from your partner when you keep banging on about wanting his baby?' He let out a manic laugh as he continued to stare manically into her eyes, that, despite herself, she could feel filling with tears.

'How do you know about the baby?' she stuttered as he let his hand relax a little, and she managed to suck in a ragged breath and get a few words out before he reapplied the pressure.

'You think I don't know what conversations go on in my own house? That I don't listen to every word that you and that fat cow of a wife of mine talk about when you pop over for coffee?' He smirked again. 'Have you never heard of bugs? Listening devices? For a lawyer, you're pretty stupid, aren't you?'

Ruby's eyes opened wide as she processed that he had been listening to their conversations. She mentally replayed the recent chats she had had with Carolyn about her planning to leave Josh, and how her plans were shaping up, and was relieved when she realised that all of them had been when they were in the sauna.

She had talked to Carolyn again about her botched abortion that had left her infertile after telling both her friends her story in the sauna—that had been a few weeks ago when she had popped over for a quick cuppa, while Josh was in London. She wondered now, with hindsight, if Carolyn had known about the bugs in her house, but then thought that she couldn't possibly. There was no way she would have encouraged Ruby to tell her the full story about Todd, and the abortion if she knew that he was listening, would she?

He released his grip slightly and shifted so she could tentatively move her legs, the cold now starting to creep into her bones from the hard ground.

'If I take my hand away, are you going to play nice?' he searched her face for assent. 'I don't want to hurt you, Ruby, but I will if I have to. I know that you're angry, but I'm going to stay away from Kira like a good boy. I'm going to go back to my life with my wife and my kids, and you and your precious friend are going to forget all about this. Do I make myself clear?'

She nodded as best she could against his hand, breathing deeply through her nose until both airways were clear.

'Yes, yes, I understand.' Her voice, to her own ears, sounded croaky and strained as she sought to reassure him that she understood. 'I'll go. I will go away, and I promise this will be the end of it.' Tears sprang to her eyes again as she desperately fought to control her emotions. 'Josh, let me up. Come on, you have my word.' She nodded at him, encouraging him to see that she meant what she said, as he climbed off her and brushed himself down, then extended both hands down to her.

'Come on then, get the fuck up. That was a nasty tumble you took there, Rubes. Want to be a bit more careful next time you go for a poke around someone's garden.' His bitter laugh rung in her ears as she hauled herself upright, shaking off his hands as soon as she had her balance.

She couldn't bring herself to speak, not trusting that she would have any conviction left to fake about leaving this situation and him alone. If anything had come from this incident, it was to strengthen her resolve to take him fucking down in any way that she could. On shaky, bruised legs, she lifted the latch to the back gate to let herself out, not daring herself to look back as Josh's voice called out behind her.

'That's it. Fuck off back to your perfect little world, you silly bitch, and stay the fuck away from me!'

It took Ruby all of 30 seconds to make it back to her car, but the walk down the driveway felt like an eternity as she struggled to process what had just happened to her. She couldn't believe that this guy, who she had met so many times before, could really be like this.

She was the first to admit that everyone had a secret side that they didn't always choose to show to the world. Damn, she was a whole different person to the one that she presented to the world now, but to fake a loving marriage and doting father when you were quite clearly a violent psychopath was another thing altogether.

With trembling hands, she climbed behind the wheel, the restraining order—crumpled and muddy—still held between her fingers as she rested her head for a second on the steering wheel. Whatever happened now to bring Josh down, she knew that she had to tell Kyle the truth, because even if Josh didn't tell him, it was the least she could do to be honest with him and help them move their lives on together.

She would be there for Carolyn—of course she would—but she had to help herself first, by coming clean to Kyle about her past and admitting that what had happened with Josh had triggered her, and how seeing Todd that summer had made her realise she couldn't keep living a lie. The only way to get what they both wanted out of life, and to build a happy future, was for them to get the treatment that they needed. Or, if she really didn't have any hope of getting pregnant through IVF, then at least they could look into surrogacy or adoption.

Ruby managed to get her breathing under control and drove the car a few blocks away from the house before she pulled over, her head pounding as the adrenaline started to wear off. She pulled her phone out of her purse, her hands only now trembling slightly, and managed to send three texts.

The first to Carolyn: 'We need to move this plan along quickly. Let me help get you out sooner. Sauna, 4 pm?'

The next to Kira: 'Hey, babe, how are things at your folks? I just wanted you to know that I'm working with Carolyn on a plan, XO.'

And the final one to Kyle: 'Can we forget the fireworks party tonight, hun? Nothing to worry about, but can we talk?'

As she pressed send on the final message, she knew then that there was no way back, that all of the truths would out, and that the ball for sorting out the Josh situation was now firmly in motion.

31

2 Months Ago
November, Carolyn

Carolyn had managed to avoid Josh for the few days between Halloween and Bonfire night. She had moved from Sarah's to her parents, and only popped home at times she knew Josh would be out, telling him that her mum still needed her as her dad was recovering from his fall.

She knew that he liked her around when he was preparing for a trip, so that she could run round like his skivvy, getting all his stuff ready, doing his washing, making sure he had stupid things like spare batteries for his head torch, or the special deet mosquito spray that she knew didn't irritate his skin. He was going to be furious that she wasn't there at the moment, but there was no way she could look him in the eye just yet, and he would see straight through her.

She knew that he had taken her for granted for years, and that he was going to realise what he was missing when she left, but fuck him. She couldn't let the few blissful early years of their relationship cloud the reality. He was an asshole, and he was going to pay. For years and years, he had behaved like a monster and had been getting away with it.

Let him sort out his own kit bag for a change; let him rummage around in the drawers under the bed through all his travelling equipment to try and locate the Swiss Army knife his dad had given him, and which he treated as a lucky talisman; let him work out where she kept the dry bags that kept all his kit dry and neatly organised; and let him sort out a lift to the airport. She was done. More done than he could possibly know.

Earlier in the day, she had checked her watch one more time and satisfied herself that at 1 pm, it was safe to return home, that he would have headed off at least an hour ago to get to the airport 2 hours before his flight. He liked to meet his crew members early and make sure that they were all ready to check in.

Yet another thing Josh demanded of her and his family was promptness. Another reason why his patience with her wore so thin, and how the twins often fell victim to his foul temper—rounding up a twosome was never going to make them on time for anything.

Carolyn thought about the last couple of days, and how the time she had spent with Sarah recently had made her realise how lonely she had really been. The tenderness Sarah had shown her had stirred something in her that she was yet to act on, and yet she felt sure that Sarah felt it too.

Carolyn had never thought of herself as someone who would be attracted to another woman, and she wanted to be sure of her feelings and that they weren't just driven by her need for someone—anyone—other than Josh making her feel needed and wanted, and most of all, safe. Sarah had never made a move, even recently when she had held Carolyn close, stroked her hair and held her eyes for a fraction too long.

Carolyn was no fool. She knew what desire looked like and felt like, and the spark was without a doubt right there in front of her—maybe just a glowing ember at this stage, but something that maybe with a little encouragement might start to flame.

Carolyn had dropped the kids at a friend's, promising to pick them up around 5:30 pm to head to the big bonfire display, and headed into the sauna to meet Ruby. She finally managed to outline the plan for how she was going to bring Josh down—all the evidence that she had started to compile in a diary of incidents over the years. Ruby had reassured her that she would help her over the next 6 weeks while Josh was away, so that she could move on her plan on the 1st January.

When she had explained to Ruby that she wanted to go through with the plan despite being scared about Josh becoming violent, Ruby had squeezed her hand hard and reassured her that she owed it to herself, to the twins, and to Kira to stand up to Josh once and for all.

It was a shock then when Ruby revealed the altercation she had had with Josh earlier that day. She couldn't believe that Josh was stupid enough to mess with Ruby of all people. Ruby had told him that she would leave him well alone if he promised to leave Kira alone, but she didn't think Josh would believe her. That he had installed listening and spy devices in their house had chilled her to the bone.

She could handle all of the overt ways her husband chose to bully her, but to find out that he was listening in on her and spying even when he wasn't in the country froze her blood. It was terrifying—what would he do next? This time it felt as if he had finally lost the plot. As usual, Rubes had been pragmatic and reassuring. Where Carolyn had wanted to rush home right then and there, and sweep the house from top to toe to find the devices, Ruby had explained that the bugs were part of their chance to prove his controlling behaviour.

They just needed someone with the right equipment to seek them out, and to document where they were and what they were doing, but without alerting Josh to the fact that they knew they were there.

It would have to wait until he was back and she was confronting him, or until he had been arrested or a restraining order had been issued, just to limit the potential risk that he posed to each of the three women, who all now had cause to end him. Ruby was sure that Kyle would help them, that he would know the best way to go about it, and that they would take the next 6 weeks to get it right.

In the meantime, they agreed that they should only talk in places where there was no chance of any bugs—the sauna or a café being the perfect places, nowhere where Josh had ever visited.

As they finished up their harrowing conversation, Carolyn moved closer to Ruby and rested her head on her friend's shoulder.

'We're all in this together now, aren't we?' she questioned.

'Yep. The three of us are going to take that bastard down.' Ruby allowed herself a small smirk. 'Let's just take it steady, gather the evidence we need and plan this properly—no mistakes.'

'OK, I know I need to be patient, but there isn't anything we can do now until he's back anyway, so I just need to get Christmas over without anything happening, and then we can do it.' She lifted her head, meeting Ruby's nod of assent.

'That's the plan,' she nodded. 'You just need to keep yourself safe now until January. Anyway, don't you have a bonfire party to go to?' She nudged Carolyn gently in the ribs.

'Shit! Is that the time?' Carolyn screeched as she hopped down from the seat. 'I have to get the kids, then meet Sarah at the gate at 6. I just hope she doesn't mind if I'm a few minutes late.'

Ruby gave a knowing smile. 'From what I've seen, Carolyn, she will happily wait for you'

An hour later, Sarah, as good as her word, had met them all at the park gate, putting her arm gently round Carolyn's waist, and ushering her through the crowds over to the brightly lit stalls selling cotton candy, toffee apples and other treats designed to make children hyper or rot their tiny teeth. Sarah had instinctively known that Carolyn hadn't wanted to talk about everything that had been happening, that she needed some distance and chance to be herself that night, and to make sure the kids had a lovely time.

When Sarah had suggested a ride on the big wheel, she had readily agreed. Packing Amber and Charlie into one carriage and hopping in with Sarah in the other, she had felt almost giddy as the ride began to turn and lift them up into the night sky. Up above the bright lights of the fairground, the air thick with the smell of bonfires and sulphur from the fireworks, the bright pinks and blues of explosions mingling with greens and yellows, she could almost forget all of the trouble she knew was yet to come, all of the challenges ahead.

Her breath came out in cold plumes in front of her as Sarah tucked her closer, her thick jacket spread out over both their legs, the soaring and rocking of the carriage lulling and calming her after the tension of the week that had seemed to last an eternity.

Grateful for those that she had by her side, and thankful that she could now see a future—and that, tentatively, it might be shared with this wonderful woman next to her, someone that was there for her, respected her, but also who encouraged her and gave her strength—she knew there was a long way to go, but at last she felt that there was some hope.

32
1 Month Ago
December, Kira

It had been a whole month since Sam had picked her up at her parents' house that Saturday afternoon. She couldn't believe that she had been so terrified that it wouldn't be really him, or that she would have been duped by Josh into giving him her parents' address. She felt foolish now, but guessed it must just be a reflection on how messed up her head was at that time—that she probably hadn't even started to process the attack or everything that had led up to it, despite the counselling she had had last year.

She knew from Ruby that Josh was out of the country until near Christmas, and that Carolyn definitely planned on leaving him in the New Year. Part of her was frustrated that Carolyn could leave it that long—why prolong the agony for herself? Why not just dump his stuff from the house while he was away and start divorce proceedings? On the other hand, she knew what he was like—that doing it that way would leave to more trauma and upset, mainly for the twins.

She had deep sympathy for her friend. She knew that despite everything that Josh had put her through over the years, he was still Charlie and Amber's dad, and that had to count for something. There was also the fear that she still felt herself, and she was pretty sure Carolyn must feel—the fear that for Josh, nothing was ever over, the fear that he had control over her and the situation, and that it was evident that he was becoming more and more volatile.

Everyone had heard the statistics and facts about women who left a domestic violence situation being more at risk of violent attack, or worse, being killed in the immediate aftermath of leaving. There had to be some safety mechanisms that both she and Carolyn could put in place before he came back, to make sure that they were both safe, that they were protected, and that he couldn't hurt them.

Kira shuddered despite the warmth of the sauna, prickles of goosebumps appearing on her arms just at the thought of what he had the potential to do; it really was terrifying. He needed to be stopped from ever being able to hurt a woman again. With Sam's support, and her blossoming relationship with her parents, she would try and find the strength and the courage to fight back and to report him.

Maybe the police would take it more seriously if she went with Carolyn, and maybe there was a chance to get him locked up for what he had done. She needed to think things through and talk to Ruby and to Sam.

She smiled to herself as she tried to relax and take her mind away from the situation by thinking about Sam. He was just the most lovely and genuine guy. That evening, when he had turned up at her parents' in his beaten-up old pickup truck, blonde hair falling messily into his green eyes and still in his red lifeguarding t-shirt and old shorts, she had to smile.

He had been so happy to see her, but also took the time to politely shake her dad's hand and ask how he was like they were old friends, not showing surprise at all when he aggressively opened the door and shouted for Kira to come confirm this guy was who he said he was. He had obviously had previous experience of over protective fathers, or at least gave a good impression of being able to handle the situation, when Kira shyly peered round her father and confirmed—yes, this was actually Sam.

He had addressed her father as "Sir" and told him he would look after her and have her home around 10 pm, despite the fact that, at 28, Kira was by no means under a curfew. It was the polite and responsible thing to do, and she could tell her dad appreciated it.

It was only later, when they sat parked up at the viewpoint, looking down at the fireworks being set off in the town below, that she found herself opening up and telling him the whole story. She could tell that the split in her lower lip and the bruises on her throat were a shock to him—that he tried not to show it as he held open the passenger door and helped her up into the truck. But she could tell something was bothering him, and that he knew immediately that she wasn't telling the truth about being off work sick with some kind of throat infection.

She could feel him glancing at her as they drove across town to pick up some coffees, his kind concern leading her to let her guard down a little and start to make small talk. He let her lead the conversation, not probing or asking questions, just letting her open up bit by bit, like a flower turning its head to the sun. They had parked up in the darkness, and he had made to turn on the overhead light when she reached out to stop him.

'Please, can we just sit in the dark?'

She knew that as she reached up to touch his wrist to stop him moving the switch, that in the dull light, he saw the bruises on her wrist. She softly lowered her hand back to her own lap and felt him looking at her again, before he reached over and very gently pulled her into his arms, wrapping them around her like a safety blanket and gently stroking her hair as she took a huge, gasping sob, her bottled-up emotions pouring out.

Once her breathing had steadied, and she had moved away a little to find a tissue in her pocket, he had then taken her right arm and softly pulled back the sleeve of her sweater, using his index finger to gently stroke the area with the most bruises.

'My ex attacked me.' She looked up at him, meeting his eyes, searching and questioning hers. 'It was the other night at Sparks, at the Halloween party,' she had continued in a flat tone, not knowing how to tell her story, but knowing that she wanted to share her truth with this lovely, kind, and gentle guy, who was continuing to stroke her arm and hold her hand in his at the same time.

'I started a relationship with this guy two years ago. It was really intense, really fast, and he wasn't who I thought he was. It was amazing at first. We met during Covid, so it felt exciting to have someone to meet up with and to plan things with, and we had this real connection, but that all ended the first time he hurt me.' She let out a long, shuddering breath, shaking her head as if still not quite believing what had happened to her.

'There were signs, before things turned violent, that things were going a bit wrong. I mean, the term "gaslighting" could have been invented for what this guy did to me, but I was so stupid and so blind—' Kira shook her head as Sam started to interrupt, 'You are not…'

'It's ok, you don't need to reassure me,' she continued. 'I know now that I wasn't really stupid, that it's what clever manipulators like him do to their victims. I know this isn't my fault.' She gave his hand a reassuring squeeze before she continued. 'He gaslighted me. He broke me down. He knew I was vulnerable after my sister had died, and he knew that she was my weak spot—using her memory to manipulate me. He played with my emotions and then started to make more and more demands on me physically.'

She could feel her heart start to beat a little faster as she continued. 'It started with sex.' She swallowed hard, not used to talking to anyone about intimate relationships.

'I had never experienced anything like it, and it was rough and exciting—not what I really like, looking back, but at the time,' Again she shook her head. 'Then it was more than that. It was pushing me on my run times in my training. It was like he became a second coach, getting me to repeat things over and over again, timing me and my transitions until I was exhausted, and then expecting me to still spend hours in bed with him.'

She let out a ragged breath, knowing that Sam was doing his best to let her continue, but she could tell by his demeanour that he was anything but calm.

'He wouldn't take no for an answer, and when I started to push back one day—I think it was the night he had pushed me into a 10k trail run, not just the usual stuff I was used to, but brutal and hard through the woods. I was so scared I was going to get injured. And when we got back to my flat, I wanted to clean up, as I had a load of scratches and cuts on my legs. He just wouldn't stop.'

'He was pushing me and pushing me into sex, and I told him "no", and that he needed to take his stuff and get out, that it was over. And that was when he got really angry.' She exhaled another long breath before continuing. 'He was trying to pin me to the bed when the neighbours hammered on the wall and said they were calling the police.' Kira played with the end of her braid as it hung over her shoulder.

'That scared him off for a bit. That was in the November. But I knew that I hadn't got rid of him entirely.' Kira had taken a moment to compose herself as Sam waited patiently again for her to continue. 'Then he started stalking me. Literally everywhere I went, there he was—outside my flat, I had changed the locks but was still scared he would find a wayin; he appeared at the studio and gyms I used to work at, peering at me from supermarket aisles, following me to get my car serviced, at the petrol station.'

She could feel Sam nodding next to her, not daring herself to look up straight away as she wanted to get the story out, before she could see the pity she would undoubtably see in his eyes.

'The last time I saw him before he popped up at Sparks this summer was on New Year's Eve last year. He came to my flat earlier that day and rang the bell—what must have been 50 times. He messaged me. He was calling me. It was just relentless. I knew that I had to get out of there, but I didn't want him to see me going, so I had to take a gamble that he would stop at some point and go away for a bit. I was used to his routine by then and thought he would go, but then come back.' She took a long, slow breath before she continued.

'I had planned to go to Ruby's to catch up with her, as we were making a plan to get me a restraining order. She wasn't going out that evening as she had a cold, and then I had a hotel booked—just the thought of being somewhere he didn't know where I was just so appealing. I know I could have called the police, but it was New Year's, and they were guaranteed to be busy. So, I waited until 30 minutes after what seemed to be his last text.'

'He had said already that he would be back, and that I had better answer my door, so I knew what his intentions were. I had probably 10 minutes as a window in which I could get out without him seeing me and to get to Ruby's. So, I picked my moment, grabbed my bag and headed out the door.' Kira felt Sam's grip get more firm, and his hand on her arm picked up the pace of its gentle strokes as her breathing started to pick up and her words got faster.

'I was literally two paces from my car, from safety, when—boom! There he is, slamming me down across the bonnet of my car.' She could hear her own voice shaking. 'And he's punching me in the back, kicking me in the legs, snarling in my face as I felt myself falling onto the pavement below.' She bit back a sob. 'He really fucking hurt me. I thought that was it. I thought he was going to kill me.'

'Come here.' Sam had moved towards her again, his movements so unlike that of Josh, soft and gentle, as he again wrapped his strong arms around her. 'You don't have to tell me tonight if it hurts too much.' She could hear the concern in his voice as he soothed her shaking body.

'No, I need to. That's the point. I've been silent for too long, and he's just been allowed to get away with it.' She felt stronger just for saying those words out loud. Looking back now, she knew that this was the turning point for her.

'So, I pushed and kicked my way back up. I must have managed to hit him in the nuts, as he went down a treat, and then I ran. I dropped everything and just fucking ran.' She let out a mirthless laugh. 'I knew I couldn't out pace him, but he didn't know the streets where I lived as well as I do. I mean, I used to train those streets every morning, so I set off at a pace and managed to lose him.'

'I think it took all my effort to get to Ruby's that night, but I made it, and then once I was there, I knew I had to set myself free from him and get the law on my side.' She wiped away a tear as it started its course down her cheek.

'I knew Ruby would want me to go to the police, but I knew more than anything she would just want to help me. Kyle was out that night, and she helped me get cleaned up and then dropped me at the hotel. She helped me with money to pay for a few more nights, so that I could move out of my flat and never have to go back.' Kira relaxed into Sam's arms.

'And then that was it. I quit my job and moved towns. I changed my triathlon club and my gym, and the restraining order was served on him. I thought I was finally free and had just started to get my life on track—new town, new flat, a job I really love, and a chance to rebuild things and work on my form, and that's when I met you.' She looked up at him, his eyes brushing hers with both compassion and kindness in their warmth.

'And that's why I wasn't ready for us to be a thing. I just couldn't let myself trust anyone, and I couldn't let anyone else get hurt after I spotted Josh at the summer party.'

'Josh?' Sam hadn't spoken in a while, and the question in his voice was evident.

'Yeah, Josh—Carolyn's husband. I didn't say at the start of this, did I? He's my ex.' She closed her eyes as she waited for him to shove her away or reject her, knowing that she had had an affair with a married man, that she had cheated with one of her best friend's husbands, but all he did was hold her tighter, his hand moving back up to her hair.

'Fuck, Kira.' Sam gently exhaled. 'That's awful. What a guy, huh?' He was shaking his head as she looked up at him. 'I can't believe you had to go through all of that. And then what happened? I mean at Halloween?'

She was happy but not surprised at the lack of judgement in his voice, that, as with everything, there was just kind compassion and a protectiveness she had never experienced in a relationship before, as he waited for her to continue, stroking her cheek as she looked up at him, the distant lights of the fireworks down below in the town starting to light up the night sky.

'It's been hell, if I'm honest.' Her mouth quirked a tiny bit on one side. 'Hey, but at least I got to meet you today because of it.'

Sam had smiled back at her then, their eyes meeting. She knew that if she had instigated it, he would have kissed her—but that he was too much of a gentleman to take the lead when she was vulnerable. She knew him well enough now to know that he would wait for when she was truly ready.

'You know if I had seen him doing that to you at Halloween, or even if I see him again, he's a dead man?' Sam growled. 'I can't help how I feel. I just can't bear to think of him hurting you, Kira. I need you to know you can come to me, that you can trust me. I will be there for you whenever you need me.' He would never know how much his words had meant to her—to know that someone had her corner as well as her parents. Maybe that was why she decided to open up to him even more.

'And being at my parents' the last few nights has been a revelation. You know I told you about my sister, Joanna, dying? Well, since then, the last few years have just been really hard between me and my parents. I think I thought that they missed her more than they would have missed me, that they were so proud of her, that the only way I could get their attention would be to win in competitions that Jo never got to compete in—but they never came along to support me.' She shrugged.

'The more I tried, the more disappointed I was. But what I didn't realise was how painful it was for them—to see me on the circuit and putting all my energy into training for something that my heart wasn't really in, trying to be something I wasn't. It wasn't about me winning competitions; it was about me being true to myself. They want to support me to set up my own fitness studio. I'm not giving up competing entirely, but I am going to try and be more myself, and that will make them just as proud as they were about Joanna.'

She found herself starting to smile once again, surprised at the strength of happy feelings creeping up her body, despite having just told him more than she had ever told anyone about herself.

'You're fucking awesome, you know that?' Sam had dropped a gentle kiss on the top of her head, as he moved his arm from around her, letting her ease back into the seat. 'After everything you've been through, you should be so proud of yourself. You have everything to live for, everything to look forward to, and if you'll let me, I want to be there alongside you.' He looked so serious then that Kira hadn't known what to think.

'I want to quit Sparks and help you with your studio. Maybe not straight away, but your gonna need staff, right? And I can help you with the practical stuff—you know, health and safety, insurances, all that business stuff. I've been doing that on the farm for my dad for years.'

'But what about your Master's?' She had been genuinely concerned. 'I can't let you quit that just because you feel sorry for me.'

He had fixed her with a straight stare, unflinching, as he said.

'Let's get one thing straight. This is not me feeling sorry for you—far from it. This is me being honest with you about how capable I think you are, how I believe in your ideas and want to be part of that success. I only have a few more months to go until I'm qualified anyway, so I can just help out between studies while you figure everything out. It doesn't have to stop me becoming a physio.'

'It wouldn't hurt for me to have a private practice too, once I finish my placements. And who knows, maybe "Kira's Studio" might expand to physical treatments one day?'

She could tell that he had surprised even himself with his rush of words. There was something about his enthusiasm and belief in her that had been palpable, that felt true and more real than anything had for a very long time. She almost couldn't stop herself then from reaching her hand up to the side of his face and pulling his lips down gently against hers. The kiss lingered—not deep or passionate, but touched with a sensitivity that she felt right down into her soul.

She waited now for the others to join her in the sauna, and to tell them about her plan—not only how she would stand side by side with Carolyn whenever she wanted to report Josh, but also her plans for the studio, her future, and her blossoming relationship with the most kind-hearted and dependable guy she knew.

33

1 Month Ago
December, Carolyn

Carolyn had heard next to nothing from Josh over the last few weeks. He had left her a shitty voice note from the airport before he had left back in November—about her lack of support before his trip, and "why wasn't she there taking care of him instead of running around after her decrepit father?" But apart from that, there had been pretty much radio silence, which suited her.

She had spent a fair amount of time over those initial weeks looking for the listening and spy devices in her house, without making it obvious that was what she was doing. At least if she knew where they were, she could make a conscious effort not to speak too openly near them; and she already had a pact with the girls that if they needed to talk about anything in private, they would meet in the sauna on the women-only sessions.

Her plans were now well underway for how she could get out of the house without Josh knowing, and actually start to make a life for herself away from him. She knew that she could count on Sarah, Ruby and Kira to support her, but she really needed a plan to be able to set herself up on her own two feet financially. She had so much going for her when she was younger. She had worked her socks off as a personal assistant, and was well on the way to getting a promotion when she had met Josh.

She didn't realise quite how much he had eroded her confidence and sense of self over the years, tearing her down, so that she didn't even recognise her own skills anymore. She knew that the committee at Aaron Sparks respected her, and that she could always pull off a blinder of an event—knowing just the right tone to set, how to make the families feel really involved, make the kids laugh, help the parents to let their hair down. But that was just superficial, right? It's not like she could actually make a living out of it. Could she?

Just that morning as she was getting ready for the day, she had looked at her reflection in the full-length mirror and had actually taken a second glance. She knew Josh wouldn't really notice the difference in her when he came back. She could barely remember the last time he had actually looked at her, but she was starting to notice a subtle change.

She was still wearing her usual "mum" outfits, but with Sarah's help, she had worked hard over the last month to clean up her diet and to start going to more classes, her confidence and fitness improving with each one. Sarah had even helped her pick out a couple of new pairs of skinny jeans (skinny, ha!) and a sparkly, slinky dress for the Christmas party, a couple of slimming cowl-neck sweaters in seasonal red and green, and her new wardrobe was nearly ready for its debut.

Ruby had definitely looked at her a little closer the other day when they met for coffee, when instead of her usual cream-and-sugar-laden latte, she had ordered a peppermint tea with no cake or biscuits to go with it. One thing she could give Ruby credit for though was that she wouldn't pry. She knew all of Carolyn's secrets and would wait for her to lead a conversation when the time was right.

As she had peered at herself again, she could see already that her complexion looked a hell of a lot better. She was less sallow, her cheeks had a slight glow to them, and her newly bobbed and highlighted hair was shiny. Her muffin top was still there a little, poking up like uncooked dough above the waistband of her jeans, but Sarah had reassured her that it was slowly evaporating and would soon be a distant memory. And the wonderful thing was that she wasn't doing this for Josh, she was doing it for herself, taking back control and becoming the person she wanted to be as she shed the darkness like a skin.

She certainly wasn't going to splurge over Christmas and ruin all her hard work, and she couldn't really give a flying fuck what Josh thought anymore. By this time next year, he would be a distant memory.

Carolyn pondered her to-do list spread out across the dining room table. She had about 2 weeks until Josh was due back, and there was still so much to do. She was heading up the committee for the Sparks "Christmas Sparks" quiz and party, and the New Year's Eve celebrations, including organising a late-night spa session for lucky ticket holders.

She had been wrangling with their insurance company to make it possible for them to stay open until 1am, with an event that gave 20 lucky people in a ballot the chance to have a champagne hot tub experience, after the clock had struck midnight on New Year's Eve. It was the duty manager's job to pull the names out of a hat at the Christmas Eve party. Then there was the rest of the Christmas shopping to be done.

Carolyn thanked God for Amazon. At least the kids were at that age now, where they had quite a clear plan in mind for what they actually wanted, and while she still had access to the credit card, she had sat down the other night and ordered a shed-ton of stuff online to be delivered over the next week.

The bit that she was still trying to push to the back of her mind was what was going to happen in the new year. Not only was she going to leave this beautiful house—the only one the kids had ever known, and where, despite everything that had happened over the years, she did have some lovely, happy memories. If she thought about it too much, it started to make her panic, the gravity of what she had planned almost too much to bear.

To calm herself down, she glanced up at the bookshelves lining the walls, all of her favourite literature stacked like a mini library up to the corniced ceilings. She looked at the stunning print of the Swiss Alps that they had bought one year during a skiing trip, spending a small fortune on bringing it home and getting it framed and hanging it in pride of place, where it took up the majority of one wall.

She looked at the dining room table, her papers all over it, the place where they had hosted sophisticated dinner parties before the children were born—where once Josh had pushed her back amongst the debris of crumbs, wine glasses and candles when their guest had departed, telling her she was beautiful before guiding her back against the table, gently pushing up her dress and making love to her.

Carolyn shivered. She had to pull herself together and not let the sentiment of those good times cloud her judgement, as it had so many times over the years. Yes, this man had given her absolute pleasure. Yes, he had had her shuddering and calling out his name. Yes, he had once brought her to orgasm so many times in a weekend in Paris that she had lost count. And yet, yes, he was a chauvinistic, tyrant who hurt women. She strengthened her resolve as she picked up the phone.

'Castle and Barret, how can I help you?' The singsong voice of the receptionist at the estate agent brought a smile to her face.

'Hi, yes, my name's Carolyn. I wondered if it was possible to make an appointment for next week to come and talk to someone?'

As soon as she started to speak, she suddenly glanced at the clock on the mantle—one of the "bugs" hiding place—remembering, shit, with a sudden jolt of fear that he would be listening. The last thing she needed was for her cover to be blown before she had even started to finalise her plans.

'Sure. Now is this about renting or buying?' the singsong voice continued.

'Um, it's…it's about donating a prize to the Sparks Christmas raffle,' she sputtered out. If Josh was listening, he surely wouldn't be able to hear the hesitation at her mistake in her voice, would he?

'I'm not sure Mr Castle or Mr Barrett would be looking to donate a prize. I'm sorry, where did you say it was for?'

Recovering quickly from her error, Carolyn was quick to turn on the charm. 'It's for Aaron Sparks, the premier sports club in Oxholm. I believe both Mr's are still active members, and the funds that we raise from the raffle actually support local children who are under privileged to attend swimming lessons at the sports club.'

She could almost feel herself injecting a smile into her voice as she continued. 'Perhaps tomorrow at 4 pm would be convenient. I would be pleased to see either of them at their offices on Mount Street. Goodbye!' Before the receptionist had a chance to reply, Carolyn had hung up.

She put the phone back in its cradle and bent her head to the table. Fuck, what had she nearly done? She needed to be more careful in future and only call from one of her friend's phones when it was something to do with "the plan". She needed another meeting with the lawyer Ruby had put her in touch with, about filing for divorce and the restraining order on the 2nd January. She would have to get Ruby to arrange that one for her when they met later.

Then there was the removals van to book, the list of things she would need to buy for the new house, and the jobs she had already earmarked on LinkedIn under a fake profile to apply for. She already had a new encrypted email address set up and all of the paperwork she needed on a daily basis was nestled neatly in a folder named "Filing for Sparks". She gave herself a mental high-five for her creativity.

She thought, *Fuck you, Josh!* She was going to get through this list of things she had to do today, and then reward herself with a mini mince pie or gingerbread with a fruit tea.

34
1 Month Ago
December, Ruby

That night back in November had been a revelation for Ruby and Kyle. It had started when Ruby had met Carolyn, and the two of them had fleshed out a plan to gather evidence about Josh, and to plan how they would go together in January to report him to the police and start the process of a restraining order and divorce proceedings. They had agreed then that they would both talk to Kira, in turn, about their plan, and that even if she decided she didn't want to be part of it, they would proceed anyway.

What they hadn't banked on was Kira rekindling things with Sam, and her parents encouraging and supporting her to take real control over her life—now that she had opened up to them about what she had endured.

Kira had eventually messaged them both ten days after Halloween, asking them to meet her at her mum and dad's house while they were out. She hadn't yet been back to work, and despite Ruby's text, hadn't been in touch with either of them. Ruby knew that Carolyn had been wary of meeting Kira—not because she had anything to hide, but because of the guilt she carried, being married to the guy who had so badly hurt her friend and not being able to stop it.

Ruby had reassured her that Kira wouldn't blame Carolyn at all, encouraging her to come to the meeting and talk through everything—just the three of them. Back then, Kira had still been a little hesitant about reporting Josh, but she told them all about the personal journey of self-discovery that she had just been on. That she had realised that what she really wanted was her own life—to stop living in her late sister's shadow, to stop trying to compete at the highest level of her sport, and to open her own studio.

She wanted to support Carolyn to get justice for the years of abuse that Josh had subjected her to, and to give Ruby the friendship she needed as and when she chose to tell Kyle her story. It had been cathartic for all of them, each of the women in tears at varying points in the night, as they sipped Prosecco around Kira's parents dining room table.

Their friendship bound together forever by their experiences—giving each other the strength to move on, to survive, to thrive. From that night on, they were back to their usual routine, each of them secure in the knowledge that there was a plan afoot and that they had each other's backs.

A month on from that night, Ruby wanted to share with them what had happened on fireworks night with Kyle. They both now knew about her run-in with Josh at the house, and how this had added more fuel to Ruby's desire to help get them both justice. However, in all their conversations, it hadn't felt like quite the right time to bring up what she herself had been going through.

Now that they had a plan, it felt like they were all on more solid ground, and she knew that if she was going to start fertility treatment in the new year, then she was going to need her friends to support her too.

As they arrived and settled themselves into their usual spots in the sauna, Ruby felt herself take a deep breath to settle herself, before launching into her own update.

'So…I told Kyle about what happened, back when I was 16.' She looked up at both of them, waiting to see their reaction. Carolyn had taken an audible breath in, and Kira had met her eyes and slowly nodded, both willing her to continue.

'It was on fireworks night. I already told you what happened with Josh that day, and that was part of the reason why I haven't talked to you both about this before now. We all needed time together to work through the Josh situation, but I also needed just some time to process how things were going with Kyle.' She looked around at both of them, waiting for them to say anything, but they were patiently waiting for her to continue. 'I had to tell Kyle because Josh knew—he knew about my infertility, and he knew about the abortion.'

'What the fuck, Ruby!' Carolyn interrupted. 'How could he know that? You don't think that I told him, do you? You know I wouldn't tell him anything personal about you.' The shock in Carolyn's voice was evident.

'No! Of course not, Carolyn. Let me explain.' Ruby shook her head at her friend, knowing Carolyn would need reassurance that she hadn't done anything wrong.

'Go on, Ruby. We're listening,' said Kira quietly.

'It was the listening devices,' confirmed Ruby. 'You know I told you about them the day Josh attacked me, and that I said we needed to leave them for now so that we had more evidence. Well, he must have been listening that day I came over for coffee, after I told you about Todd.' She looked between her friends as the penny dropped.

'He must have heard through one of his microphones all about it, and how I was keeping it from Kyle, that I might not be able to have children because of the dodgy abortion after the rape. So, that's what he threatened me with when he attacked me at your house, Carolyn.' She grimaced as she continued. 'I had to make a decision—either wait and see if he came good on his threat, or tell Kyle myself. To be fair, it was time. I know I should have told him sooner, so despite what that bastard did to me, he actually did me a favour.'

Ruby's outward sigh sounded more like relief to her two friends, so they were surprised when she carried on.

'There's also more to it than I've ever told you both. It felt only fair that I talk to Kyle about it all—everything, the good, the bad, and the ugly—before I spoke to you guys, and before I went to get some help.' She had looked around again then, picking out the puzzled look that Carolyn had thrown Kira.

'We're here for you, Rubes. We're listening.'

'So, you both remember that guy that freaked me out back in the summer? Todd?' she continued. 'And that I told you, when we were sitting in here, about what had happened to me at the party at his house? That I was raped, and that it led to me getting a really bad abortion—one that left me with damage to my cervix so that I wouldn't be able to maintain a pregnancy?'

Ruby knew that her bluntness now, about something she had been so emotional about before, might be confusing for her friends, but it was the only way she knew how to get through what she had to tell them.

'That wasn't the worst of it. The reason why I haven't ever felt able to talk about any of this is partly about the abortion and what that night did to me, but more to do with my family and my background. You already know I changed my name from Ruth, but I never told you my surname.' She bowed her head. Despite her bravado of a few moments ago, the realisation of what she was now vocalising for only the second time in her adult life finally hitting her.

'Rubes, you're not making a lot of sense, love. What are you trying to tell us?' As always, Carolyn wanted to rush to the crux of the story, to speed it up so she could be part of any solution.

'Carolyn, let her take her time,' Kira urged her friend to be patient.

'My name is actually Ruth Merrimore-Chilcot. I'm the daughter of Judge Chilcot, the QC that you've probably read about in the Sunday papers growing up. The lenient judge who was known for frequently siding with men, enabling rapists and sadists to walk free—the one who allowed a legal loophole from 1824 be used in court to free Damian Trestcoe, when everyone knew he was guilty of those kidnaps and sexual assaults.' She looked in turn at each of them.

'He's the judge you hope you get when you've committed a really heinous crime, as he's known for his leniency and ability to turn a blind eye to the victims, who, in most cases, are women just like me,' she spat out, the venom in her voice clear in the darkness of the sauna. 'I'm his only child—a child he disowned when she came to him the day after she had been brutally raped, at a party by a guy from her high school.

'The same father who, when I turned up on his doorstep a couple of months later and begged him for help when I found out I was pregnant, told me that he "didn't have a daughter", before spitting in my face and slamming the door on me. The same father who told my mother that if she had anything to do with me, he would cut her off too, and my mother being the door mat that she was choosing him over me, as she did every time he was cruel or bullied me during my childhood.'

She paused for breath, knowing that she had just stunned them into silence. Everyone had heard of her father and knew his reputation. She didn't need to know that this revelation alone would be a shock to them.

'Oh, Ruby!' Carolyn didn't know what to say as she moved closer to take her friend's right hand. 'That's awful. Seriously, I can't believe it.'

Kira moved down from her place on the top row to Ruby's other side, softly picking up her left hand.

'We're here for you, Rubes. Jeez, I can't believe what you've been through!'

'I've wanted to tell you both for such a long time, and that's the point. I've been holding onto this for so many years, not telling anyone I got close to, holding a part of myself back because I was so ashamed. Not just of what happened to me and how I felt disgusted about allowing myself to be abused like that, but because I was ashamed to be his daughter.'

'Telling Kyle and you both is the start of my future. I can't expect the two of you to be brave and stand up to Josh if I'm not prepared to be brave myself. I know none of this was my fault. I have nothing to be ashamed of.' Ruby could feel her voice getting stronger as her confident grew in telling her story.

'So, what did I do? I had been told over and over again what I should be, how I should look, how I should behave so that I could snare myself a decent husband and support him—one that would bring more money and prosperity to our family name. No one cared about what I wanted, or how I felt.' She paused. 'I was lucky I had a friend—well, not a friend as such, but he became that for the short time it took to help me find a place to stay and get myself on my feet. That was Todd.'

'Todd!' Carolyn exclaimed, clearly puzzled. 'The guy that freaked you out at the summer party? I thought he was the guy that attacked you?' she finished.

'I should have been clearer before when I was talking about him, but I hadn't had a chance to really process everything before, and I needed time to work through my feelings. But no, Todd was a good guy,' she paused and emphasised, 'is a good guy.' Ruby's mouth tilted into a small smile before she continued.

'So, the party that night was at his house. He was the cool rich kid who was allowed to do pretty much whatever he liked, mainly because his parents didn't give a shit about him either. As long as he did well at school, he could always walk into a position in his father's firm. No worries about grades or reputation, he had it made. But what people didn't know about Todd was that he was actually incredibly kind, that he saw things that other people didn't, and that he felt guilty for his privilege.' Ruby sighed as she took a sip of her water.

'Nothing that happened at his house that night was his fault. He had tried to get me to drink some water at his party, tried to get me to stand up and get fresh air. But then one of the other guys threw a punch and a fight started in the pool room. That was when I went looking for the bathroom, and one of the other guys found me. You know what happened next,' she shrugged. Now that she had told the story, its power over her had seemed to slip away.

'Todd had his suspicions about what had happened to me at his house that night. He had seen me stumble out of his bathroom and saw Serena get me into the taxi, but he didn't know what to say or do.' She took another sip of water and cleared her throat. 'He was the one who found me down at the marina the day I told my father about the rape and he kicked me out. He was the one who let me stay on his parents' yacht for months.

'He helped me find somewhere to get the abortion and then find somewhere a bit safer to live. He gave me money, clothes even, and then he contacted his wonderful godmother, who was a librarian at Oxford University, to ask if she would help me.' Ruby warmed to her topic.

'Juliet was an angel. She basically became my fairy godmother. She had a spare room and friends who needed a babysitter, so I could earn a little money,' she smiled. 'She helped me enrol at a local college to finish my A-levels and get into university to study law.' Ruby shook her head, still unable to believe that this wonderful woman had taken a chance on her. 'Honestly, I don't know what I would have done without her.'

'The day I moved into halls at uni, I cut off my long blonde hair into a short bob, dyed it bright red, got my ears, nose and lip pierced, and got my first tattoo. Todd had kept in touch, and he helped me move into my first student house, but then he moved, and I changed. I guess I wanted to push away the past, and that was the last time I ever saw him, until this summer,' she smiled sadly.

'I feel now for the way I reacted when I saw him. He was nothing but kind to me,' she gave a sad smile.

'It was the shock, Rubes, that's all. I bet if you saw him again now, that you can talk about this, that he would be glad to hear from you.' As always, Kira wanted to reassure her friend.

'Seriously, Ruby, that is an amazing story! What did Kyle say?'

Ruby took her time then and explained how Kyle had been incredible—that he had taken her in his arms as she relived some of the toughest times in her life and held her close as he told her how proud he was of her, how strong she was, and that no matter what life threw at them, he wasn't going anywhere. She had broken down with relief to hear him talk through his emotions.

That he was disappointed that she hadn't told him from the start, but that he understood how latent trauma could affect the ability to talk about something so incredibly painful. That he was sorry for pushing her to have a baby, and that they could give it as much time as she needed to work out what they wanted to do. That again, he wasn't going anywhere, and he loved her and would always stand by her side.

Kira's audible sniff next to her brought her back to her surroundings, as both women moved from their spots in the sauna to sit either side of her—Carolyn wrapping her arm round Ruby's waist, and Kira one round her shoulders.

'Fucking hell, Rubes. Well, that tops our bloody stories, doesn't it?' Carolyn, never one to mince her words, wheezed out a laugh.

'Ruby, you're awesome,' sobbed Kira. 'I can't believe you had to go through all that alone. I mean, it's been hard for all of us these last few months, but you've been carrying this around with you for years—your parents, the attack, all the stuff you just told us. I just can't believe a person can be such a success carrying all that baggage!' She swiped the tears coursing down her cheek away with the back of her hand.

'Ladies, if this has taught me anything in life, it's that we women are the true heroes. We are resilient and strong and can get through things. It's also taught me that people deserve to pay for their wrongs. There needs to be retribution, to make things right that have been done wrong,' Carolyn proclaimed, giving each of their hands a squeeze.

'Well, I'm up for making people pay!' Ruby agreed with enthusiasm.

'That's probably why you're such a shit-hot lawyer, right, Rubes? You're fucking marvellous at making people pay,' Carolyn chuckled, as she nodded along with Kira.

'Ha, yeah, something like that,' Ruby smirked.

35
2 Weeks Ago
December, Kira

Kira sat waiting in the coffee shop for Ruby to meet her so they could do some last-minute Christmas shopping, and as usual, Ruby was running late. Kira didn't mind, as it gave her time to sit and reflect on how much her life had changed in the last 6 weeks. She stirred sweetener into her matcha latte and almost gave herself a pinch to check she wasn't dreaming.

It had been amazing with Sam since the night of her revelations, as they had sat on the top of the hill and watched the fireworks below them. She had felt like another huge weight had lifted off her shoulders as she confided in him.

They had sat for another hour or so after that. He had opened up to her about the pressure his dad had put on him, as the eldest son, to take over the farm. But now that his younger brother had started to grow up a bit, it was obvious to the whole family that he was more of a natural fit to take on the role. And that his dad—albeit reluctantly—had said he would support Sam in whatever career he chose.

They had shared more about their families and growing up, both laughing when they realised that their families both used to go to the same beach in Devon at similar times each year—and perhaps they were destined to meet? As the night had grown darker as the fireworks had faded away, he had started the engine and taken her back to her parents' house, and made sure she was safe before he drove away with a promise to call the next day.

There had been no playing it cool for either of them this time around—no saying he would call the next day but leaving it a bit longer. He was as keen as she was to see where this would go—not only for the business, but for the both of them. It was like the missing piece of the jigsaw had finally found its place at just the right time. He had picked her up at her parents' the next afternoon and taken her on a magical hike round his parents' farm.

They primarily focussed on sheep farming, but had acres of arable land too that they used for all sorts of crops. Some of their land was surrounded by a pine forest, which they had explored as Sam made her laugh with stories about the escapades he had got up to with his brothers throughout their childhood. It was in these woods that the atmosphere had changed. He had taken her to a clearing where a gamekeeper's hut still stood, a plume of smoke gently curling from its chimney and mingling with the aromatic smell of pine all around them.

She had looked at him curiously, as he explained that this was where he and his brothers had been allowed to camp out in the summer holidays, and that they kept the hut now as a place of respite away from the farm. He told her how he loved to come up there after a hectic day, light the fire pit, open a cold beer, and just take some time to look at the stars.

Sam had hesitantly taken her hand then and asked her if she wanted to go in, making sure she knew it was entirely her choice. She could see he was so consciously trying to consider her feelings, that she had to take him by the hand and lead him over to the low wooden door with the metal latch. He took his keys with the big "S" keyring and held it out to her for her to make the decision. She gave him a reassuring smile that told him that she was perfectly happy to take a look at the cabin.

Inside, the hut was cosy and dark, the log burner was warm and inviting, and a kerosene lamp hung in a corner, casting a soft light over the stripped wooden planked walls. Sam explained to her that he and his brother had tidied the interior up over the last few years, adding the sagging sofa covered in sheepskin throws and the daybed that was pushed up against the far wall. His mum had helped with the curtains, and they had added a primus stove, so that they could stay overnight and cook somewhere other than on the fire pit.

Kira couldn't help but express her surprise that two guys had made the place so cosy and welcoming, as she reassured Sam again that she was glad to be there with him and for him to share this with her.

At first, they had sat on the sofa in front of the log burner, drinking coffee and warming their feet in the heat as the light outside had started to fade. Sam had kept a respectful distance again all that day, occasionally taking her hand to help her over a style or broken branch, and once brushing her hair out of her eyes, his hand lingering on her cheek as their eyes met for more than a couple of seconds.

There was something though, that she hadn't expected or experienced the last time they were seeing each other—a kind of magnetic pull, where she couldn't help but move closer to him when he spoke to her. It was like she could feel herself leaning in closer, wanting to be drawn more into his strong warmth.

Even now, as she daydreamed about that day, she remembered the feel of being wrapped up in a soft, fleecy throw, as she had watched him kneel in front of the fire to stoke it. She had admired his strong physique, honed from years of tossing hay bales on the farm and training in the pool to support his lifeguarding.

At six-foot-two, he was much taller than her, and yet never made her feel as if he was forcing himself into her personal space in the way that Josh used to do, stretching out his six-foot frame to make her feel small. If anything, Sam tried to make himself smaller, tilting towards her to make her feel enveloped by his warmth and strength.

Kira hadn't planned what had happened next that night in the cabin, but as the darkness continued to fall, they had moved closer together on the sofa. She had leant her head gently onto his shoulder, as he reached out a hand to play with her hair as it fell across her cheek. She had looked up into his forest-green eyes, as they seemed to darken despite the light of the fire dancing in them. He moved so his forehead was just touching hers, looking for permission.

And this time, he had taken the initiative, kissing her gently at first, then deepening the kiss as he felt her moan into his mouth. He had pulled away slightly then to whisper her name, questioning if she was ok. She had answered then by pulling herself round and up onto his lap, straddling him.

She knew that he was still holding back, that despite what she could feel from the hard ridge of him against her inner thigh, he was still enough of a gentleman to not take it further without her explicit permission. Kira had known then that this experience with this sensitive, strong and beautiful man would change her life—that he would teach her how a man is supposed to love a woman, and that he would make her feel strong and incredible.

She didn't want him to pull back now because he thought she was fragile, so, in one swift movement, she shucked off her fleece, pulled her tank top over her head and moved against him. There had been no mistaking her intentions as she had pulled him into her again, her mouth hungrily seeking his, gently taking his bottom lip in her teeth, teasing his tongue with hers as he opened against her.

'Sam?' she had whispered huskily against his neck. 'You don't have to be so gentle with me, you know. I'm not going to break. I want you—all of you.'

This reassurance was enough to make him moan with relief as he gently lifted her from his lap and pushed her back down into the fleeces, slowly taking time to peel off his hoodie and t-shirt, eliciting a delighted gasp from Kira, who—despite having seen him in the pool so many times—hadn't had the pleasure of witnessing his sharp hard lines this close up before. He reached then for the buttons on her jeans.

As she lifted her arse to help him peel them off her, she could feel the warm pleasure pooling against the fabric of her panties, as he moved his fingers gently along the fabric covering her. Things had seemed to both slow down and speed up then all at the same time. Once she had nodded permission for him to remove them and told him that as long as he was clean, she was on the pill, he had sated himself on her.

His mouth had elicited her first climax, followed by his hands. She had helped him out of his jeans then, unable to wait any longer, needing to feel him fill her and take her wholly. The third time had come later, their bodies covered in a sheen of sweat in the firelight, as he had guided her back down onto him, watching her arch her body in sheer pleasure.

After, as the fire had burnt low and Kira's stomach had started to rumble and make them both laugh, Sam had extracted himself from where they lay in a tangle on the floor and helped her dress, warming her hands between his as they walked back through the woods towards the farmhouse—each of them grinning and unable to keep stopping for one last quick kiss before they made it inside. She had been right—that night had changed her life, and only for the better.

The sound of a coffee mug hitting the table brought Kira back to earth with a bump. She had looked up at Ruby then and caught her eye as Ruby eyed her suspiciously. There was no hiding anything from that woman.

'I know that look! That's a "I've-just-had-a-hot-sex-flashback" kind of look,' she said and started to crack up. 'You can't deny it, girl. I've seen it too many times before!' Ruby's wicked laugh rang out across the quiet café.

'Rubes!' Kira coloured, her cheeks flaming. 'Keep your voice down, seriously!' Despite her initial embarrassment, she was pleased that she was noticeably happier to Ruby after the drama of the last year. She had told the girls about how she was now back together with Sam, but hadn't gone into any detail about the more private aspects of it to date.

'Ok, so you're right. Yes, I was having a bit of flashback, if you must know. And yes, it was very lovely, and that's all you're getting, ok?' She couldn't hide her grin any longer as Ruby flashed her a wink.

'I knew it! Come on, spill.'

'He's just lovely, Ruby. I just can't seem to get enough of him,' Kira let out a contented sigh. 'He has just been so supportive. There's no pressure there, Rubes. He hasn't made me tell him anything, but I've wanted to tell him everything. His family are also really nice. They have that big farm out on Five Hundred Acre Hill—the one with the little farm shop? It's so peaceful out there. It just feels like whenever we go there, I can just breathe again.'

Kira let out an audible sigh of contentment. 'Don't get me wrong. I know this isn't over yet. But I think that as long as I can get through the next couple of weeks—and I've got you all on my side, and Sam looking out for me—I can actually see a future, that I can actually be happy again. I seriously can't thank you enough.' She looked up to see Ruby blushing, the red of her face nearly matching the bright tones of her hair.

'Ah, babe, you don't need to thank me. And you're right—this isn't over yet. Yes, you have the support you need now, but we need to finish this and get this guy out of all of our hair once and for all. We need justice, and I don't care what that looks like. The way he's hurt all of us and the pain he's caused to people over the years, it's not fucking on.' It didn't take long for Ruby to get ramped back up again, but in true lawyer style, it also didn't take her long to calm back down as she picked up the menu.

'So, enough of that shit today. What looks good?' She looked up to see the young waitress approaching.

After they had ordered, Ruby wanted all of the details of what Kira's plans were.

'Well, let me start with the less X-rated stuff, Rubes,' she started. 'Sam has helped, of course.' She couldn't help the involuntary quirk of her lips whenever she said his name. 'We're going to spend Christmas and New Year together. He's working a bit over the break at the pool, and I'm covering a few extra classes to make up for those that I missed. He wants to make sure he's with me when I'm coming to and from work, you know?' She didn't miss a beat as Ruby raised her eyebrows.

'It's not like that, Rubes. He's not being possessive or saying I can't do things without him. He can just see how scared I am sometimes.' Kira searched her friend's face for understanding. 'I'm going to get some more counselling in the New Year. I know I need it, but I need to do it when I know he's in a place where he can't hurt me anymore.' She couldn't bring herself to say Josh's name out loud anymore.

'I get it, don't worry. We all know Sam is a good guy. In fact, Kyle has been exactly the same—so protective of me and getting me to text so he knows where I am and that I've arrived places safely. He knows that Josh will be back soon, and I think he just worries that he'll do something stupid. He's met guys like him before—we all have,' she reassured Kira.

'So, what's on the agenda for this shopping trip then?' Ruby could tell she needed to lighten the mood, and there was nothing like buying a load of Christmas tat for people who already had too much stuff to take her mind off this conversation. 'Socks for Sam? Or a copy of the Karma Sutra maybe?' She winked at Kira across the table.

'Well, I did hear that Anne Summers was having a mid-winter sale,' Kira shyly whispered.

'Well then, chick,' Ruby winked, 'get that drink down you and let's go check it out!'

36
2 Weeks Ago
December, Ruby

It had been a satisfying few weeks for Ruby. Since she had found the strength to be open with Kyle, they had talked and talked, often staying up into the night with a pot of tea and a box of biscuits, going into more detail about both of their pasts than they had ever explored before. Ruby felt as if a huge weight had been lifted off her shoulders. She was almost kicking herself for not trusting her instincts to open to Kyle before.

She guessed it did have something to do with the shame she had still felt until recently—that somehow this was still all her fault. It was only now, she reflected, that she realised how much her secret had been pressing down on her and preventing her from really moving on with her life. There was still an uphill struggle ahead with the plan to deal with Josh. Like Carolyn, she was trying to put this to the back of her mind until after Christmas, when she could actually start to put the plan that they had agreed in action.

There was almost no point in dwelling on that until then. She knew that Kira was in a safe place, staying back at her parents', and with Sam making sure that she wasn't on her own, or checking up on her and meeting her to and from work to ensure her safety—it felt like one less job for Ruby to take care of.

She had met with Carolyn yesterday after her shopping trip with Kira, catching her for a quick sauna before Carolyn had her final committee meeting about the Christmas Eve party. Seriously, the amount of organising that had gone into that thing was quite something! She had chatted to Carolyn about a job she had seen advertised at a local festival and events management company one of her ex-clients worked for. They had a vacancy for a part-time events coordinator that would be right up Carolyn's street.

She knew that one of her friend's greatest regrets had been putting her career on hold to support Josh and bring up the kids. She didn't resent the time she had been able to be a full-time, hands-on mum, but Ruby knew how much Carolyn thrived on being able to be creative and to drive forward a project.

She had listened with interest every time Carolyn had told her about her PR job back before she met Josh, and all the things she felt she had missed out on— not only her independence financially, but also the freedom that being a working mum gave you. Time away from children to have adult conversations, a chance to put skills to good use, to feel like you had really achieved something in your own right by the end of the working week, being thanked by clients, feeling you had made a real difference.

Ruby knew better than anyone how hard women had to fight to just be themselves, to be able to make a living, support and provide for their families if they chose to do so, to not rely on a man to complete them but to complement them. She wanted this for Carolyn more than anything, and she knew that when her friend was strong enough to get there on her own, she would. But right now, she just needed a little help from the sisterhood to get the plan over the line.

Ruby had been thinking about her own plans for the future. In the last few weeks, with things going so well with Kyle, they both felt like the new year was a fresh start for them and their relationship. They had always had an intense physical connection, but now they had a deep emotional connection too. They were openly talking about starting a family in a really positive way, and they were both entirely open that they were 100% committed to each other. Ruby even felt that Kyle might want to take it a step further and get married.

Sure, they had bought a house together last year after Kyle had moved in with her a few months after they first started dating, and some might say that three years in was still fairly new in any relationship to feel completely committed, but for Ruby, there was nothing more apparent that her love for Kyle and his love and respect for her.

And yet. There was still one thing that Ruby had an itch to do, one more door that she needed to close on her previous life so that she could start the new year afresh. There was no way to know if Todd would be receptive to seeing her— supposing she could even track him down—but she needed to apologise. She was the one, all those years ago, who had cut him off, who had turned her back on him after he was the only one who helped her when she was desperate.

He hadn't deserved that, and he certainly hadn't deserved her reaction to him back in the summer when she had bumped into him at the summer party. Ruby knew that what she was going to do was a breach of GDPR. It was really unethical, and if she got caught, she would be in serious trouble. She might get banned from Sparks or even reported. However, it was worth the risk to ease her conscience.

Yesterday had presented the perfect opportunity to work on her plan for tracking Todd down, as she sat with Carolyn in the café after their sauna. Ruby had noticed on a few occasions that Sue from reception disappeared from her post, for a couple of minutes to get a coffee refill in the café every hour or so. From where Ruby normally sat in the lounge area, she had a clear view through the café bar to reception and had observed that not only did Sue leave the reception unattended, but she left her staff key pass there every time.

The key passes were kind of an access-all-area for the building, but also swiped access to the various computers and tills around the building. They were clearly coded to each person, but there was some kind of reset swipe pad behind the reception area, that meant that any card could be swiped and re-coded to a new employee. She remembered Kira telling her about it after she had lost her original card and freaked out about getting a replacement.

All Ruby needed was a quick peek at the membership database to see if she could find the records from the summer party. All members had to sign in day visitors using an electronic guest pass. Ruby guessed this was some kind of fire safety precaution or something. She knew where the database was found on the system. Carolyn had access to some of it on her laptop as part of social committee, but there was a locked area with personal details in that she couldn't access with her pass. Only a staff pass could get into the folder.

Ruby knew that the building was also covered by CCTV, but unbeknown to most of the punters, it was having intermittent faults that had got worse over the last week. They were still waiting for the engineers to come and repair the cameras in the reception area, and the ones that covered the main corridors to the changing area and pool. She also knew that today was her one window of opportunity to nab Sue's pass, as she grabbed her third Americano of the day around 3 pm, and to try and access the database.

She just needed to get one of the café girls to keep Sue talking for a few extra minutes to give herself enough time. Luckily, 3 pm was precisely the quietest time of the day at Aaron Sparks. It was the week before the kids broke up from school, so they normally arrived with their parents from 3:15 pm, when school kicked out for after-school club and swimming lessons. The older generation had already finished their senior tennis, aqua aerobics and late lunches and had headed out, and the PTs were on their breaks in the staff room.

The last thing Ruby wanted was to get Sue into any sort of trouble. They had become friends over the years, and she had helped Sue with her divorce a few years ago. Sue was also friends with Carolyn, sometimes looking after the twins from school. She would have to be careful and quick.

'Hiya, Sue, how's things?' Ruby blipped her pass and made her way into reception, waiting for Sue to stand up from behind the desk, only the top of her head visible from the front entrance.

'Hello, lovely! My day is much better for seeing you here, Rubes!' Sue greeted her with a wide smile, as she turned round to reach for a towel to hand over. 'So, what's the plan today, my love? Are you in the sauna meeting the girls, or is it catching up with emails?' she eyed Ruby's laptop suspiciously.

'Yep, you've got me, Sue. I have a ton of case work to catch up on, and a load of reports to write. I can't say it's going to be a particularly fun afternoon, but it does pay the bills,' she grimaced.

'Well, you have to keep the wolf from the door, don't you? Well, you go grab yourself a table, and maybe you'll get to use that towel later for a nice relax, once you get all your work done?' Sue encouraged.

'Will do. Thanks, Sue. Always nice to see a smiling face!' Ruby walked on through to the café, careful to choose a table on the other side of the room, but with a clear view of the reception desk when she sat down.

She couldn't actually see Sue from where she sat, as there was a pillar and a low wall blocking her view, but she could see the sliding doors that separated reception from the café, so would spot Sue as soon as she made her way into the café. She just needed the second part of her plan to work now—to make sure Sue got distracted. There was nothing Sue loved more than chatting to the guys in the kids' club. She had seen Sue admiring their handiwork as they prepped for the next influx of children.

As predicted, there was Billy and Candice in their bright orange T-shirts, "Little Sparks" logos emblazoned across their chests, sat about 50 yards away from her table. Ruby set up her laptop, ordered a sugary mocha treat and a slice of cake, and made her way over.

'Hey, guys! Show me your latest creations!' she enthused, hoping the pair of them wouldn't think it too strange that she was suddenly showing an interest in their "art", when (a) she didn't have a kid, and (b) had never really talked to them before in her life. Luckily, the boredom of the afternoon seemed to be showing on their faces, and they seemed only too keen to engage her in a chat.

'Hiya, you're Ruby, right? Want to grab a chair, and we can show you how to make a three-balloon Santa?' Candice held up a phallic-looking balloon pump and waggled it in her general direction.

'No, Candice, she wants to learn how to make a four-balloon Reindeer!' Billy shoved a handful of limp, straggly, deflated modelling balloons up towards her face, clearly proud of his modelling prowess.

For a second, Ruby was a little taken aback by their enthusiasm, but also their competitiveness. However, she could see now how this could work even more to her advantage.

'Um, actually, guys, I was chatting to Sue on reception, and she told me how much she was looking forward to seeing your latest creations! You know how much she loves to take the balloons that you practice on to her grandson?'

'Really? I knew she liked our stuff, but she hasn't asked to see anything we've been making for Christmas yet.' Candice and Billy exchanged a grin. 'We've got some pretty special stuff for the kiddos this time,' he continued enthusiastically.

'Yeah, we've been watching crap loads of YouTube and stuff,' interrupted Candice.

'Ah, man, you've got to stop cursing!' he nudged her, causing her to let go of a bright yellow balloon, which went sailing off over their heads with a strange farting sound.

'Billy!' she whacked him over the head with a green balloon she held in her other hand.

'Candice!' he grabbed a red sausage-shaped balloon and chucked it at her, giggling.

'Um, ok, guys,' Ruby interrupted their impromptu balloon fight, 'so I was saying, maybe Sue thinks you're too busy to show her? You'll have to call her over next time you see her and show her your amazing talents!' *There was nothing like flattery to win the heart these two clowns*, thought Ruby.

After she had filtered through another ten or so emails back at her seat, she had spotted the top of Sue's head as she stood up from the reception desk and started to make her way on cue into the café. Ruby had taken a step back behind her, and as Sue walked through, Ruby made her way behind the pillars and chest-high screen that ran around the bar. She knew Sue would be distracted needing her caffeine fix. She also knew she had around 10 minutes if Billy and Candice managed to lure her in.

She got to the desk, lifted the part that allowed staff to enter, and easily found Sue's pass hanging on the hook. All she needed was a quick blip of the QR code on the pass on the computer's scanner, and she would be in to the system. She had just made a start when she heard footsteps approaching.

'I knew I had left my phone somewhere!' Sue's distinctive local accent was unmistakable. 'Let me just grab it, and I can show you the Christmas decorations I've been getting our Alice to make when I look after her.'

As she drew nearer, Ruby's heart felt like it was beating in her mouth, as she crouched lower behind the desk. She spotted Sue's bag, and luckily, there was her phone in the side pouch. Ruby grabbed it, thrust her hand up above her as she squashed herself under the desk, and hoped that Sue would merely lean over instead of coming back round the desk to find it.

'Oof, forgot how tall this bloody desk was.' She could hear Sue groan. 'Ah here it is. Must remember to stick it in my pocket,' she muttered to herself, her footsteps retreating.

Ruby let out the breath she had been holding and pulled herself up into a shaky crouch, her limbs feeling as if they were vibrating with adrenaline. She had less time now as she tried to punch in Todd's name in the search bar. Luckily, with such an unusual surname, it took her all of 2 seconds to find the entry and to take a quick snap of the screen on her phone, before she caught a glimpse of what looked like Michael, the duty manager, over by the café bar, about to head her way.

'Fuck.' She shrunk down behind the counter again, absentmindedly slipping the pass into her pocket. She crawled backwards to the hatch and slithered her way out, bottom first, into the lobby area in front of the entrance gates, just as Michael approached. For the second time in less than 5 minutes, her heart was giving her palpitations. She had to think fast. As she reached up and, under the guise of a sneeze, unhooked her left earring and shoved it under her leg.

'Oh, Ruby! Are you ok down there? Have you fallen?' There was no mistaking Michael's concern as he leant down over her to see what she was doing.

'Oops, no, Michael. Sorry to give you a fright. My earring fell out as I was coming back from the car park,' she answered brightly, proceeding to scrabble around on the floor on the pretext of finding her earring, which at this point was now digging into her left knee.

'Well, let me help. If you shuffle back that way a bit—ah, that's it; back a bit more,' he encouraged.

'Oh look!' she exclaimed. 'I'm kneeling on it, silly me!' She held out her arm for him to help her up. 'Right, that's me sorted. Sorry for surprising you. Back to the emails. Have a lovely day and all that,' she garbled, hoping that he would mistake her flustered appearance for nothing more than the fact that she had been crawling around on the floor, and not that she had been up to no good.

She sat down heavily on the bright Sparks green sofa, trying not to draw attention as she spotted Sue still engrossed in a demonstration about the correct way to tie off a modelling balloon. She took a swig of her now-cold mocha and opened a browser, as she reached into her pocket for her phone. She recoiled in horror as she realised she still had Sue's pass in her hand.

There was no way she could give it back to her now without looking like she had deliberately taken it. Sue was now engrossed in a conversation with Paul, who had called her over from the bar area to ask her about some paperwork. She had nodded and smiled at Ruby as she had taken her coffee back over to the desk.

Ruby slammed her laptop shut, and scooped her paperwork off the table into her cavernous bag. She had to get out of there before Sue realised the pass was missing. Spotting Sue still engrossed with Michael, she had walked confidently out of Aaron Sparks and slipped behind the wheel of her old battered purple Beetle. As she pulled out of the space, she suddenly spotted Sue's distinctive yellow Cinquecento a couple of cars up, when a thought hit her.

She knew that, as well as her regular caffeine breaks, Sue also popped out for a sneaky vape near her car, out of the eyes of the CCTV cameras. Without thinking too much about it, Ruby cracked her window an inch and flung the pass out, gasping at how well she had aimed when it bounced off the bonnet of the little yellow car and slid down under the front wheel. Hopefully, Sue would just think she'd dropped it. As she sped out of the exit, she didn't see the dark blue Tesla pulling into the space she had just vacated.

37

2 Weeks Ago
December, Carolyn

Carolyn had had a productive couple of weeks. She had successfully completed most of the jobs on her list of things she needed to get her split from Josh under control. She had met with a couple of estate agents, getting Ruby to arrange the appointments for her, along with the consultation with Ruby's close colleague—an expert in family law and messy divorces like the ones Ruby dealt with herself.

Despite her friend offering to represent her at first, they had agreed that as Ruby was likely to also file a complaint against Josh relating to his assault on her at Carolyn's house, that it was probably a conflict of interest, and they needed to keep things clean. She had every confidence that Peter Humbett would do what Ruby instructed him to do—get her a temporary restraining order while she went to the police, and then start immediate divorce proceedings and a request for full custody of the twins.

Her parents had been shocked, but incredibly supportive when she had told them her plans over a cuppa in their cosy kitchen earlier in the week. Her mum had cried and said that she had known for a long time that Josh didn't treat Carolyn as he should do, but that she didn't want to interfere. They would also be happy to help in any way that they were able. Her dad, despite his Parkinson's and physical limitations, had paced the kitchen, angry that he hadn't seen what was under his nose all these years with how Josh had treated his daughter.

Carolyn didn't want to burden them, especially as stress aggravated her dad's condition, but was grateful for their support and their offer to help. They finally agreed that on New Year's Day, her mum would take the kids to their house, and then onwards to Carolyn's sister house on the coast for a few days to give her the space she needed to speak to the police, and getthe restraining order in place. Who knew if the police would arrest him straight away?

And the last thing Carolyn wanted was for Josh to retaliate by taking the kids—something she could definitely see him doing out of spite. She also needed time to pack and get out of the house so that, as soon as he was served the order, he couldn't come for her.

The plan was that, as soon as she had the restraining order in place, she would go and stay with Sarah for a few days, while they all figured out what was going on and saw how Josh reacted. Her new place would be ready mid-January. Carolyn had finally settled on renting a small two-bed flat for six months. She had reasoned with herself that she was happy to sleep on a camp bed in the living room area for that amount of time, if it meant never going back to the house she lived in with Josh again.

It also meant she could start to move on as the legal processes got underway, and afford to pay most of the solicitor's fees from the money her parents were kindly lending her. It was all she could afford for now, but she was hopeful that the contact that Ruby had put her in touch with would confirm if she had the job and could start in the New Year. It was part-time to start with, but at least it was a regular income.

Carolyn had also been extremely touched when Kira had taken her to one side the other night after their sauna, and told her excitedly more about the plans that she and Sam had for opening her own studio, and how she was going to need someone super organised and exceedingly bubbly to help with the initial marketing, but then to manage the studio itself.

She hoped that Carolyn would consider it when the time came. It may not be soon, but Carolyn was Kira's first choice, and she had made that clear. Just knowing that her friends had her back had given her a real boost. She knew that she could get through this.

Carolyn was still trying to get her head around her friendship with Sarah. She had let Sarah comfort her and soothe her, but she had also felt herself growing in confidence as Sarah also supported and encouraged her. She had never been attracted to women before, but it didn't mean that she wasn't willing to open herself up to what this could mean. It just all felt a bit soon when she was still so raw from the revelations about Josh and Kira.

She knew she probably had to have a chat with Sarah sooner rather than later, and make sure that they were on the same page. The last thing she wanted to happen was to raise Sarah's expectations when her head was all over the place at the moment.

One thing that she knew that she definitely did have with Sarah was protection. There was no denying that she was a strong woman, and not just in the emotional sense. She benched 130kg recently, a club female record. She was also tall and muscular, having honed her body coaching high-intensity spin classes six times a week, taking clients on as a personal trainer the rest of her time, her speciality being getting women into weights and lifting.

When she had pulled Carolyn in for a hug the other week, she had almost crushed her rib cage. Carolyn had given a yelp before asking Sarah to remember that she was just a normal woman, slightly squishy around the edges, and not one of her gym bros.

Another thing that she had with Sarah was trust. She felt there was nothing she couldn't say to her about her relationship with Josh, nothing that would shock her or make her want to push Carolyn away. They had talked at length about Josh's job and how discovering new plants was more interesting to him than his own family. She trusted Sarah so much that she had brought her over to the house on a few occasions recently, under strict instructions not to say anything incriminating because of the bugging devices, as she had needed her help to get a few things out of the attic before Josh came back.

They had communicated in whispers and hand signals, with Carolyn warning her not to go anywhere near Josh's study, as this was where he kept his specimens from his trips including deadly ones he wasn't supposed to have, and that he would blow a gasket if he could tell anyone had been in his private space, before they moved into making small talk about the children's art work on the fridge, the best Christmas dinner ingredients, and how is it possible to wrap something as complicated as a push bike.

They had exchanged furtive glances and smiles as they shared the burden of taking the boxes up and down the stairs, before Carolyn slipped out up the garden to take a call and left Sarah to it. As good as her word, not only had she found all the bits of paperwork that Carolyn had been looking for in one of the boxes, but she had then carted them all back up to the attic, before putting the kettle on when Carolyn came back into the kitchen.

Shit, Carolyn thought she must remember to give Sarah back the silver "S" keyring she had found on the floor outside Josh's study. She must have lost it while they were lugging boxes around. Yet another thing to remember.

Yes, Sarah was a wonder. As Carolyn pulled up outside her house, she just hoped that she would react well when she talked to her about where this was all going, and hoped that she would be patient. She had dropped the kids off at her parents', and was just bracing herself for what had the potential to be a really awkward conversation.

Before she had time to knock, the door had swung open to reveal Sarah in her customary outfit of running shorts straining over her solid quads and a faded "Tough Mudder" t-shirt, rolled up on the shoulders to expose a serpent tattoo design on her left shoulder, complemented by a brightly coloured phoenix on her right arm, its fiery tail feathers reaching down to her elbow.

'Hey, babe.' She pulled Carolyn in for a hug, more carefully now since the rib-crushing incident. 'Come in, come in. Have I got a feast for us tonight!'

That was yet another thing Carolyn admired about this wonderful woman— she could certainly cook up a storm in the kitchen. Not only were her recipes super tasty, but more importantly, they were healthy. No wonder Carolyn had been steadily losing weight recently, despite it being the run-up to Christmas. The more time she spent with Sarah, the more her good habits seemed to be rubbing off on Carolyn.

As they made their way inside, Sarah had turned to her, gently taking Carolyn by the shoulders. Before Carolyn could say anything, Sarah had said gently.

'Look, I know that you're going through a lot right now, and I know that being more than friends with me may or may not be something you want to explore at some point. But I just wanted to say to you right now, so that there isn't any confusion, I really like you, Carolyn. But whatever does or doesn't happen, one thing I always want us to be is friends.' She bent a little at the knees, pinning Carolyn with a firm but soft stare, ignoring the blush creeping up Carolyn's face as she opened her mouth to reply.

'I don't want you to ever feel awkward or pressured or unsure, ok? There isn't anything you can't say to me, you hear me? And I will respect you no matter what. You deserve to be treated like a queen, and even if I only ever get to do that as your buddy, then that will make me happy.' She sighed. 'Lord knows you've been through enough crap. I just want to be here for you.' She beamed down at her as she pulled Carolyn in again for another gentle hug.

Carolyn had sighed then as she had eased her arms around Sarah's solid bulk, contented in the fact that she hadn't had to raise the subject, but also happy to know that no matter what happened, she had another person looking out for her—

another person who wanted to love and protect her, that she could rely on. And that no matter what did or didn't happen next, this was more than Carolyn had ever hoped for since she had married Josh.

38

1 Week Ago
Christmas Eve, Ruby

There had been something off with Kyle all week. It was subtle, but nonetheless, Ruby had felt the almost imperceptive shift in the atmosphere in their house—something brewing that she just couldn't seem to grasp. Kyle had been so supportive about everything she had told him about Todd and her fertility problems. And they had spent so much time talking about all the options over the last few weeks, that it just didn't feel right that there was now this undercurrent of something she couldn't quite grasp.

They had discussed what they would do if IVF didn't work—that they would look at adoption or even fostering in the new year. But now, there was this weird atmosphere, and Ruby didn't know what to make of it. She was fairly certain it wasn't a reaction to her past. She didn't think Kyle was fickle enough to say he was fine about something so important to her and to their future, and not then be honest to her face. If there was something Kyle prided himself on, since getting clean and leaving his old life behind, it was honesty.

The only thing she hadn't told him was about going to meet Todd last week. She knew that keeping it to herself was going back on their agreement about complete transparency in their relationship, but this was something she needed to do for herself and by herself—she had to get closure. But maybe someone had seen her? Or he had found out somehow and thought she was doing something she shouldn't have been doing?

Ruby hadn't wanted anyone else's opinion about whether she was doing the right thing in tracking Todd down, and mostly she didn't want to have to confess to how she had tracked him down in the first place, which is why she had kept it to herself.

She had wanted to tell Kyle about her meeting with him straight afterwards, but she knew she needed time to process her feelings on her own, and then with her therapist to really understand how she felt about everything that had happened to her in the past, and to find the strength to move forward with the new phase of their life—potentially with children.

The meeting with Todd was everything she expected for the both of them. He had been surprised when she had turned up at his house out of the blue the other week, but had, without hesitation, welcomed her in with the agreement that they needed to talk. His house was nothing like Ruby had expected. With Todd's privileged start to life, she had imagined him working in finance somewhere, or for one of his father's companies, and living the high life in London or maybe even abroad.

What she hadn't expected was Todd explaining how the incident at that party all those years ago, and then the after-effect of helping Ruby get back on her feet, had influenced his path in life. He had explained to her over a pot of Chamomile tea in front of his cosy log burner, that what had happened had opened his eyes to his family's privilege, and how, despite all of their money and material possessions, no one in his family or immediate friendship group seemed to be happy. They had everything that they wanted and yet still took more.

Todd had chosen to study social policy at university, while volunteering each summer for humanitarian projects all over the world. Much to his father's disgust, he had then used his trust fund and some inheritance to set up a small charity for homeless young people, seed-funding the development of supported accommodation and support workers—a project that had now helped over 200 young people a year.

Ruby had been taken aback by the passion with which Todd spoke about his work, and to learn about how her story had been part of his decision to break ties with his elitist past. She had explained to him what had happened to her after she broke off contact with him all those years ago—the pain she felt at being rejected and not believed by her family, and how she felt the only way to cope with that was to reinvent herself, to become someone new.

But she realised now that running and hiding didn't resolve the feelings that she still had deep inside, and one of those was regret for how she treated Todd. He had been magnanimous and understanding, something Ruby initially didn't feel she deserved, but as he put it to her:

'You can only move on when you forgive yourself, Ruby. And from what you tell me, you want to look forward now in life. There are exciting things on the horizon, so let yourself look forward, but be true to yourself. You have nothing to hide, nothing to be ashamed of, and one day whoever did those terrible things to you at my party will pay for what they did.'

They had hugged goodbye then, with no promises to keep in touch or meet again, but both with a feeling of resolution.

Ruby had continued to think over what Todd had said to her, as she slipped into one of her favourite Christmas dresses, smiling to herself at her choice of festive greens and reds of her fitted halter-neck '50s-style prom dress. Kyle had called earlier with instructions to meet him at their local bistro, as he wanted to talk to her. Maybe now she would find out what had been bugging him all week, and she could use the opportunity, while they were alone, to tell him about Todd.

It was so out of character—Kyle booking a table and then not coming home to meet her first—that she couldn't help but worry. He had said on the phone that he didn't have time to come home first, as he needed to drop Christmas gifts off at suppliers, but even that sounded shifty to Ruby. She had helped him with the gifts days ago, and couldn't think who else he may have needed to buy for.

Well, come what may, if she was ever going to truly move forwards, she had to stop worrying about confronting things and running away from them. If Kyle had changed his mind—about the baby, or even about her—she could deal with it. She was stronger now than she had ever been.

As she nervously pushed open the door to the restaurant, she glanced about in confusion. The whole place was in darkness, with the exception of one lone table lit softly by candlelight. As Kyle stood to greet her, she noticed that instead of his usual scruffy jeans and t-shirt, he was wearing a smart shirt and trousers. If she was worried before, her nerves had now ramped up to a billion percent. What was going on?

39
1 Week Ago
Christmas Eve, Carolyn

Carolyn had known for a few days what Kyle had been planning. Most guys were pretty good at keeping secrets. She had first-hand experience of that and how that could turn out, so she was really pleased when Kyle had confided in her about his plans—especially as Ruby had admitted how worried she had been this week about Kyle's strange behaviour. She had bumped into Kyle as each of them had braved the icy walk between the spa area and outdoor heated pool at Sparks on Monday morning.

They both laughed as they braved the first dip into the deep blue water. Lit from underneath, it did look inviting with the steam rising up into the dark morning air. They had made small talk for a bit after they had each swum a few lengths, before Kyle had said he wanted to ask her opinion about something and also ask for her help.

Her immediate thoughts had sprung to the Ruby's recent revelations about her past and not being able to get pregnant. She almost giggled as the thought that he might ask her to be a surrogate popped into her head. She had shaken herself mentally and told herself not to be so daft, as Kyle launched into a speech about how much he loved Ruby, and cared for her, and wanted to be there for her.

Her mind wandered, as the cynic in her thought, that six months ago, she would have delighted in Kyle's revelations and his open declaration of love for Ruby, but now, all she could think about was—is this a load of bullshit? Her faith in men being truthful had been severely jeopardised by recent events, but as Kyle continued, she realised that his heartfelt speech was genuine. He had looked at her intently then and waited for her to reply.

It had taken her a minute to realise that he had asked her if she thought Ruby would marry him if he asked, and would Carolyn help him set up the proposal on Christmas Eve? She remembered that she had shaken her head then, pretending to shake water out of her ear to give her time to compose her thoughts and reply.

'Kyle, if you're half the guy I think you are, and you truly mean what you say about your feelings for Ruby, then I am 100% with you. You know I've had a shitty couple of months, and there's more of that to come, so I might not be the best person to comment on relationships at the moment. However, I want Ruby to be happy, and I think that you are the person to do it. I may not believe in marriage anymore, but I do believe in you, Kyle. So, yes, of course I'll help you!'

She almost shocked herself with how passionately she had spoken, and even Kyle had looked slightly taken aback, stuttering out a thank you before explaining the plans he had in mind. He had asked Carolyn to meet him in the car park after their swim, so that she could look after the ring, then bring it to the restaurant for him on Christmas Eve, asking her to make sure that the waiters had his and Ruby's favourite song ready to play, along with champagne and roses.

So, this was how Carolyn found herself at 7 pm on Christmas Eve, hiding in the kitchen of La Botellino, ready to hand over the ring and issue instructions to Josepe and his waiting staff. What Kyle probably hadn't considered when he asked her for her help was just how difficult this day was going to be for her—the mother of twins on the eve of their last family Christmas as they knew it.

The tension in the house that day had been palpable. Josh's presence had put her on edge ever since he had walked back through the door last week. There had been something animalistic about his presence, an undercurrent of danger and threat lurking just under the surface, waiting to explode.

She could usually judge his moods, and work out the best way to diffuse a situation before Josh even realised that she was playing him at his own game. Years of experience had taught her that there were moods that were dealt with through silence and avoidance—the less she said, the better. Any retaliation against his demands or unreasonableness would just add fuel to any fire. Then there were the outright fiery, hot-tempered moods.

These were the worst in some ways, as they nearly always lent themselves to someone or something getting hurt—the bruises on her body always in places that no one could see, her full swimsuit ensuring that even her closest friends in the sauna didn't have a clue of how bad it had got in more recent years.

The moods that lasted the longest were the ones that bubbled along for days. This was when he would be highly critical of everything she or the kids did, nitpicking over and again at how she looked or how she kept the house—a glass on the shelf with a smear, make-up accidentally trodden into the bathroom carpet, his favourite shirt not laundered as quick as he desired it. These were the tricky ones, where placating and trying harder just drew more of his attention.

Ignoring wouldn't work either, as that would show that she didn't care or wasn't an attentive enough wife, unlike his colleagues and friends whose wives all had various attributes that she obviously didn't have. Then it was just a waiting game—who would burst the cloud first, and what form would it take? Sometimes the tension could last for days. The longer it went on, the worse the consequences.

She had honed ways of diffusing the tension through trial and error—the technique was hit and miss. In recent years, she had found that if they were interrupted as things were reaching boiling point, some of the heat was taken out of the situation. Sometimes, she had found herself breaking the tension and snapping first, that this actually resulted in less collateral damage. She had bitten a number of times, snapping back at him when she could see that the kids were safely out of earshot, occasionally throwing things.

The first time she did it was with a tea towel. This just drew a snide remark about her throwing skills, which turned into laughter. The second time it was a mug. The dent it made as it crashed into the worktop was still visible. That time he had grabbed her arm and dragged her down to the floor while telling her pick up the pieces. It had hurt, but at least the tension had been broken.

This pattern had lasted a number of years now. She tried to pick up on what kind of mood he was in as soon as she heard his footfall across the threshold. Ultimately, there weren't any winners in any of the "playing of the moods" game—she ended up wounded one way or another, whether it be physically or emotionally, the impact added up to the same. So, when he had stomped into the kitchen earlier that day with Kyle's ring between his thumb and forefinger and shoved it in her face, she was ready for him.

'What the actual fuck is this? What's going on, Carolyn?'

His hand was so close to her face that she could see each individual hair on his fingers as he continued to shove the stunning ruby, embedded in a platinum band, in her face. She nearly broke into a smile. Rubes would be thrilled with Kyle's choice—she had no doubt about that. It had taken all of her strength to compose herself as she thought, *This will be one of the very last times I have to go through this shit*, before calmly replying.

'Ah yes, that's Ruby's engagement ring. Can't wait to see it on her ring finger.' The calmness of her reply belying the butterflies that were creeping up her stomach.

'What are you on about? Why have you got Ruby's ring? I'm surprised that fat bitch could fit this on her finger.' As usual, Josh had to be as venomous as possible.

'I'm safekeeping it until tonight. Kyle wanted someone to look after it before he proposes to Ruby. I'm dropping it off to him later when you take the kids to your parents' for Christmas Eve hot chocolate. They know not to expect me.' Her nerve threatened to break as she held contact with his eyes, hoping something or someone interrupted their exchange soon to break the tension.

'What the hell are you doing? Blowing off my parents for Kyle? Huh? They are expecting you. We always go over there on Christmas Eve.' His voice was dangerously quiet now as he hissed in her face.

'Well,' she had continued calmly, 'I spoke to your mum the other night, and she said it would be fine if I didn't come with you, as they are coming over to ours on Boxing Day anyway. I've also got to go and pick up Charlie's new bike and hide it before you all get back. I've then got steak for supper and a nice bottle of that Port you like,' she replied quietly, no longer defiant and meeting his eyes, subservient and cowed, just as he liked her.

He had slammed the ring down on the kitchen counter then, and reached up to grab around the back of her neck, bringing his face down closer to her, forcing her gaze up to meet his eyes, violence threatening. Before he could speak another word, the doorbell had rung. She had just got lucky that Josh's brother had chosen that moment to arrive.

There had been no guarantee that he would time it to coincide with Josh's outburst, but Carolyn knew that the less she and her husband were alone over the next week, the better, so she had spent more time than usual planning visits to and from their family and friends.

As Josh's hand had dropped from her neck, she had reached up to rub the sore spot where she still felt his fingertips. It was amazing what a little planning could do—leave the ring where he would spot it, make sure Mike was due to arrive around a certain time, etc. She really was great at playing this game now.

She had followed the sound of the door opening and the back-slapping man hugs, between her husband and his equally handsome brother into the hall, sighing in relief that by the time she came back later, Josh would have calmed down and forgotten all about their spat. With any luck, he would already be stuck into the Port—the one drink that actually made him more mellow and less likely to start a fight. If anything, it might make him want to have sex and even cuddle—the thought of which had made her cringe.

She had left them as they were rounding up the kids to head out together to their parents' house, Mike explaining that Laney, his wife, wouldn't be there that evening either, as she was going to some church choir thing, and that their kids were already at the grandparents. Carolyn had breathed a sigh of relief for Mike—he was always so calm and jovial and seemed to bring the best out in Josh. She hoped that, with any luck, the buoyant mood would carry over to Christmas Day when her parents were joining them.

Now, as she peeked out of the kitchen door into the restaurant one more time, the smell of delicious sauces and grilled meats making her mouth water, she watched as Ruby, with her vibrant red hair and incredible, startling outfit, made her way from the bar with a look of confusion on her face. She looked so expectant, so radiant, so willing to trust Kyle and why he had asked her to come meet him with no explanation.

Carolyn felt a pang of envy, and then the hard lump of emotion in her throat, followed by the sting of held-back tears. It was beautiful to watch this man, who loved her friend so much, put his heart on the line tonight and say what he needed to say to her—maybe love could conquer all? As Kyle stood from the table to greet her, he nodded discreetly to Carolyn in her hiding position, his arched eyebrow conveying the message "all set?" as she nodded back at him.

As Kyle led Ruby to the table, Carolyn set her phone to video mode and started to record as Josepe and his wife, Talia, started to slowly approach the table from behind where Ruby sat, with champagne on ice, a bouquet of roses where the ring lay nestled within the petals of a central closed bud. As Kyle dropped to one knee in front of Ruby, the first bars of Metallica's "Nothing Else Matters" started to play over the sound system, as Ruby's face turned as red as her hair.

'Ruby, I know that you hate grand displays of affection, that you are the consummate professional when it comes to your job, and that you hate showing any vulnerability—but just on this one occasion, I hope you will indulge me. I have loved you from the very first moment I spotted that crazy red hair across the room at that tattoo convention. I knew from that very second that you were the only person that I would ever want to be with forever—my kindred spirit.'

Kyle took the bouquet from Talia and lifted out the single full-bud rose, opening the petals to reveal the ring. As he lifted it with a shaking hand, he continued.

'You are the only one I trust to be my whole self around, and after the last few weeks, I think I'm that person for you too. Ruby, the love of my life, my world, my future—will you marry me?'

Carolyn had looked at her friend then to see tears pouring down her face, as she appeared to be lost for words. Ruby looked down and met Kyle's eyes then, before dropping to her knees with him on the floor as she took him in her arms.

Her cries of 'Yes! Yes, yes, yes!' rang out across the restaurant as the small crowd of kitchen staff broke into applause, the cacophony drowning out Ruby's words as she whispered into Kyle's neck, 'Oh, Kyle, I never thought you'd want to marry me. After me telling you I can't have kids, and you wanting them so much, I thought that this might be over.'

'You need to get a little faith, Ruby Lou. Why the hell do you think I've been off over the last couple of weeks, you daft moo? I've been shitting myself that maybe you didn't want me! I couldn't have stood it if you hadn't said yes. Honestly, Ruby, you're my absolute world.' He rocked her back and forth so hard that the pair of them nearly tumbled to the floor.

Carolyn bent close to the happy couple, holding out her hand to Ruby first.

'Come on, up you get. There's champagne here getting warm!' she beamed at her friend.

She knew in her heart of hearts that Kyle was a good guy—that he was one of those that would go out of his way to love and protect Ruby and any children that they did hopefully manage to have in the future. As the scene calmed down, and Josepe brought their starters, Carolyn knew it was time to make her excuses and leave before Josh and the kids got home. She would endeavour to be jovial, putting out a carrot for the Reindeer, and then a whiskey for Santa, which Josh would no doubt neck as soon as the kids had trod on the first stair up to bed.

She would feign tiredness then, hopeful that they would both get a decent night's sleep, before the inevitable early morning wake-up from the twins. As she blipped the lock to her car and opened the door, she felt the vibration of her phone in her bag—caller ID showed it was Kira. *Ah, perfect timing*, Carolyn thought. She bet Ruby had already texted her to share the good news, and Kira wanted a debrief. As she sat down into the driver's seat, she pressed the green button to answer.

'Hey, babe! Let me guess, Rubes has messaged you?' The sound of hiccupped breaths and obvious crying filled her ears. 'Kira? Kira, what on earth's wrong?'

40
1 Week Ago
Christmas Eve, Kira

Kira's day had started so well. She had woken up with a feeling of excitement for Christmas that she hadn't felt in years. Just knowing that she had Sam by her side and plans for the future mapped out, filled her with joy. Kira had always loved Christmas Eve as a child. Growing up, she and Joanna had always been filled with anticipation for what Santa might bring from their Christmas wish list.

They had both known from an early age that Santa wasn't into big, ostentatious presents, but the things that he did bring were thoughtful and considered, even if they were not big and flashy. The thing that they had both loved the most, though, was the festive feeling of home. Their parents had never had a huge amount of money, but they did have an abundance of love that they showered on both of their girls. Their mum had also been an absolute genius when it came to arts and crafts.

There was the year her mum had spent hours with them, stringing together freshly popped corn to create garlands to hang over the tree. The tree itself was a cheap, synthetic thing from Tesco instead of one of the big, beautiful fir trees, but theirs always had the best and most innovative decorations. One year, they even had dried orange slices and chillis in the oven, and once they were varnished, they had sprinkled them with glitter to create pretty garlands that could hang across the mantlepiece.

They had regularly made cookies and gingerbread to take with them to junior running meets and to relatives' houses in lieu of gifts, each of them spending an inordinate amount of time carefully decorating the baked goods with red, green and yellow icing, before impatiently waiting for them to dry, so they could package them up in paper bags they had decorated with potato-cut prints in stars and snowflakes. Just thinking about how Christmas had been in the past, and how it might be again now in her future, gave her a warm, fuzzy feeling.

She knew it was early days with Sam, but there was already a deep connection between them. They had spent hours lying on the day bed in the cabin, or sat by a fire pit out front on the edge of the woods with a glass of mulled wine, just talking and talking. He was the first person she felt she could be completely honest with about her hopes and dreams for the future.

Kira had been upfront in their discussions. Ideally, she would like to spend the next few years growing the business, once the studio was up and running, and maybe one day look at a franchise or expansion of the business model if it went well. There was a real appetite at the moment for wellbeing and healthy living, and that meant they could be on to a real winner. Kira also wanted to address early on her feelings about family and children.

Despite her current feeling of contentment and the happy memories she had of her own childhood, she knew in her heart that a traditional 2.4 children lifestyle wasn't really what she wanted for herself. She wanted to be successful in her own right with the business, but she also wanted the flexibility of making her own choices about her working patterns—to be able to travel and see the world, to have the opportunity to bring new ideas to her work, but also to not be tied to just doing the same thing all her life, to be able to take risks.

The time had come around quickly as her relationship with Sam had intensified, to tell him that, in her future, she really didn't want children.

As Kira stretched out and reviewed her notes for her next session in the Sparks changing room, she thought back to the conversation she had had with Sam the day before—one that still gave her a real glow of satisfaction and contentment, where she knew she had made the right choice to be open with Sam from the start. They had been in one of their favourite spots on the farm. They had followed the sheep track up the hill to one of the highest points, the pastures that would be full of lambs in the spring, empty in the winter months.

The views were breathtaking. As they leant on a five-bar gate, huddled together looking down at the frosty landscape below, they had bundled up in their thick winter jackets and held hands through their knitted gloves, as they had watched the lights come on all over town. She had broken her grip from Sam for a moment to reach round to pour them both some more hot chocolate from the thermos she had packed to bring with them.

Handing a steaming mug to Sam, she had met his eyes and knew that the time had to be now to have the conversation. They were heading into spending one of the most important times of the year together, and it felt now that there were things that couldn't just remain unsaid. She had taken a deep breath and met his eyes as he crinkled his forehead into a look of mild concern.

'That breath sounded like you're going to say something serious?' he questioned as he carefully put down his cup on the cold, hard ground.

'Ha, um, yeah, there's something I think we need to talk about. I'm not even sure that my timing is right, but I think things are going well between us, and I don't want to think that there are things on either of our minds that we don't feel able to share with each other.' She had already felt in that instant like a weight had been lifted. The fact that she felt strong enough now to even have this conversation was significant progress. She took another breath before she continued.

'You know that I'm really serious about us, Sam? That I want to make this work, and that I can't thank you enough for how patient you have been with me.' She faltered over her words a little, nerves making her stumble as Sam interrupted.

'You're not breaking up with me, are you?'

'No! No, sorry, that speech probably sounded a bit ominous. No, it's just I need to tell you something, and it might change your opinion about me, about us.'

Sam reached up to smooth her hair behind her ear, caressing her face with his hand.

'There is nothing, and I mean *nothing,* that would make me change my mind about you, Kira.' He had tilted her chin up to face him then and dropped a warm kiss against her cold lips.

'Well, you don't know that yet. Let me tell you, and then you can make up your mind.' She braced herself before blurting, 'I don't want kids.' She looked at him then. 'And I mean ever. This isn't a "oh, she'll change her mind because she's still young" kind of situation. This is the reality. I have never felt maternal, never felt that pull that other women have about children. About animals, definitely. I would love a load of rescue cases one day, but just not of the humankind.'

She frowned then as she realised that her babbling seemed to have shocked Sam into silence.

She continued, determined to make her point before he could speak.

'So, if kids are something you always saw in your future, then I'm really sorry, but I just can't change how I feel. And what I'm really saying is, if you think we have a future, then I wanted you to know where I stand on the matter.' She paused. 'Urgh, I'm waffling again. Sam, say something please. You're making me anxious. I need to know what you think.'

'Well.' Sam had taken a deep breath as he had composed himself. 'It's a lot to take in, but before you start to think that I'm not up for considering this, then you're wrong. I guess I always thought that my future would have children in it—you know, the kind of conventional route that we're all sort of conditioned to follow? I think I just assumed that that was right for me too, but I really don't know if it is, Kira.'

He had reached out and taken her hand back in his then.

'What I really want is someone that really gets me, that wants all the sort of things that I want in life, and that I can explore the world with. And I think that might be you.' The earnest expression on his face had nearly brought tears to her eyes then, as he had raised her gloved hands up to his lips.

'I don't want us to chuck all this away just because I've been conditioned to think there's one path for me in this life. I've already defied the odds by not becoming a farmer like my dad wanted. I'm pretty sure I'm liberal and flexible enough in my own thinking to make this work with you—if you're willing to let me give it a go?'

She had leant in then, and this time, she had taken his face between her hands, bringing her lips to his, first, gently, and then with more heat as they leant into the gate, the passion and electric running between them giving him the answer to his question.

Kira sighed in pleasure at the memory. Her heart still felt like it was going to burst with pride, that she had been fierce enough to have such a brave conversation that could have ended it for them. For having the courage of her convictions to say what she really wanted, what she really needed for herself and for her future, knowing that if he hadn't been willing to give it a go, she would be on her own again. It was a risk she had had to take, and it had been worth it.

She was so looking forward to Sam being with her tomorrow at her parents' for Christmas dinner—being able to have that special day with her family and with this guy that she was falling in love with. She just needed to get through this final evening class. As usual, it was over-subscribed with people trying to pre-empt the amount of crap they were no doubt going to overindulge in eating over the holiday, by casting off some calories—or at least tightening their ab muscles to hold it all in—in one last Pilates class of the year.

She checked her watch one more time as she put in the combination of her padlock and slid it from her locker, dragging her kit bag out onto the floor. She did a double take as she reached into her bag for her towel, when the first thing her hand touched was a rectangle of red card. As she pulled it out of her bag, she frowned. She couldn't remember anyone giving her a Christmas card today as she arrived at work. Maybe she was distracted.

She had certainly had a lot to think about over the last twenty-four hours, but then, there was no writing on the card—which was strange. Maybe she had picked it up by accident as she had shoved her stuff into her bag after her 2 pm class? She wondered if someone was missing it. Well, there was only one way to find out if the card was meant for her, as she slid her finger under the lip of the sealed envelope.

She pulled the card out, peering at the cute picture of two penguins holding hands, as the humorous caption on the front made her chuckle; and she wondered if Sam had managed to slip the card into her bag without her realising. As she slowly opened up the card, her blood ran cold as she read the message:

Don't ever forget who you belong to. If I can't have you for Christmas, then by New Year, no one will.

Kira had let the card fall to the floor as she felt herself sliding onto the nearest bench on shaking legs. There was only one person who would threaten her like that, and only one person who she was convinced would actually follow through with the threat.

The hope that she could move on and into the New Year for a fresh start was instantly shattered, as she scrabbled in her bag for her phone. With clammy hands hitting the speed dial button, she was grateful for Carolyn picking up on the third ring. As she struggled to get her words out, she could hear Carolyn's panicked voice.

'Kira? Kira, love, what's going on?'

As she steadied herself, she knew that she just needed the answer to one question to confirm her worse fears.

'Is Josh back?'

She could hear her own voice shaking, the blood rushing to her ears almost drowning out Carolyn's whispered answer.

'Yes.'

41
The Day Before
30 December, Carolyn

Carolyn didn't know how she had managed to keep it together over the Christmas break after Kira's panicked phone call on Christmas Eve. Luckily, thanks to her immaculate planning, she had arranged to keep her family occupied all week. The house had been pretty much full of visitors; with kids fighting and food and drink flowing, it had meant that she and Josh had barely had a moment alone.

From the outside, Christmas at their house could have looked just like anyone else's festive break. The one thing that marked it as different was the knowledge that she was just a couple of days away from ending this fake reality. The pretence that her marriage was absolutely fine, that she was a devoted wife, that Josh was a loving husband, that things were just peachy, thank you very much.

The worst thing about knowing that she had only had to put on this front for just a little while longer, meant that it felt like the hours were dragging along, despite being surrounded by people for most of the week—first Josh's brother and his family, then his parents, then a day trip to her cousins for their turkey and tinsel buffet, and now they had friends of Josh's from university visiting.

It still felt like she was wading through treacle. Hour after hour, she watched as the clock ticked down its countdown until finally, finally, she could put her plan into action and be free.

By some miracle, Josh had remained in a fairly amiable mood throughout the festivities, but the pressure of holding everything together and his better-than-average mood, and the way things had been going so uncharacteristically well, had put Carolyn even more on edge. From first thing this morning, she could feel that the atmosphere was changing. Just from the way she had caught Josh looking at her this morning—there was an eeriness to the way he stared at her today.

She had started to doubt herself as she went about her morning chores, questioning herself as she went back over her plans in her head. She had been meticulous in her planning—she hadn't made any phone calls about the plans while in the house, she had given Ruby all her paperwork to look after, she had kept the bag of clothes she would need in the immediate aftermath at Sarah's. There was no way he could possibly know, was there?

There had also been something about the way Josh had looked at her during the toast on Christmas Day, when they had all held their glasses of champagne up "to the future" that had chilled her, his crystal blue eyes seeming to bore straight into her thoughts, seeing how she was planning to betray him.

Then again, last night when they were getting ready for bed—Bejamin, his uni friend, and his lovely wife, Trudy, had just got settled in the guest room down the hall, when Josh had come up behind her when she was taking off her make-up in the mirror in their en-suite bathroom. He had gently smoothed her hair down with one hand and placed his hand on her shoulder, while encircling her waist with the other hand, snaking round to her newly trim stomach, and caressing her through the old UCL t-shirt she had chucked on for bed that evening.

'Have I told you how fucking sexy you're looking at the moment?' he had asked her reflection as he met her eyes in the mirror, before pulling the neckline of the t-shirt to one side and dropping an open-mouth kiss on her exposed shoulder, taking her involuntary shiver as a signal of her desire for him.

She had held back from saying anything, knowing that he was in one of those moods where she could easily say the wrong thing. He had been shooting back whiskey less than an hour ago with Benjamin, so he was already volatile by her standards.

She had weighed the options up in her head then, her whole body screaming that she couldn't bear for him to touch her, that she needed to get away from him. Maybe she could gently remove his hand and say she was tired, and hope, because they had friends staying, that he would take this with good grace and leave her alone?

She knew better though. From so many times before, this approach was not likely to be a winner—that if she resisted or showed hesitation, he would make her pay for it. It was amazing how many ways he could find to hurt her without making a sound, knowing she wouldn't risk crying out or involving anyone else in their personal drama. A hard pinch on her rib cage, a sharp bite to her breasts as he pinned her down to the bed, a rough grab of her arse with the threat of something more personal, more intrusive, more violating.

There was only one other option, one that would end with him falling into an orgasm-induced sleep, with the promise that he may actually sleep later than her in the morning and give her time to plan another busy day to keep him occupied. She had felt sick to her stomach as she had reached her hand behind her, as he had continued to kiss her neck, his tongue and wet lips leaving a cold, damp trail down her throat.

She had fought the nausea rising in her throat as she had placed a firm hand over his growing hardness and whispered what she knew, after all these years, would still get him going.

'Want to play mummies and daddies, Joshie? I can be the naughty little girl and you can tell me what my punishment is?'

He had audibly growled into her neck then and spun her round to face him, hungrily devouring her mouth with his hard, frantic kisses.

She had despised herself right then. She knew that women did desperate things like this every day to gain a little respite from their abusers, to give themselves back a feeling of power and control when really had very little. She was a cliché at that very moment, but she was a cliché with a plan that would finally rid herself and the other women he had abused of this terrible man thrusting into her once and for all.

The morning had come all too soon, and as they didn't have any pre-made plans for the day, Carolyn was up well before Josh, quietly slinking down to the kitchen to put on a pot of coffee for their guests. They had to leave early to drive cross-country to Trudy's parents, so had already planned to pick up breakfast on their way. She had sat for a quiet hour and mentally gone through her checklist again as to what she had to do from the first of January.

She had found her notebook and pen and the checklist for the NYE party at Sparks. She was on top of most things, but she still needed to pick up the balloons later for the decorative arch that guests would walk through on their way in.

She needed Josh's car to collect them. She didn't want to call Sarah to help with her 4x4. They had agreed to try and keep some distance from each other just during this Christmas week, until she was ready for Sarah to come get her on New Year's Day.

The last thing she wanted was to draw Josh's attention to anything to do with her friends, while he was stuck with her at home, knowing that he would want her undivided attention, and that she didn't want or need him to scrutinise anything she was doing. Especially after the way he had looked at her as he had poured himself a coffee before heading into his study.

She knew what she would do—she would suggest that she popped out to do the balloons while Josh got the kids ready, and she would propose they went for a session at Ninja Warrior, followed by late afternoon pizza and a movie. Josh could never resist the opportunity to show off his physical prowess in front of the other dads, trying and failing to fling themselves up the "wall", when Josh made it look just so easy.

The smugness she would get from him later as he berated the other unfit and fat dads, laughing at them for their pathetic attempts, would be worth it for yet another day, where they didn't get into a fight.

She was surprised half an hour later, when they had finally waved Benjamin and Trudy off from the front porch, when Josh had come back into the kitchen with two fully-dressed kids, complete with backpacks and snuggle blankets.

'So, I called your mum and she's going to have these two monsters for the night. I thought it was high time we had some time together before I head off to Borneo next week.' She knew with the look he had given her then, that it was game over. The cold hardness of those eyes she once considered the most beautiful she had ever seen now sent fear straight to her heart. He knew.

'Well, she's having them quite a lot over the next few weeks before they go back to school, and she's got Dad to worry about. Why don't we just call her back and cancel? I thought we'd go to Ninja Warrior today. You'd like that, wouldn't you, Charlie? Amber?' She could already feel the prickly sensation of tears forming at the back of her throat, and the feeling of dread trickling down into her stomach.

'Dad?' Charlie looked to Josh, always deferring to his father, while Amber had looked at her.

She knew then that the battle was lost. Whatever was going to happen today between her and Josh did not need to be played out in front of the kids. They didn't deserve that. They needed to retain their innocence for as long as she made it possible.

'It's fine, kids, we can go to Ninja Warrior another day when Daddy hasn't arranged a lovely trip to Grandma's for you. She'll be so pleased to have you tell her all about what you've been doing since you saw her on Christmas Day.' She reached over to give each of their shoulders a squeeze as the doorbell rang.

'Quick, give your mum a kiss then grab your stuff. Amber, don't forget your water bottle. Come on, get a move on.' He herded them towards the door as she had kept step behind him.

'But, Mum, this one's Charlie's!' Amber moaned.

'You can't even tell which one's which—they all look the same.' Charlie nudged his sister towards the door.

'Well, your one has a little chip out of the drinky bit, idiot!' she retorted, as she pushed him back.

Before more chaos could descend, Carolyn's mum interrupted.

'Well, what a lovely surprise, my little angels!' Her mum was always pleased to spend time with her grandchildren. She may now be a little frailer and tired now that she had to care more for Carolyn's father, but she was still a bundle of energy when it came to the kids.

'Is this all their stuff? Wonderful! Well, Charlie, Amber, Grandpa can't wait to hear all about your new bike and your new art stuff. Let's give your mum and dad a chance to breathe again, after running round after you two for the last week.' Her mum had smiled a tight smile at her then, looking at her standing behind Josh and yet to speak.

As she met her mum's eyes, there was a spark of something between them, an unspoken connection that was almost telepathic, that could only happen between mother and daughter.

'So, I'll bring them back tomorrow before the Sparks party. That's ok, isn't it, Josh?'

And before he had time to respond or to contradict her, she had given a firm nod and met Carolyn's eyes again. Reaching down to grab the two backpacks, she had walked briskly back to the car.

As the door slammed shut, Josh was already spinning round, grabbing her by the throat. He threw her up against the wall as her head cracked against a picture that Charlie had painted of a rainbow. It swung above her for a second before dropping to the ground in slow motion, the glass shattering as Josh leant into her face, his voice strangely even for someone quite so filled with rage.

'So, when the fuck were you going to tell me that you're leaving?' He pulled his fist back and slammed it straight into her stomach.

The next few hours were a blur. There were blows, punches and pinches, while she was lying on the hall floor, before Josh went to get another drink. She had pulled herself upstairs then, any way she could to get as far away from the kitchen—anywhere safer than where knives and other sharp objects were kept. Even at the height of his previous rages, Josh still knew where and how to hurt her so it wouldn't show.

She had thanked God for that small mercy then, as she thought about what the twins would think if they saw her bruised and bloodied. Even if Josh was a monster, he was still their father, and she didn't want them to understand this terrible truth. If he was planning to kill her, then he wouldn't care where he hurt her though, would he?

All she had to do was make it through the night, and somehow get through the day until her mum dropped the kids off. She knew that her mum knew that she was in trouble. However, as she hadn't ever admitted the extent of Josh's violence, she could only assume her mum thought that she and Josh needed time to talk.

And that despite their silent communications, she was doubtful that she would come back earlier than planned or organise any other sort of help. Carolyn groaned as she rolled onto her back and tried with all her mental ability to use ESPN to convey this across the county to her mum, or Sarah, or anyone—*please know I'm in trouble and help me.*

Carolyn heard footsteps on the stairs creeping slowly towards her. She knew that Josh wasn't drunk enough to stop, nor had he got the answers he was looking for. Despite the hurt he had inflicted on her earlier, she had continued to deny that she was leaving—just that she needed a little space and was planning to stay with her parents while he was away in Borneo.

Maybe if she just came clean now, she could try and reason with him, tell him that she was mistaken, that she was wrong to think about leaving, that they were meant to be together forever, weren't they?

Before she had chance to think about what to say, Josh was right there beside her, dragging her off the bed by her arm towards the en-suite bathroom.

'Look at you, you fucking snivelling mess,' he had spat at her. 'No one else will ever want you, Carolyn. You know that you got pretty fucking lucky with me, don't you? You're definitely punching well above your weight.'

As he continued with his vicious words, as he man-handled her into the bathroom, the force making her trip and fall to the floor, she missed the corner of the tub by a few inches. Forcing herself up into a sitting position, she jumped in surprise as the bathroom door slammed behind her, followed by the sound of a chair being forced under the door handle from the outside. She silently cursed herself for ever having designed a house, where a door didn't open inwards as normal doors do—now she'd been made a prisoner.

'Josh?' She could hear her voice sounding ragged and strained. 'Josh! What are you doing? You can't keep me in here! Seriously, let me out and we can talk. I can explain.'

His muffled reply came from the other side of the door.

'But you can't, Carolyn, can you? You can't explain why you thought you could get away with this, that you stupidly thought I wouldn't find out until it was too late. Who the fuck do you think I am, you stupid bitch? One of your silly little friends? That fat cow Ruby? The one who's helping you plan all of this? Or maybe that skinny runt Kira?'

Carolyn took a sharp intake of breath at Kira's name. She still wasn't sure if Josh knew that she knew about the affair.

'Yeah—Ruby. She isn't as clever as she lets on, is she? All this act of being a hotshot lawyer when she leaves your paperwork just lying around on her kitchen table. Well, just shows what sort of friend she really is—she's a snake. I'm going to go pay her a visit after this and teach her and that tattooed prick of a boyfriend a lesson once and for all.' His voice continued to rise as he continued.

'And you can cut the act, Carolyn. I know that you know about Kira. You'd actually be doing us a favour by leaving me—you know that, don't you? All the time that Kira was pretending to be your friend, all the help you think you've given her—well, think again, you stupid dumb slut. She's been playing you all along. We're together. That's right—me and Kira, ARE TOGETHER!' Josh screamed, before letting out a crazed laugh.

'I'm going over there right now to tell her that the coast is clear, that we can build our life just as we imagined it. I just had to get rid of you first.'

To Carolyn, he sounded insane. She thought finally he'd lost the plot—he's deluded. She didn't know how she was going to get out of here or how she could warn her friends. Any hope she had of them all getting out of this unscathed has now gone. She knew someone was going to get hurt.

42

The Day Before
30 December, Ruby

The last week had been pure bliss for Ruby and Kyle. They were so deeply in love and head over heels about the prospect of getting married and starting their future together. Ruby had been walking around with a huge grin on her face; the proposal at the restaurant had taken her by surprise, but had certainly explained Kyle's strange behaviour. As she had always known, she had a great guy who was a keeper. She just wanted to sing from the rooftops about how happy she was and how much she was looking forward to their future together.

The night of the proposal they had got home late. High on champagne, they chatted about dates and venues, and whether to start the adoption process before or after they were married, how they were so excited they didn't want to wait for either. The anticipation of Ruby's response to the proposal had spiked Kyle's adrenaline, and Ruby could tell he couldn't wait to get his hands on her as they moved into the kitchen.

As she reached over to plug her phone in to charge before bed, he had grabbed her hips from behind. Without any subtlety, he had ground himself hard against her soft arse, his hardness against her crease giving a clear indication of his desire. She had turned then as he drew her in for a long, lingering kiss before he bit her gently on her bottom lip.

She smiled to herself now as she remembered thinking at the time, that there was no way that they could have made it all the way upstairs that night. With the passion burning this hot between them, they were just about to combust. A pleasant shiver ran down Ruby's spine, as she remembered how he had slipped his hands under the full skirt of her Christmas dress and grasped the elastic on her panties, as he had pushed her back against the kitchen cupboards.

Ripping them clean from her body, he had used his hand to circle her most sensitive spot before dropping to his knees to work her into a frenzy with his firm mouth. When she had felt her legs shaking and that familiar tingle start to grow to a crescendo, he had swiftly stood, lifting her with him to balance her on the countertop as he made short work of his belt and zip. The sight of him semi naked was too much, as she grabbed him and pulled him into her, reaching her climax almost as soon as he filled her.

As she held on to him with one arm, she had used the hand that wasn't tangling in his hair to scoop up the files and paperwork littering the worktop, and had flung them haphazardly onto the dining room table next to them as he had sated himself on her.

As she poured herself a cup of coffee, she blushed. She could almost see scorch marks burnt into the counter—such had been the ferocity of their passion that night. She sighed contentedly as she remembered how she had cried out his name as he brought her to orgasm for the second time that night; his stamina was just one other thing she loved about him.

In true Ruby and Kyle style, they had agreed later that night when they had finally tumbled into bed that they needed to cement their commitment to each other immediately, agreeing to get matching tattoos on their wedding fingers as soon as the tattoo shop was open. The design would then be covered with bespoke rings at their wedding service. Ruby glanced down at the delicate etching of black ink with their initials and the date of the proposal inked in tiny italics around her ring finger and smiled to herself again.

God, she was one lucky girl. However, she needed to get a grip of herself; she had stuff to do! After the last few days spent lounging around the house, ordering take out, gorging on chocolates, and watching crap on Netflix between being hauled back to bed every five minutes by Kyle, she knew she had to pull herself together and get organised.

Carolyn was counting on her to be there and ready when they went to the police on New Year's Day. She also had a few new clients that she needed to schedule into her diary for initial meetings in early January.

Then there was the New Year's Eve party. Carolyn had put her in charge of printing off the quiz question sheets, and checking in with the kitchen to make sure the buffet was all under control for those that had paid for a ticket to the official function. Sparks was due to close at 5 pm tomorrow night, so that the majority of the staff could take the evening off. The managers had agreed that the volunteers could take control of most of the activities, as long as a skeleton staff stayed behind to cover health and safety.

Sam had volunteered to be on lifeguard duty as he wanted to stay close to Kira, who was in charge of getting the spa areas ready for the midnight candlelitpool dip. James was working the bar, whipping up his famous cocktails with Keely and Ed, both uni students who never turned down a shift on double time.

Ruby had Sue on her list as reception cover to check everyone's tickets, and hand out towels and robes. Sarah was the designated first aider and would also double up as DJ for the evening. Ruby had no doubt that she had a set list of absolute bangers planned; her spin classes were still legendary for getting people up and moving. Then there were the volunteers, along with herself and Kyle, who were there to help with the quiz and to keep everyone organised.

They had six others coming along to run various other tasks for the 50 guests, and then the lucky 20 that had won the ballot to access the spa at midnight. Then, of course, last but most importantly, chief organiser Carolyn, the queen of the committee, was in charge of balloon archway and general joviality.

As Ruby poured herself a second cup of coffee, she tried Carolyn's mobile again. She had already rung twice today and then sent a couple of WhatsApps, but was still waiting for the little blue ticks to appear to show that her friend had read the message. Shaking her head, she cut herself a generous slice of Christmas cake, and approached the dining room table to make herself comfortable before starting on the next couple of calls on her checklist. As she went to take a seat, she did a double take.

She knew that when she chucked the pile of folders from the counter to the table on Christmas Eve, she had made a bit of a mess, but the folders from her memory had stayed in relative order—the pile had slid to one side and the odd bit of paperwork had stuck out here and there from the manila cardboard folders.

What caught her eye now was that Carolyn's paperwork was on the top of the pile, its contents still neat and tidy in contrast to the other folders. Surely Kyle wouldn't have touched her paperwork, would he? Although he was incredibly supportive of her career and showed an interest in all of her cases, he had never once moved or touched any work that she had brought home.

The one time she had asked him to shift a pile of folders for her from the table into her study, he flat out refused, politely explaining that he was clumsy and didn't want to be responsible if he tripped and dropped them, or made a mess of them in transit.

No, it couldn't have been Kyle, so how had this happened? She was pretty certain that she hadn't touched those folders at all, since the passionate kitchen encounter nearly a week ago. As she opened the outer folder now to check the contents inside the manila cover, the first document on the top of the pile stood out. This document had been secure in a separate envelope and in the middle of the folder when she had last looked at it last week.

There was no way in the world that it would have been able to get to where it was now without someone purposely putting it there. As Ruby picked up the copy of Carolyn and Josh's marriage certificate, she gave a shudder. Why wasn't Carolyn answering her phone?

43

The Day Before
30 December, Kira

With Sam's help, Kira had managed to get through Christmas Eve and Christmas Day without having an anxiety attack. Just having him close was enough to make her feel safe and secure, so that she could still enjoy herself. The thought of Josh accessing her locker and putting that card in her bag had made her feel physically sick, especially when Carolyn had confirmed that—yes, he was back for Christmas.

Carolyn had messaged Sam for her as soon as they had hung up, and he had arrived within 10 minutes, lying to Sue on reception that Kira had hurt her back and needed him to go into the ladies' locker room to help her. Sue had shown her usual concern, as she would for any of the employees when she thought that they were hurt. Although Kira felt terrible for deceiving her colleague, there was no way she wanted Sue or anyone else to know why she was incapable of leaving the locker room unaided.

Sue's continued fussing and offering to carry Kira's bag and take her stuff out to Sam's truck hadn't helped her anxiety, as she had continued to shake, the tremors not leaving her body until she was safely in Sam's strong arms on the driveway of her parents' house. He had quite rightly wanted her to take the card straight to the police there and then, but Kira had placated him once more by explaining the plan and why it had to wait until New Year's Day to be executed.

The last thing she wanted was to bring any more drama to her parents' door step when things between them all were now finally back on track. She wanted Sam to experience the warm and loving family Christmas of her childhood, and for them to be able to wake together on Christmas morning wrapped in each other's arms the same way millions of other couples did. The last thing she needed was to be stuck in a soulless police station until God knows what time waiting to have her statement taken.

No, she had made the right decision—she would keep hold of the card, slipping it into a sandwich bag to preserve any fingerprints or fibres as soon as she got home. It may or may not serve as evidence, but she wanted to capture as much as she could to help tell her story. The plan would go ahead in the new year.

The week that followed had actually been lovely. Sam had been caring and attentive to her all day at her parents' house, helping her mum in the kitchen on Christmas morning to serve up scrambled eggs and smoked salmon along with Bucks Fizz. He had patiently waited, while Kira had worked with her mum to create a sumptuous feast for their Christmas dinner. Her mum had certainly pushed the boat out this year now that she had her daughter safely home and once more happy about her future.

Then there had been the board games—if anyone could survive a three-hour stint of Monopoly with her dad, then they were definitely the man for her. She wasn't sure if it was Sam being polite and deferential to her dad, but it seemed suspiciously like he had let him win—the amount of hotels her dad had seemed to accumulate not quite within the rules of the game, overlooked by Sam as the banker. Well, if it kept both of them happy, then she was happy too.

Later that night, as she and Sam sat side by side in her bed sipping on a nightcap of Baileys, he had taken her hand in his and gently stroked up and down her arm. She had leant into him then, snuggling up against his soft plaid shirt as she started to drift off.

He had taken the glass from her hand and placed it on the nightstand, before he had gently moved them both down the bed, tucking the covers over them as he had held her close. Her last thoughts before she drifted off into a dreamless sleep had been that she had never felt so safe and so contented.

They had spent the next days in a post-Christmas haze. She had met Sam's huge extended family at their annual Boxing Day buffet, the table in his parents Bill and Susan's delightful farmhouse kitchen groaning under the weight of home-cooked hams, fresh crusty bread straight from the Aga, a huge selection of gooey, rich cheeses and a massive fruit cake.

Kira had always felt nervous in situations where she was confronted by such temptation; every choice she had made for the last 10 years had been about what fuel she had put into her body for optimum functionality, a careful balance of protein versus carbs on a daily basis.

Since her own revelation that she didn't want to compete competitively anymore, and the realisation that she had to live her own dreams and not just try and live for Joanna's memory, she had been letting herself ease into a new mindset. There was nothing wrong with trying all these delicious foods, just because she had consumed more than her usual calories, and apart from a few hikes on Sam's farm, had done very little exercise. She no longer felt the need to punish herself physically or mentally.

Sam had helped her carve a thick slice of juicy ham from the joint on the table, and had saved her favourite truffle in the box of chocolates handed around the sitting room in front of the fire, as the family settled in to watch the Boxing Day film of choice. This was her life now, her choice, and she had this great guy by her side with which to share it—it beat podium places and medals any day.

She had also enjoyed watching Sam with his family over those days spent on the farm. He was so happy to help out his dad. Any tensions about Sam not wanting to take on the farm had seemed to melt away, when it was clear that Phillip, his younger brother, clearly had a real passion for the place.

His dad was no longer resentful that Sam wanted a different career, and had taken to winding him up about his lack of stamina when shifting hay around the barns, or being a lightweight when Sam wanted to stop for a coffee after they had brought the livestock into the barn.

Sam's family had made her so incredibly welcome; his mum had presented her with a lovely gift of thick, fluffy, hand-knitted socks made from wool from their own sheep that she had dyed herself. Kira was so touched that despite hers and Sam's slow start, she was clearly being embraced by his family. She knew that this bliss couldn't last for much longer, and that the spell needed to be broken so that they could get on with their real lives.

In the New Year, they would start to ramp up their plans for the studio. It was going to be a lot of hard work, but she knew that they had the passion and commitment to really make a go of it. She just had one more evening here that she and Sam were going to spend hiking up to the cabin in the woods, with a bottle of wine and some steak to grill on the fire. Kira had got used to the solitude of being up in the woods, even though it was still disconcerting not to have a phone signal—she wasn't used to being totally cut off from the world.

Kira picked up her phone to make a few calls before they left for the cabin. There was no way she wanted to rush to get out of bed with Sam later to find a signal—she had some very hot plans for that man! She gave her mum a quick call to catch up on what they had been doing over the last few days, happy to hear about a New Year's party her parents were planning to attend, and that her mum had actually splashed out on a new dress in the winter sales. She checked her emails before her thoughts turned to her best friends.

Carolyn had messaged her once briefly on Boxing Day to wish her a Happy Christmas. They had agreed that they would try and stay out of contact this week. Carolyn knew that she had Sam with her, and that they had been planning on lying low for the week at both of their parents' houses. They had agreed Carolyn would call both her and Ruby tomorrow about the final arrangements for the quiz and the midnight dip, so she wasn't surprised at all about the lack of radio contact.

She just hoped her friend was ok, and that her week hadn't been too hard. She knew better than anyone what would happen if Josh found out about their plan. Maybe she would just drop Carolyn a quick text now to say—did she need any more help with the plans? It would be innocent enough if Josh happened to see the text, or better than that, she would call Ruby and see if she had heard how Carolyn was getting on and maybe get her to text—that way it kept Kira's name out of the equation.

'Hey, Rubes!' Kira was glad her friend had picked up on the first ring, as she knew Sam would be keen to get going to the cabin as soon as he was packed. 'Just checking in with you and seeing if you had a lovely Christmas?'

'Kira, so lovely to hear from you, sugar. It's been such a nice break. How have you been after getting that card?' It was so nice to hear the happiness in Ruby's voice.

Kira also answered with a smile in her voice.

'Rubes, it's been fine. Honestly, I couldn't give a damn about the card now. The last few days have been bliss, and we're nearly on the home stretch, so really it feels like New Year is really about new beginnings and all that. That's partly why I'm calling. Obviously, it's lovely to chat to you, but I just wondered if you'd heard anything from Carolyn at all? I know we're supposed to be keeping things on the down low for a few days, but I just worry about her, you know?'

She fought hard to try and keep some of the emotion out of her voice. As soon as she started thinking about any situation that might involve Josh, her power of rational thinking went out the window, and she started to have mild palpitations. She knew that Sam worried that she may have a form of PTSD that she needed to get checked out, but for now, she needed to keep it together.

'Well, it's strange actually. She had messaged a few times nearer Christmas to say all was well, and that they were really busy with family and friends visiting and that, but she was supposed to check in with me today about this balloon arch thing and quiz sheets, and I haven't heard from her yet.' Ruby paused, and Kira could hear her take a steadying breath. 'And something weird happened earlier, so I tried calling her and there was no answer.'

'What something? What do you mean it was weird? Ruby, you're scaring me now.' She could hear her voice escalating up an octave as the fear she had been trying to suppress started to rise in her throat.

'Well, I went to sort some work stuff out in the kitchen. I needed to sort out all my piles of paperwork for my cases to get them in some sort of order for the new year.'

'Seriously, spit it out, Ruby. I don't need a full explanation,' she ordered impatiently. 'Sorry, sorry, I didn't mean to be rude. Carry on.'

'Well, the top file was Carolyn's,' she took another breath, 'and it wasn't when I stacked them like that. It had been moved to the top, and her marriage certificate had been taken out of the envelope I had put it in and placed on the top of the paperwork.'

'So, Kyle moved it maybe? Is that what you're saying?'

'No, he didn't. That's the problem. Neither of us touched it, and we haven't had anyone over since before Christmas.' She heard Ruby blow out a big breath. 'I think Josh got in our house somehow and found it, and now I can't get hold of Carolyn.'

'Oh shit,' Kira exclaimed quietly. 'So what do we do?'

'Well, I wasn't supposed to hear from her until the morning, so to be honest, I'm worried that messaging her or calling her again might be an even worse call than leaving it and keeping to the plan. I mean, it could just be my mind playing tricks, right?'

It was the first time Kira had ever heard doubt creep into her friend's voice. Ruby, who was normally so assertive and sure of what to do and how to do it, was doubting her own judgement, and that made Kira nervous.

'So do we leave it?' Kira looked around the farmhouse kitchen, suddenly aware that Sam would be back any second and expect her to be ready to go. She owed him so much for his support this week, that she was desperate not to let him down on this last night at the farm, but she couldn't shake the fear that Carolyn might be in danger. She heard the beep beep of Ruby's phone in the background.

'Hang on, Kira. I've literally just got a text.'

'Read it to me,' she hurried.

'It says, "all good, babes; see you tomorrow". Hmm, well, that's something. But it doesn't really sound like one of her texts, does it?' she questioned.

'I don't know. Maybe she's busy with the kids and couldn't text properly? Maybe he's stood next to her?' Kira sought reassurance. 'I don't know what to do, Rubes. You're the one with the plans. I know what we agreed, and I don't think Carolyn would want to change anything. We have a plan—we stick to it?'

'Yeah, I know, Kira, you're probably right. But if I haven't heard from her by 11 tomorrow morning, I'm going over there,' Ruby was adamant.

'I'll come with you. We're off up to the cabin now, but I'll make sure we are back here by 9 so I have a signal again. So call me when you want me to come with you—unless, of course, you hear from her again, ok?'

As they hung up, Kira felt uneasy. She knew how dangerous Josh could be, but she was also confident in Ruby being able to make an informed judgement about sticking to the plan. As far as they were both aware, Carolyn and Josh had the kids with them today. She was still due to run the NYE party tomorrow, and the plan would come together like they agreed. She just couldn't shake the feeling that there was more to this than either of them imagined. She just hoped that tomorrow wouldn't be too late.

44

12 Hours Before
New Years Eve, Carolyn

Carolyn had finally dropped off to sleep sometime in the early hours of the morning. Josh had been suspiciously quiet for an hour or so. She could no longer hear him pacing around outside the bathroom, so she assumed he must finally have gone downstairs. She had curled up on the floor under her dressing gown and a pile of towels and tried to get some rest. Around 4 am, she woke with a start, realising she hadn't heard any bangs, slams, things being smashed or broken since she had previously checked a few hours before.

She had wondered what on earth he was up to and how long he planned to keep her in here. She winced as she had rearranged herself on the bathroom floor, knowing from previous experience that she was likely to have at least one broken rib among the many scrapes and bruises down her back, on her arse and along her arms. At least it was cold outside, so she could get away with long sleeves and covering up for some time.

She had wondered if her waterproof foundation might actually stick to the bruises on her arms, so that she could at least still participate in the midnight dip at Sparks later—presuming that she actually got the hell out of this bathroom. He knew her mum was bringing the kids back later. There was no way he could just keep her captive here when people were expecting her, would he?

The frustration at being locked in the bathroom after everything that she had planned over the last few weeks was almost overwhelming. The plan was meticulously in place. He just had to go and find out and spoil everything, hurting her along the way. She was pretty confident that he didn't know that she was planning to go to the police. He knew about her leaving, and that was it. She just needed to get some more of the twins' stuff ready and put it in the boot of her car.

If only she could persuade him to calm down and let her out, give him the platitudes he needed to believe her, so that she could escape. The twins were being collected by a friend's mum in the car park at Sparks before the party later, and she was keeping them at her house for a sleepover along with 4 other kids from scooter club, assuming she could get out of the bathroom in time to get everything ready. Urgh, it was so frustrating.

She settled back down into the nest she had made, trying reluctantly not to succumb to the tears that threatened. She knew they would only make her headache worse. The best thing she could do now was get some more rest and reserve her strength for the morning and whatever that may bring.

As Carolyn woke again from another uncomfortable sleep, she opened her eyes into the glaring day light and pushed her hair out of her eyes. She gave herself a mental shake. She had to think logically. There had to be something in the bathroom cabinet that could help her undo the lock that Josh had jammed from the outside, or even undo the hinges of the door so she could escape that way.

The only challenge was, if he was still in the house, what he might do to her if she tried to get away? How long had she been out for? She glanced at her watch then, shocked to find that it was nearly 11 am. It must have been the serious adrenaline crash that had knocked her out for so many hours. Ouch, her body hurt.

She eased herself up off the floor, grasping the side of the bath and the vanity unit to steady herself, her one leg feeling a little numb from lying for so long on the hard surface. She was due to meet Ruby soon. Surely if she didn't show, that would have sparked something off in her friend's consciousness?

Carolyn may be a little scatty, but she always fulfilled her duties when it came to her friends and to the Sparks committee. She could only wait and see as she wondered how was she supposed to get everything sorted and herself out of this mess before the Sparks party. She had responsibilities.

The twins would be back later, and the last thing she wanted was for them and her mum to find her in this state. She could already tell from the way that she had looked at her yesterday that she was worried. Her mum and her dad didn't need the additional stress of supporting Carolyn in this predicament.

She shook her matted hair out of her eyes, pushing it back behind her ears, and cringed as she felt another lump burgeoning under her scalp on the back of her head. That must have been when he had pushed her up against the wall in the hall, and the frame on poor Charlie's painting had dug into her. She shuddered at the memory and the thought of what destruction was on the other side of the door.

The attacks and abuse she had sustained over the years had been vicious, but had never really resulted in Josh damaging their own property. Sure, a few plates and glasses had become victims of heated disagreements over the years, but from what she heard last night, Josh seemed to be on a rampage. Not only smashing stuff down in the kitchen, but hurling things against the bathroom door while slinging insults at her. The only mercy being that he had seemed to not want to take her physical punishment any further.

She could only assume that in his deluded state, he didn't want to get into any trouble, so that he could pursue his fictional "life" with Kira. Maybe she had his delusions to thank for the fact that despite the cracked ribs, she had actually got off lightly, as she had absolutely no doubt in her mind that Josh was capable of murder. Her concern was less for herself now and more for Kira. Josh wouldn't take her rejection well, and he had already threatened her life.

As the feeling came back in her legs, she started to flex out the rest of her body, getting used to where the pain was and how she could control her reaction to it. She dug inside one of the bathroom cupboards and pulled out the packet of paracetamol and some ibuprofen, sliding her head under the tap to swallow down a couple of each. She hoped they might at least take the edge off some of the pain and bring the swelling down for now.

She stretched up and opened the small top window as wide as she could. The others didn't open at all since they last painted them, as both she and Josh had been wary of the twins accidentally opening them too wide and climbing out if they were unsupervised—something she was regretting now. She climbed up on top of the toilet, and balanced one knee on top of the counter as she heaved herself up, so that she could stick part of her head out the window, grateful for the kilos she had recently managed to shed.

She knew that if she could twist herself slightly to the left, she should be able to see if Josh's car was still in the driveway, and with any luck, work out if she could complete her plan to get out of there. There was no way she could squeeze more than her arm and part of her shoulder out of the actual window, so that wasn't going to be an option for escape. As far as she could tell, she couldn't see his car.

There wasn't any glimpse of its distinctive bright blue paint emerging from the corner of the porch or reflecting off the wind chimes that were hanging from the magnolia tree. She was about to climb down and start rummaging through the contents of the bathroom cabinets for anything resembling a screwdriver, when she spotted a bright purple Beetle heading into the drive, the gravel crunching loudly under its tyres.

There was no way that car belonged to anyone other than Ruby. This had to be the way that she got out of there. She trusted her friend to do the right thing and to have her back. Now she just had to get her attention.

She started to shout and holler as loud as she could to try and get their attention, knowing that the window on the side of the house wasn't properly visible from the front driveway. She knew she had to do something fast, otherwise they would head to the front porch and wouldn't be able to hear her. She looked around frantically to see what she could grab to alert Ruby to her predicament. Then she spotted the loo roll.

She scrambled down off the counter and grabbed the nearest full roll, unravelling the end slightly and doubling it up so it didn't break. She launched the roll out of the window, almost giggling to herself as it streamed out and into the wind, making it career down towards the driveway. Just as she started to doubt her actions, she felt a distinct feeling of relief as she spotted Kira and Sam climbing out of the car after Ruby.

Even if they did make it to the door, and even if Josh did happen to be home, he was outnumbered. Just as she was about to reach down and launch another loo roll, Sam glanced up. He did a double take, as he then walked quickly round the corner and smiled up at her.

'Carolyn! I believe I might be your knight in shining armour!'

45

6 Hours Before
New Years Eve, Kira

It had been hours since Sam had heroically smashed the lock off the front door of Carolyn's house to break in, and Kira still felt jittery and shaky. Seeing her friend wince with pain as Ruby bowled in and grabbed her into a hug, after they had helped her escape the bathroom, and then helping Ruby assess the damage once Carolyn had allowed them to help her into the shower and then into fresh underwear, was painful.

Ruby had insisted on photographing the bathroom, and then gently took pictures of Carolyn's injuries before they had helped her to wash and change. Ruby had calmly instructed Sam to take a walk around the house and to film the destruction on his phone, asking him to immediately email it to her at her chambers and her personal email address as more evidence.

Kira had helped find Carolyn's gym bag and a small suitcase, and started to pack more clothes to tide Carolyn and the twins over for a few extra days. She had had no idea if what she had packed would be the right things, but at that moment in time, she wasn't thinking about fashion choices, more about practicality. The one thing Carolyn insisted on was that she still wanted her new glamourous party dress packed along with her stunning new stiletto heels.

They had both shaken their heads at her as she insisted on scooping up her make-up and her decent Dyson hairdryer into the overnight bag, both in awe of her composure. She had assured them that the worst was over for her now. The only thing she had to do was get the hell out of the house, put on the best night ever at Sparks, and hang on in until they met with the solicitor in the morning at the police station. There was no point in trying to do any of it quicker now; the solicitor was away tonight, and everything was arranged.

Carolyn had called her mum and asked her to take the kids out for the day, before dropping them with the twins' friends. She hadn't told her mum the whole story, but Kira had heard her saying that it wasn't safe to bring them back to the house, and that it was best they stayed away from their own home, just for the day, as she didn't think Josh was in a fit state to see the kids today.

Her mum had understood what she was saying; and Carolyn told her that Sam would text her the address to take the kids, as she was still sure that her phone and the house were bugged, and she didn't want Josh—wherever he was—to know their plans.

Kira had been touched by Sam's concern about dropping her off at Sparks, while he went back to the farm to grab some of the decorations that Kira had left there over the Christmas break. She had agreed to order them on her Amazon account, but in their frantic rush this morning to get to Ruby's and then over to Carolyn's, when neither of them had got any answer from their texts and calls, she had forgotten to grab them.

She needed to get the pool area strung with fairy lights, and the path marked to the outside pool with hurricane lanterns and tea lights, before attending a quick team briefing at 7 pm. Sam would only be thirty minutes tops, so she felt comfortable being on her own for a short space of time. She would just pop round the pool area, then back through the staff corridor to reception to catch up with Sue. Sam would be back with her before she knew it, and there were plenty of people around now to call on if she felt unsafe at any time.

She just couldn't wait for today to be over, the weight of it was hanging heavily over her now. All she wanted to do was go back to the farm with Sam tonight, as soon after midnight as was polite to leave and after they had tidied up, so that she could collapse in his arms, ready for the big day ahead.

Compared to this morning, the weather had come in thick and fast. There had been storm warnings on the radio since Ruby had bundled them into her Beetle, and she had felt the wind rocking Sam's truck as they had sat at the traffic lights. The rain was lashing down, and she seriously wondered how many people would actually bother to come to the quiz tonight—or if they did, how many of them would actually stay for the midnight dip?

There were also warnings of power cuts and trees down. People may be put off coming along if they hadn't already pre-booked a taxi, as she doubted many of them would be working that night. It just didn't seem worth their while.

She shivered as she made her way in through the automatic doors, a gust of wind sending leaves whirling around her feet as she made her way over to the desk.

'Hello, my lovely!' It was always nice to be greeted by Sue's smiling face. If there was one thing that could be relied on, that was Sue being her usual cheerful self in the face of any adversity. 'Well, what a storm, hey? I'm kind of hoping it puts a lot of the punters off this evening, if I'm honest. It would be nice to have more time to chat to everyone, and you never know—if there's less competition, I might even win the quiz,' she chuckled. 'Anyway, how was your Christmas? Tell me all about that lovely man of yours and what you got up to?'

Kira was grateful for the distraction for the next few minutes, as everyone knew there was one thing that Sue excelled in, and that was the ability to chat and gossip. Kira found herself relaying the story of Sam letting her dad beat him at Monopoly, and all about the cabin in the woods—well, maybe not all about it. That would have been too much detail. She grinned to herself.

'You'll be glad you're not in that cabin tonight, my love. Probably best not to be around potential falling trees. We've enough problems here with the flipping power keep tripping, and that backup generator still being a bit dodgy. I told Daniel it might even be better to cancel this shindig, but he won't listen. You know these manager types—guess he's scared to lose out on revenue or something.'

Kira nodded in agreement.

'And apparently, there's some issue with the filter on the hot tub now, so we have to put the "Out of Order" sign on it. That's not going to go down well with whoever wanted to go in there after the midnight dip.'

Kira shook her head at Sue's exasperation, knowing in the next breath she would be as cheerful as ever. However, Sue's next question had knocked her off balance just for a second.

'So, when does Carolyn's plan come into play?' Sue faced her in deadly seriousness.

'I'm sorry?' Kira asked sharply. 'What plan?'

They had been meticulous in keeping everything amongst the three of them for now. With the exception of Kyle, Sarah and of course Sam, no one else was privy to their plans.

Sue smiled at her then.

'You know,' Sue met her eyes and held them for a second, before continuing, 'the plan to hand out fortune cookies for everyone, with a prophecy for their new year?'

Kira let out the breath she didn't know she was even holding.

'Oh, um, yeah. I'm sorry, Sue. I didn't even know that's what she was planning! You know Carolyn—she always has these amazing little twists to these events.' She smiled back at her. 'You can ask her shortly. She should be here soon with the balloon arch that she's gone to collect in Sarah's van.'

'Fab stuff. I'll see what her plans are and if she needs a hand. I think those fortune cookies might be just what we all need. One thing we could all do with next year, and that's good fortune.' She leant over then and gently squeezed Kira's hand. 'You three in particular,' she winked as she turned her attention away to the pile of freshly laundered towels and started folding them.

'Thanks,' Kira mumbled, frowning slightly as she tried to interpret what Sue meant.

Kira made her way to the locker room to dump her bag, saying hi to a few people as she went. She walked out to the spa area. As she got up close to door of the plant room where the lanterns were stored, she noticed the keypad lock hanging slightly to one side. The staff and managers were meticulous about making sure this door was always locked shut. The big hazard sign on the outside declaring "Hazardous Materials" and "Strictly No Entry to Non-Trained Staff" stating the obvious.

The room contained the plant for running the sauna, steam room and hot tub, along with pool chemicals, and storage boxes with things like the lanterns Kira needed and inflatables for the pool parties. She must remember to tell Michael as soon as she got the lanterns in place that someone needed to get it fixed. The last thing they needed tonight was some stupid punter accidentally stumbling into the plant room after a few too many vinos.

Kira dragged the first box of storm lanterns out across the tiled floor of the pool area, sliding it carefully along the walkway next to the sunken hot tub, and used her butt to push open the patio doors leading to the outside pool. Despite the terrible stormy weather, the outdoor heated pool was going to look spectacular when it was all lit up later, with the steam pouring off into the gloomy night.

As she started to lift the first two lanterns out of the box, a gust of wind caught the edge of the pool cover, making it unravel slightly and flap out onto the pool. It needed to be fully secured by two straps, especially on a night like this, so it wouldn't unroll—either one had come loose, or someone hadn't been doing their job properly.

As she moved further into the shadows to find the end of the tie to pull it into place, her spider senses kicked in. The hairs on the back of her neck stood up as she crouched down to secure the cover. She almost couldn't bring herself to look round and over her shoulder.

The outdoor pool was surrounded by a high fence and artfully placed foliage. Some of the bushes were blowing like crazy in the wind, so maybe it was just the shadow of one of those that was making her feel like someone was there, watching. She eased herself up onto her haunches—the stance she would take when she competed in sprints rather than distance—knowing that if it came to it, she was better off in flight rather than fight mode.

She slowly turned her head in the direction of the far corner of the pool, the darkness enveloping everything around her, the howling wind buffeting the pool loungers, leaves swirling up around her. For another second, she held her breath. Surely there wasn't anyone there?

She shook herself. She knew she was on edge after today's events. It was just shadows. She needed to pull herself together—she had a job to do. Just as she was about to straighten up and go back to the lanterns, she saw the slightest movement of a shadow growing from a crouching position to the height of a person, hidden in the gloom behind the foliage. There was no mistaking that there was someone there, and if they were hiding, then they couldn't mean well.

Before she even had time to think, she leapt to her feet and sprinted back inside the safety of the building, slamming the door behind her and dashing to the bar to find the others.

46

3 Hours Before,
New Years Eve, Ruby

As soon as Ruby had walked into Sparks around 6 pm, Sue had grabbed her and pretty much frog-marched her back behind the bar area and into the kitchen. There she had found Kira sitting just inside the stockroom on an upturned bucket, holding a glass of brandy in her shaking hand. Sue had just shrugged and discreetly left them to it, as Ruby dropped the bags she was carrying in shock and crouched down beside her, pulling Kira in close, asking her with concern.

'What's going on?'

'I saw something,' Kira stuttered out, 'by the outdoor pool, in the dark; there was a man hiding in the shadows.' She continued through shallow breaths, 'Rubes, I'm sure it was him!'

Ruby held her tighter as she continued to shake.

'Look, it's been a really fucking stressful day, Kira. It's stormy as hell out there at the moment. Are you sure it's not just your mind playing tricks? I mean, what we had to deal with earlier with Carolyn and the threat that Josh made to you—it's probably just overloaded your brain.' Ruby hadn't been prepared for Kira's almost violent reaction as she forced Ruby's arm away from her, slamming the glass down so hard on the kitchen floor that Ruby was surprised it didn't shatter.

'I know what I saw, Ruby! This wasn't just some figment of my imagination! He's out there, he's coming for me, and you know it. I don't know what he's planning, but I want to call the police now! I can't play this waiting game any longer. This can't wait until the morning. Something bad is going to happen, I just know it!'

She had stood up then and started pacing the length of the stockroom.

'All along, I've been patient—waiting until Carolyn was ready to tell her story, waiting for Carolyn to get her plan in place and get her shit together. But we can't wait any longer. Can't you see, Ruby? He's coming for us!'

Ruby had risen to stand in front of Kira as she struggled to contain her emotions. She almost agreed with Kira. This couldn't all be about Carolyn; there were other victims of Josh's violence in this equation. But then her rational brain kicked back in. A few hours, and this would all be over. What could happen to them from inside the safety of the club?

As soon as Carolyn arrived, they would all be together in one place. Sam would be here, Kyle was coming for the quiz, Sarah was due to arrive any minute with Carolyn, and there were staff and members milling around all evening. They needed to hold their nerve a little longer and calm down. Getting hysterical was when mistakes were made.

'Look,' she faced Kira, reaching out to hold onto each of her arms, forcing Kira look at her. 'I believe you, ok? I believe you, and I know that you're scared.' Kira had met her eyes then. 'But the best place for you right now is right here with us. No one is going to get to you with us all around. It's just a few hours, and then we can put the plan in place, and it will all be over, and he will never be able to hurt you or anyone else ever again.'

She had nodded at Kira, who mimicked the motion. 'So get this brandy down you. I will come with you to the locker room while you get changed into your New Year's outfit, and then we will get James or one of the other guys to sort out whatever jobs you were supposed to be doing.' Kira had given her a weak smile. 'I will stick to you like glue, missy, ok?'

Kira gave another weak, unconvincing nod, before reaching out and taking the brandy from Ruby, downing the fiery amber liquid in one before turning to march out of the kitchen.

As they walked past a concerned-looking Sue, Ruby had turned to give her a reassuring grin and a discreet thumbs-up. Ruby helped Kira stow her stuff back in her locker and waited, while she changed into a smart black jumpsuit and reapplied her eye make-up and lipstick, while she stowed her bikini and towel on the top of her bag in the locker, ready to change into later.

Part of the plan tonight was when the quiz was done, and the punters were enjoying cheese and biscuits and a glass of Port or two, they would have a final debrief in the sauna before the midnight dip.

The next couple of hours had been flat out. As well as helping make sure that all was in order for the quiz, Ruby had been keeping one eye on Kira the whole time, making sure that she wasn't left alone. This was easier once Sam had arrived, and she had seen the two of them quietly chatting in a corner as glasses of fizz had been handed round as people started to arrive. She knew that Kira was all about openness and honesty, so she would have told Sam everything that was on her mind.

At least that had meant that he was now stuck to her like glue. Ruby had also been concerned about Carolyn, who had showed up just after 7 pm with Sarah, huge gold and red balloon arch in tow. She needn't have worried though. There was one thing that Carolyn was an expert at by now, and that was putting on her game face.

She had breezed in wearing her new black dress with long sleeves, accentuated with diamantes, make-up applied carefully so that no one could see the dark circles that Ruby knew were hiding under her eyes, and barking instructions to, 'Move the buffet tables to the left a bit so there's more room to dance,' and, 'James, add a little more cranberry juice to the Midnight Punch. You don't want them all sloshed before they eat.'

Ruby had caught Sarah's eye for a second, and almost laughed when Sarah gave a two-handed shrug. They both knew what Carolyn was like—she was resilient through and through.

The quiz was just about to kick off at 9 pm when Kyle finally walked through the door. Ruby had deployed him to do a drive-by past Carolyn's house after her chat with Kira. She wanted to know if Josh's car was back there, and if there were any lights on. At least if they knew where he was, then it would rule out where he wasn't and give them all a little more peace of mind. Kyle had shepherded her by the elbow out into the reception area, where they could be alone for a minute.

'So, did you spot him?'

'The car was there, but there were no lights on,' Kyle had shaken his head. 'So, I don't really know what that means. I was going to take a look through the windows, but a cop car drove past, and I thought you wouldn't have appreciated me getting arrested for looking like I was casing the joint.' He pushed his windswept hair back across his head. 'Sorry, Rubes, I don't know what else I can do.'

Ruby sighed as she reached out to squeeze his arm.

'It's fine, babe. There isn't anything anyone can do now. We just have to hope things go our way.' She pressed her forehead against his as she added, 'You're amazing, Kyle, you know that? I'm so lucky to have you. In a few hours, this will all be over, and we can get on with our lives.'

As she kissed him gently, they were rudely interrupted by the sound of screeching feedback from Sarah's microphone.

'Ladies and Gentlemen, it is my pleasure to start this final quiz of the year. As you know, we love a good theme to our quizzes, and we have Ruby to thank for this one. The theme tonight is "FRESH STARTS".' The microphone gave another high-pitched squeal. 'Eyes down, question one…'

47

1 Hour Before
New Years Eve, Sauna

Despite the tensions of the day and the general feeling of unease, the quiz had actually been a blast; even the dreadful weather hadn't put people off attending. The numbers of people for the midnight dip were still depleted, but that just meant that there would be higher bar sales that night, and that there was less decanting of drinks into plastic cups for taking out by the pool—so less mess to clear up the day after.

James had been round both the indoor and outdoor pool areas, to sort out the lamps that Kira had abandoned and to string up the fairy lights by the spa area. Even in the winter gloom, with the storm raging outside, the three of them had to admit that it looked really pretty and inviting.

It had taken Ruby and Carolyn some convincing to get Kira in the mood for joining them both in the sauna. After the exhausting day and her scare earlier by the pool, she wasn't happy about leaving the safety of the bar area where she was surrounded by a crowd. Even the promise that Sam would be on lifeguard duty next to the main pool, or that Sarah had promised to help watch the CCTV on reception while Sue took a break, gave her any reassurance.

Eventually, after an extra-strong mojito and a stern talking-to about needing to regroup, she was convinced into changing out of her New Year's outfit and into her bright halter-neck bikini. She grabbed her Sparks water bottle and filled it at the water fountain, suspicious that Carolyn's bottle actually contained something other than water, as she had spent a strangely long amount of time next to the punch bowl before they had come into the changing room.

Ruby led the way, with Kira in the middle, and Carolyn bringing up the rear, her towel bound tightly around her swimsuit and her arms held closely to her side to mask the sight of the worst of the visible bruises and scratches on her arms. She planned to be well out of the spa area way before any of the members came pouring in after Big Ben had struck midnight.

The last thing she wanted was to answer any awkward questions. She had also promised Sarah that they would leave as soon as possible after midnight, so that she could try and get some decent sleep before the big day tomorrow.

The familiar warmth and smell of cedar mixed with the heat from the coals in the dark, womb-like sauna was enough to trigger Kira. As soon as she walked in, all of the trauma of the last couple of years came flooding back to her. All of the times she had spent in here, building new friendships, pouring out her truth to her friends, and them helping her put herself back together, was just so overwhelming.

She had collapsed heavily onto the middle of the wooden bench and put her head down onto her knees, covering her head with both her arms as sobs wracked her body. Ruby and Carolyn were at her side immediately, enveloping her in a three-way hug, arms and hands grasping each other as they let each other pour out the emotions that had managed to keep contained all day. It was only when Kira had gone in for a particularly strong arm around Carolyn's waist, and she elicited a squeal that they let one another go—first Ruby, then Carolyn descending into a mild case of hysterical laughter. Kira had looked to her left at Ruby and shook her head before turning to Carolyn, who had tears of pure release pouring down her face.

'Seriously, ladies, you are all completely insane!' A small smirk played at the corner of Kira's mouth as she fought the urge to join in. 'Why, um, what? I don't get…' She couldn't finish, as the urge to giggle got the better of her and she chortled along with them.

It took a few minutes for them to get over their hysterics; each time Ruby tried to get a word out, she couldn't catch her breath and started to chuckle all over again. It felt so good to be here with one another and, within minutes, break the tension that they were all feeling. When Carolyn finally managed to squeak out a fully coherent sentence, she turned to the ladies sitting next to her.

'Right, now we've got that out the way…ha, ha, sorry, let me get control of myself. As I was saying, now we're here, we are safe, and we are literally right on the edge of our future.' She steadied her breathing.

'I just wanted to say to you ladies, to my very best friends in the whole world, just how grateful I am for your support—for everything you have done for me, for your patience, your bravery, the chance you are taking with me after the clock strikes midnight tonight—when everything we have worked towards will make our future together so much better and what we deserve.'

Carolyn absentmindedly wiped another tear from her cheek as Ruby joined in.

'I want to second that. In the last year, with your support, I have confronted my worst fears. I have laid some ghosts to rest that I wanted to keep firmly in the past, and I have seen what true friendship can mean when you learn to trust people who put their trust in you.' She nodded along with each of her own affirmations, finishing in a whisper, 'I owe you guys. I really do.'

As Kira opened her mouth to speak, ready to join in with the positiveness of the occasion and wanting to share her gratitude to these wonderful, strong women she sat next to, Carolyn had held up her hand and interrupted her, her face distinctly redder than it had been a moment ago.

'Ladies, is it me or is it getting significantly hotter in here?' The sweat was now pouring off her brow as she stood up to look at the thermometer on the wall.

'It's saying it's already 98 degrees in here! How didn't we notice that when we walked in?' She looked between the others for acknowledgement.

'Well, I guess we had our minds on other things,' smiled Ruby. 'It's fine. We'll just take one more minute, then we better get out. The last thing we need now is to get a dehydration headache from sitting in this heat too long.'

'Yes, let me just have my say, ladies, and we can go and sit on the loungers for a bit before the others join us. Or maybe one of us needs to go tell Michael that there's a fault with this as well,' joined in Kira.

'As well?' asked Carolyn.

'Oh yeah, didn't I tell you the hot tub is out of action? There's some fault with the filter cover or something. We must have walked straight past the sign as we came in here. That, and the lock on the plant room door—shit,' Kira cursed herself. 'I meant to tell Michael earlier that the lock was broken off! I completely forgot after seeing that person in the dark out by the pool.'

'Bloody place is going to hell in a handcart!' Carolyn exclaimed. 'Well, there's fuck all we can do about that right now. I'm sure someone will sort it in the morning. Seriously, I'll be glad when you get your place up and running, Kira, and I start putting my energies into making that place run smoothly, instead of helping the management here stick plasters over all the bits that are falling off.' She smiled at Kira, nodding at her to continue. 'So, Kira, you were saying?'

'Yes, sorry, so, I just wanted to join in with saying how grateful I am—'

'Did you see that?' Ruby interrupted this time and jumped off the bench. 'That temperature gauge just shot up past the 105 degrees mark, and I swear I'm starting to have palpitations.'

'Ok, so I'll be quick—'

'Fuck that, Kira. You can do your thank you tomorrow.' Carolyn fanned herself with her free hand, the other tapping the mercury on the thermometer, as Ruby slid past her to push open the door.

'Let's get some air in here, ladies, then let's get a cold shower.' She paused, her hand firmly on the door. 'What the fuck! It's stuck.'

'What do you mean it's stuck?' Carolyn stood next to her. 'Stop messing around, Rubes. Give it a shove.' She placed her hands next to Ruby's, and they both tried the door once more before Carolyn turned to Kira. 'She's not wrong—it's stuck!'

'So hit the emergency release button then!' The panic in Kira's voice was palpable.

Ruby slammed her hand on the red emergency release button at the side of the door, wincing as the button dug into her hand. 'It's not working!'

'So, hit it harder,' Kira snapped.

'Kira, love, I've hit it three times now and tried the door. You've just watched me. I'm not messing with you. It's stuck. We're locked in.' She glanced back as the red line on the thermometer continued to rise, now hitting the 125-degree mark, each millimetre signally more discomfort.

'Ok, let's not panic. We've only been in here a short time and we have water. The others will be coming in shortly, so we can bang on the door and someone will let us out.' Carolyn tried to rationalise, despite the sweat now pouring down her face. She abandoned her towel and used it to mop her brow. 'Except, I didn't put water in my bottle. Like an idiot, I topped it up with punch!'

Ruby grimaced as she caught Kira's fear-struck face.

'Yep, just as I suspected,' she shook her head. 'Ok, well, we can just ration out ours. It won't be long until the others come.' It was then she looked down at her watch. 'Shit, it's another 40 minutes until midnight, and look at that gauge now.'

The others followed her as they crowded around the wall as it hit 130, the arrow on the gauge firmly into the dark red "EMERGENCY" area of the thermometer.

'How long can people survive at these temperatures?' Kira asked shakily, as she turned to Ruby as the perennial voice of reason for reassurance. She frowned when she saw that her friend's face was the same colour as her bright red hair—Kira's concern increasing as Ruby answered in a small voice.

'Not long.' The terror they all felt was evident in that tiny statement.

'Help! Help!' They all used as much of their remaining strength to pound and hammer on the door. 'Help! We're stuck! Anyone? Help us!'

'Maybe I can break the glass panel in the door with my water bottle?' Kira grabbed her stainless steel bottle. 'Stand back.' She smashed it as hard as she could against the reinforced glass panel that was face-height in the solid cedar door—smack, smash, over and over again as the heat continued to rise.

'Ruby? Ruby!' Kira turned to see Carolyn help a stumbling Ruby, as she collapsed onto the nearest bench.

'Kira, I think she's going to faint. She's got some kind of heat shock.'

'Quick, pour some water into her mouth from your bottle, wet the towel a little and put it on her head.' She helped her friend lie Ruby down across the slats. 'You look after her. I need to keep trying. Sam's out there. If I'm loud enough, I'm sure he will come.'

Even saying this out loud to herself gave her the strength to try one more time, hoping the sound of the gurgling, malfunctioning hot tub wasn't loud enough to drown out the noise of her hammering the door down with her bottle.

'SAM! SAM! HELP!' she yelled with all her strength, the bottle reverberating in her clenched fist. 'SAMMMMMM!' The sweat poured into her eyes; her hair was plastered to her face. Just as she was about to slump down and admit defeat, she saw a flash of yellow at the corner of her vision—Sam must be near the edge of the pool, on the edge of the spa. She inhaled one last hot lungful of air and let forth with a near-deafening scream, 'SAMMMMMM!'

A few long seconds passed. Her vision started to blur as the exertion of hammering on the door caught up with her. Her body started to fall limp as the mercury hit 140. As her back hit the wall and she started to slide, a gust of cool air washed over her and Sam came into view, swooping down to catch her just before she hit the floor.

48

30 Minutes Before
New Years Eve

Kira had helped Sam drag Ruby out onto the tiled floor of the spa, before he had returned to help Carolyn up from where she had collapsed onto the bench at Ruby's feet. He had run into the plant room and grabbed a bucket that he dunked into the main pool, and had then proceeded to dump the entire contents all over Ruby, bringing her round with a shock, but cooling her down in the process.

He kindly repeated this for both Carolyn and Kira until the three of them were able to explain to him what had happened, and Ruby had been helped up to a sitting position against the wall.

'What do you mean the door wouldn't open and the emergency release was stuck?' He held Kira's hand in his, as he crouched down on his haunches to speak to them. 'I swear on my life they were fine earlier. It said so on the health and safety card when I took handover.'

'Well, quite obviously something broke, didn't it?' Sam looked up in surprise at Carolyn's tone. 'Sorry, Sam, I know it's not your fault. I just think the three of us have had a massive scare tonight, and there isn't a straightforward explanation for it.'

'It's fine, Carolyn. It's seriously scary what just happened to the three of you. I'm just glad this one here has a powerful set of lungs on her.' He looked affectionately at Kira, who raised her eyebrows at him, the colour in her cheeks finally returning to something like normal.

'Do you think someone did it on purpose?' Ruby looked to Sam for answers.

'What, like sabotage?' he frowned. 'Who would...oh shit, you mean Josh?' He stood then, raking his hands through his hair as he struggled to comprehend. 'But how would he have got in here? And got past me?'

'Well, Kira thought she saw someone earlier outside, didn't she?' said Ruby.

'And the plant room door is broken,' Kira joined in.

'And there was a power cut around 7 pm, wasn't there?' Carolyn continued. 'Isn't there a back gate into the pool area from out by the bins?'

'Yeah, but you need a staff pass to access it. It might just be a coincidence, maybe?' Ever the pragmatist, Sam was keen to reassure them that this was nothing but an unfortunate series of events. 'Look, I'm pretty sure it's almost impossible to override the emergency buttons on these things. It would need someone who knew electrics, for a start.'

'You do know that Josh was in the army before he pursued his botany career, don't you?' Carolyn looked at the group around her. 'He had to learn a trade as well as being a commander on expeditions. It's not like you can operate in the army on map-reading skills alone. That guy knows electronics, I'm telling you!'

'Shit, Carolyn.' Ruby took another sip of water from the bottle Sam had just filled for her. 'I forgot about that. But how would he have got in? Surely the CCTV would have picked him up?'

They looked at one another then, as Carolyn and Kira said in unison, 'The power cut.'

Just then, the lights flickered as the power once again threatened to trip.

'Fuck this, I've had enough of this tonight.' Sam looked shocked as Kira, who rarely swore, let out a curse. 'Why don't we all just get the hell out of here? We don't know if Josh is here, or if he is, where he is. It's terrifying. Why don't we all just bundle into Sam's truck and get to the police station right now?'

Carolyn had shimmied along the wall then closer to Kira, water still dripping down her cooling head as she levelled with her.

'Love, I know this is a lot, and I know that you think that this might have been Josh, but seriously, we only have a short time to go and then we are home free. We have guests ready to come out to the pool at midnight. I just need this one last thing to go to plan, then we can get out of here. Will you do this for me?' Her look beseeching Kira to agree. 'Please?'

Kira let out a long sigh as she looked between her friends and up at Sam.

'Fine. But we stick together, ok? No one gets left on their own.'

As they eased themselves up from the floor, Ruby addressed them all.

'We have 30 minutes to get ourselves sorted and pull of this event. Thanks to Sam, we can get through this, just a bit longer.' She pushed herself off the tiled wall behind her, her hands still a little unsteady as she braced herself against the wall to catch her breath. 'I know you said we need to stick together, but I need to go check on Kyle. None of us have our phone, and I want to go and get mine, ok? So I'll meet you in the lockers in 10 minutes.'

They watched as she gingerly picked her way across the sodden floor and back towards the women's locker room.

'Well, if she's carrying on in the face of adversity, then I guess we better make up the numbers, hadn't we?' Carolyn looked to Kira, who couldn't meet her eye. 'Come on! We can do this.'

It took all of Kira's strength to hold back from what she was really thinking. Could they really go through with the plan? What was going to happen to them afterwards? Was it really as watertight as they hoped it would be? They didn't even know where Josh was when they needed to. As she let Sam lead her away from the hot tub, he turned her just before the ladies' changing room, pulling her to stand in front of him.

'I've got you. You know that, don't you?'

She leant into his arms, his strong biceps enveloping her, his one hand on her waist steadying her as he moved his other hand to tip her chin up towards him.

'Not long and it will be done.' He kissed the tip of her nose before releasing her from his embrace, so she could follow Carolyn back to the lockers.

Just as they reached the door, and Sam turned to head out through the male locker room, the lights faltered again as the wind outside howled around the building. Rain thrashed the windows as a sudden gale-force gust of wind whipped through the line of hurricane lamps, extinguishing them, as a dark shape stepped out from the shadows.

49
10 Minutes Before New Years Eve

'We're going to call off the midnight dip.' Michael called the staff and volunteers to one side in the area to the side of the bar. 'The weather out there is absolutely atrocious, and I don't want to be responsible for any accidents that might happen from flying debris or someone tripping in the dark. I'm really sorry, but it's just not worth the insurance hassle.

'Sarah, can you go tell the others? I think they're still out in the locker room. And James, if you can tell the rest of the guys—maybe grab Kyle and get him to tell Sam that we'll be closing down the pool now, just after midnight.'

A relieved sigh was audible across the room as the staff realised that they wouldn't have to change into their swimwear, or spend time after midnight cleaning up by the pool; they would get back to their loved ones sooner after midnight than they imagined.

As the storm continued to rage and lights across the town flickered off, as power cuts started to hit and powerlines came down, the figure slipped unnoticed through the doors into the candlelit spa area.

50

5 Minutes Before New Years Eve

'I've just heard that the swims off,' Sarah came barrelling into the ladies' locker room. 'So I guess you guys just wait midnight out in here then?'

The three of them looked at each other and nodded in agreement.

'Well, I guess I'll see you all on the other side,' she grinned as she took the staff exit from the lockers into the corridor that linked to the family changing.

'Fuck that. I don't care what Michael says. I'm getting in that pool. We always said that would mark our fresh start,' Carolyn stood up.

'Seriously, Carolyn, do you think that's a good idea? We've just been trapped in the sauna. The weathers awful. Can't we just wait it out here? There's only a couple of minutes to midnight now. It's not like we have ticket holders we need to manage now, is there?' Kira reasoned.

'It would be kind of memorable though, wouldn't it? What a way to kickstart the New Year—a big fuck you to the year and a chance to celebrate how awesome we are.' Ruby took Kira's hand. 'We can do this. Fuck him, fuck things holding us back. What can he do to us now?'

'So, this is it then?' Kira looked between her friends as they grasped hands and the crowd from the bar started the countdown to midnight from twenty seconds. With one last look at each other, they stood up.

'Let's do this.'

Carolyn was the first to leave the changing room. As she stepped out onto the tiled floor and began the walk back to the spa area, the shadow moved as the electric finally succumbed to the power cut, and the backup lights went out, plunging the whole area into darkness.

Kira was the next to leave. Emerging into the gloom, with only a few candles still lit, she could barely see as she moved towards the hot tub.

Ruby paused at the door before turning back quickly to grab their towels, following a minute later.

As the backup generator kicked back in, the twelve strikes of midnight could be heard from the loudspeaker in the bar. The gloomy green emergency lights illuminated the pool, and the hot tub spluttered and gurgled back to life. All of a sudden, the cheers of the crowd in the bar were drowned out by an ear-splitting scream.

51

Now

Midnight, Ruby

The scream that had emerged from her throat had been so vociferous that Ruby had nearly deafened herself. She couldn't comprehend what was happening, what she was seeing right in front of her eyes. Between the swirls of steam and the frothing bubbles, she could see a dark shape. She could feel her chest heaving and her heart pounding—how could this be real? The jets went silent as the motor cut out when the power cut out again. The shape rose up to the surface, parting the foam.

As she got closer, she could see more clearly—it was hair, it was a head. What the fuck? Why were they face down? Why were they not getting up? And then the jets kicked in again, the waterfall function cascading and pouring down, making the shape bob up and down creepily in the dark hot tub. She could just see a hand floating under the water, a finger breaking the surface as if pointing at her. Where were her friends? Who was in the pool?

Just as she got a grip on herself, from the corner of her eye, she could see someone flying towards her, screaming, slipping across the wet tiles past her, plunging down the steps into the heat of the pool. And there was Carolyn, sliding into the pool.

51

Now

Midnights, Carolyn

'Josh, Josh, oh my God, oh my God, Josh!' Carolyn didn't understand how she had managed to propel herself at such speed across to the pool and jump in, nor did she remember the words she shouted or the keening wail that started to emit from her chest, as Kira appeared behind her on the steps, and they, along with Sam and Sarah, who had just appeared from the plant room, started to drag him up the pool steps.

52

Now

Midnight, Kira

Kira couldn't catch her breath; she literally couldn't breathe. The scene in front of her was like something out of a horror movie. Her body felt like it was made of lead, and she couldn't make it do anything that she wanted it to do.

She could barely comprehend that the sodden body lying prone on the wet tiles was Josh, the man who had tormented her, hurt her and violated her. She couldn't process that Carolyn was screaming and crying, hanging onto Josh and begging him to be ok—this man who had caused her no end of pain and suffering.

She paused for a second, waiting for her brain to catch up, taking a deep breath before she could react to the scene unfolding in front of her. Despite the horror of the situation and the visible outpouring of grief and shock from Carolyn, if truth be told, all she could feel once her head started to clear was absolute relief.

'Josh, Josh, oh my God, oh my God, Josh!'

The sound of Carolyn screaming his name as she continued to grab at him and hug him on the tiles snapped Kira back into the moment as she turned to Sam to ask him to help.

53
Now

Carolyn couldn't understand at first what Sam was saying, as he tried to gently move her away from Josh. All she could think of in that moment was that her children would be without a father; she would be without a husband if he didn't pull through.

'We need to give him CPR,' Sam commanded again as he started to explain his lifeguard training.

She continued to pound on Josh's chest, crying, shouting, 'You can't leave us, Josh. I'm so sorry, I'm sorry I'm not a good enough wife, a good enough mum. No, no. No, please, don't do this to us!'

As she continued to grab at his body, Ruby had joined her on the floor then, taking part of the weight of Josh's limp body into her arms as she tried to calm Carolyn.

'We've got him, Carolyn. Sam knows first aid, don't you, Sam?' Ruby looked up and saw the panic in his eyes. 'Don't you need to do mouth to mouth?'

'We don't do that anymore. Protocol is to get the heart going first. You need to let go, Carolyn, so we can lay him flat and we can do chest compressions.'

Ruby had moved out from under Josh then, laying his limp body back on the wet, cold tiles as she tried again to get Carolyn to move.

Ruby leant forward and spoke quietly in Carolyn's ear, 'He isn't breathing, so you need to let go of him now so Sam can help.'

Carolyn had slowly extracted herself from under his body. She looked up at Kira and held her eyes for what felt like an eternity. She said quietly, 'We better call an ambulance. You know, let the professionals deal with this,' before looking at Ruby for confirmation.

Ruby had given a small nod of agreement as Sarah turned to Sue, who had just appeared from the changing room. 'I'll go raise the alarm.'

'The phone lines are down,' came Sue's stuttered reply. 'I just came to tell you before I left.' She dangled her car keys by the letter S keyring in her hand as she took in the scene in front of her.

'Well, let's hope I can find my mobile quickly then,' Sarah said as she moved slowly towards the changing rooms.

54
After
New Years Day

As Sue and Sarah collected up the towels and the ubiquitous Sparks water bottles that had been left scattered by the hot tub, and Sam draped foil emergency blankets around their shoulders, the three women slumped back against the damp tiled wall. In the gloomy green glow of the emergency light, they reached for one another's hands as they watched the paramedic declare life extinct and place his high-viz jacket lightly over Josh's cooling body.

Ruby turned first to Carolyn in the centre and gave her hand a squeeze.

'It's over,' she spoke gently, as Carolyn nodded and turned to Kira on her other side, speaking the same words. 'It's over.'

Kira let the tears pour freely down her face as she nodded with relief. Leaning forward, she reached across Carolyn for Ruby's other hand to complete their circle. As she too nodded, closing her eyes for a second and feeling the strength of her friends next to her, she too spoke the words they all needed to hear.

'It's over.'

55

After

1 Week Later, Sauna

The week after Josh's demise had been a whirlwind of police interviews, dodging the press, and for Carolyn, breaking the sad news to the twins that their daddy had been in a terrible accident in the hot tub, and that he was dead. The friends had had little time to meet, but as they sat in their usual spots in the warmth and safety of the now re-opened sauna, they each gave a contented sigh as they sank back against the hot cedar slats.

Carolyn was the first to speak. 'The police say that the club could still be sued for the broken lock on the plant room and not fixing that filter in the pool—the one they say his swim shorts were stuck in.' She looked between her friends as Ruby joined in.

'Well, the officer I talked to said something about the generator being to blame. They say it could have been tampered with, so it didn't work properly when there was a power cut. I guess that explains the lack of CCTV on the night?' She paused. 'At least that means that they didn't keep Sue and Sarah in questioning for long. They could hardly monitor CCTV that wasn't working, could they?' she paused again 'and they didn't even question Sam thankfully'

'Also, the fact that we were by the pool didn't help, I guess. I mean, with none of us having phones close by to call for help?' Kira added. 'I know Sam tried CPR, but it did take ages for the ambulance to get here.'

'Shame that.' Carolyn met each of their eyes as she looked down at the ugly bruises now fading to yellow on her arms.

56
After 1 Year Later

The three women stood side by side as Carolyn smoothed her sleek blonde bob down around her ears, before returning her hand to Ruby's, as the cold winter wind whipped Ruby's bright cerise coat tighter over her burgeoning baby bump. Ruby reached for Kira's right hand, as Kira glanced down at her other hand, smiling to herself as the weak winter sun glinted off the diamond sparkling on her ring finger, the feeling of it still new to her.

They watched as Amber and Charlie stood quietly at their father's graveside on New Year's Day. They looked the perfect picture of grieving children, their heads silently bowed in thoughtful contemplation, as they bent in unison to place a small posy of winter flowers on the mound of mud at their feet.

As she checked to make sure that her mother was out of earshot, Amber turned slightly towards her brother, leaning into him as he put his arm gently around her shoulder. To any bystander, his concern would have looked touching. If they had been closer, they may have heard Amber say quietly, almost under her breath.

'I always knew he would take that drinks bottle if we left it in his gym bag long enough.'

Charlie nodded in agreement. 'He always was too lazy to sort his own stuff out. He would have just thought Mum had packed it for him—stupid idiot,' he smirked, as Amber giggled.

'Yeah, it was handy that Sparks gave us all matching ones. People never noticed if they got swapped and people always just left them lying around didn't they?' Charlie smirked. 'Oh, poor Daddy, if only we'd paid attention and stayed away from those horrible poisonous specimens in his office!' Charlie warmed to his theme.

'If only he hadn't lectured anyone who would listen about how they were undiscovered, and if only he had handed them in to the research centre when he was supposed to?' She paused as Charlie took her hand and they slowly turned to walk back to the car where their Mum was waiting for them.

'We couldn't have done it without the others though, could we?'

Charlie gave his sisters hand one last squeeze as he muttered sadly.

'If only he hadn't been so evil'.'

Epilogue

Extract of Interview/s with witnesses, as told to Sheila Leech, journalist, Evening Argus

Peter, 58

I heard that they can't prove fowl play, that even if they wanted to look at a manslaughter charge they couldn't prove anything. The club couldn't help someone's stupidity could they? Going into the spa pool alone when it was obviously under maintenance, and I heard that he had alcohol in his blood.

Gillian, 72

Well, I heard that his board shorts—you know, those silly long things with bright colours that blokes like to wear—well, they got stuck in the filter or something in that hot tub and he drowned! I never did trust that hot tub thing. Urgh, think about all those bodies in there, just boiling off their skin like lobsters!

Lottie, 33

I have good sources, you know. I heard from Jen, who knows Cathy who cleans the gym on weekends, who knows that Claire from spin class, that there were too many chemicals in the hot tub, and that he was poisoned. The staff here are brilliant though—so meticulous, always coming round with their little clipboard and testing pH levels or whatever it is that they do. Someone's going to be in serious trouble.

Miranda, 68

It's probably one of those kids they employ as lifeguards fault. I mean, who are they kidding? There's this one lad who looks like his legs are made of pipe-cleaners. If me or my hubby—Stan—I think you've spoken to him already? Well, if one of us fell in the pool, he would have no chance of hefting either of us out with those twig legs! Maybe they couldn't get him out fast enough?

Carl, 28

. The thing is, I don't understand why he was in there in the first place. We all knew that the late-night candlelit swim had been cancelled, because of the weather. He should have listened to the rules. I mean, we were all disappointed but we all obeyed them. Someone did tell me that he was meeting someone, so maybe he was pushed?

Aneka, 27

Well, I heard from Dan from HiiT that he had been accused of having an affair or something, but I think his wife heard it in the locker room. I feel for the wife and kids I really do but we all know guys like that, don't we? What do I mean by guys like that? Well, you know, the ones that look at you a bit too long and get too close—we all saw him do that around the club.

Amy, 34

Someone told me that he was abusing his wife but that could just be gossip, she was always so on top of things with the committee and all that. The kids always seemed happy too, but if it was true, then maybe the bastard got what he deserved?